Alex Kava is the author of the Maggie O'Dell series. A former PR director, Alex dedicated herself to writing full-time in 1996. She lives in Nebraska, USA. Find out more at: www.alexkava.com.

Also by Alex Kava

Alex
KAVA
Breaking
Creed

sphere

SPHERE

Published in the United States in 2015 by G.P. Putnam's Sons,
a division of Penguin Random House
First published in Great Britain in 2015 by Sphere
This paperback edition published in 2015 by Sphere

1 3 5 7 9 10 8 6 4 2

Copyright © S.M. Kava 2015

A CIP catalogue record for this book
is available from the British Library.

ISBN 978-0-7515-5581-3

Printed and bound in Great Britain by
Clays Ltd, St Ives plc

Papers used by Sphere are from well-managed forests
and other responsible sources.

MIX
Paper from
responsible sources
FSC
www.fsc.org   FSC® C104740

Sphere
An imprint of
Little, Brown Book Group
Carmelite House
50 Victoria Embankment
London EC4Y 0DZ

An Hachette UK Company
www.hachette.co.uk

www.littlebrown.co.uk

FOR MY BOY, SCOUT

March 1998–May 2014
Miss you like crazy, buddy.

AUTHOR'S NOTE

From the time I was able to crawl, I've been enamored with dogs. I even have a few scars that could have and probably should have discouraged me. My earliest memory is of the day I decided to follow our two farm dogs anywhere they went. They were my constant companions when my older brother and sister were in school and my younger brother was too little.

On this day I remember joyously trotting along with the dogs until I glanced over my shoulder and saw that our farmhouse was quite tiny in the distance. I must have been three or four years old at the time, and, of course, I don't need to tell you that my mother was frantic by the time I wandered back with my two friends.

For years now I've included dogs in my novels, but I've been itching to create a character who, not only shared my love and my awe of dogs, but who would be truly happy and most comfortable living in the company of dogs. And wouldn't it be interesting to have the dogs be strong characters, as well? As much as I love research, finally I would be writing about a subject I knew quite well.

Needless to say, I'm excited about this new series, but never once did I realize nor could I predict how very difficult it would be to write about dogs while losing one of my own. And not just any dog, but my sixteen-year-old buddy, Scout, who had been at my side – literally sitting next to me – while I wrote all fourteen of my novels. He even waited until I finished this one before telling me he'd had enough of fighting kidney disease for two years.

My good friend Sharon Car said it perfectly: 'Big personalities leave a big hole, and I'm sure Scout has left a crater in your heart.'

That, he has certainly done. But one of the privileges of being a writer is finding some small way to honor those we love. At the end of the book, you might notice that Jason names his puppy after Scout Finch from *To Kill a Mockingbird*. But in truth, Jason's dog is named after my Scout who was actually named after my favorite literary character. In future books you'll get a glimpse of my Scout's quirks, like chasing his tail, giving kisses on demand, and making everyone – including the other dogs – laugh . . . a lot.

In addition, this book is dedicated to my boy, Scout. And although he was a West Highland terrier, something tells me he would have approved of being represented by a Labrador. His spirit is definitely big enough.

1

BARRANQUILLA, COLOMBIA

Sweat slid down Amanda's back. Her stringy hair stuck to her forehead. The room was stifling and reeked of greasy fried pork. She felt nauseated, and the smell wouldn't let her forget the slimy soup she had been given to coat her throat. A small dish of the golden liquid sat in front of her, its surface beaded with oil. The soup was for her benefit, Leandro had reminded her.

'It contains a special medicine.' His tone was always so gentle and reassuring. 'It will be good for your throat and make your task much easier.'

Amanda knew he was right. Last week, when she

did this for the first time, she didn't even feel what she was swallowing. It was as if her entire mouth had gone numb, just like in the dentist's office.

Still, she stared at the remaining balloons piled up on the scarred wooden tabletop, and she couldn't shake the sick feeling in her stomach.

Last time she had swallowed fifty-one balloons. Leandro had been so proud of her. And every single one had come out without any problems – well, no problems meaning none had ruptured. The coming-out part had not been pain-free as Leandro had promised. But Amanda had been so relieved that she didn't mind the pain.

This time she had downed only thirty-six before the nausea hit her.

Leandro would be disappointed. How could she disappoint him when he had given her so much? When he had been so good to her.

She watched him fill the last of the balloons. He had explained to her that he used only the strongest condoms available. He told her he did it for her benefit, because he cared so much about her and because this would eliminate the risk of a balloon rupturing while inside her stomach.

Amanda had asked what would happen if one of the balloons did break, but Leandro had waved his hand at her as if he were swatting flies. It was a gesture that was becoming familiar, and it was usually accompanied by his favorite phrase: 'This is something you do not ask. This is something you leave to Leandro.'

But now, as Amanda watched his slender fingers stretch the condom over the top of a glass vial, she wondered what would happen if one of the balloons broke inside her. Is that why she was feeling sick now? The thought made her shiver, and she forced herself to sit up straight, as if that would give the balloons in her stomach more room.

She tried not to think about it. Instead, she continued to watch Leandro as he carefully spooned the cocaine into each condom. When the latex tip bulged out a half inch to an inch in diameter, Leandro tied a knot, keeping it small and tight. Then he trimmed it close and neat, so there was less to swallow. When she'd watched him last week, he had explained that this, too, was another detail he did out of concern for her.

She glanced around the room. The three swallowers and Leandro's partner, the old woman they called Zapata, paid no attention to Leandro. They all were focused on their own tasks in front of them. But Amanda watched how his muscles bulged under his T-shirt and yet how gentle his fingers were. He was focused on making everything easier on her, and it made her love him even more. He would never let any harm come to her. And certainly she could ignore a little stomachache.

She licked her lips and realized she couldn't feel them. Instead of panicking, she quickly reminded herself that it was only the special medicine in the soup. She must have gotten some on her lips. She tried not to think about it. She needed to calm herself. Her stomach probably wouldn't be upset at all if it weren't for the new girl. And now Amanda realized that her discomfort was definitely the girl's fault.

She'd been crying since they brought her into the room, even while she ate the greasy soup. Pathetic sobs, all soft and quiet except for that irritating hitch to her breathing.

The girl was a year older than Amanda. She'd heard Zapata tell Leandro that the girl was fifteen. She sure didn't act like it. She was probably just faking to get Leandro's attention, because now suddenly he left his work of filling the balloons and went over to her.

'Lucía,' he said gently.

Then he put his hand on the girl's back, almost a caress. Amanda stopped breathing, straining to listen as Leandro bent over and whispered something to the girl. His lips almost touched her ear. Amanda couldn't make out the words. She didn't know enough Spanish, but she couldn't help noticing that Leandro's tone sounded soothing, as if he were coaxing and persuading Lucía that everything would be okay. It was the same tone he used with Amanda.

Amanda grabbed another balloon from the pile. She dropped it into the small dish in front of her and rolled it around in the greasy liquid, using her fingers and not caring that they became slick, too. Then, still watching Leandro, she put it quickly into her mouth. Her throat was still numb, and she swallowed it with no problem.

She took another and followed the same process, just as Leandro had taught her. Then she did another and another, letting her anger sweep them down. Already her nausea started to leave. Before poor Lucía had cried and choked down two balloons, Amanda had added a half dozen. And her reward was Leandro looking over. He raised his eyebrows in surprise, then a smile transformed his entire face. By the time they were ready to leave for the airport, Amanda had swallowed two more than last week, while Lucía – still crying and now grasping her stomach – had managed to get down only twenty-five.

Amanda found herself silently telling the girl that she would never win over Leandro with such a pathetic performance. Although the older girl was so very pretty, with long, silky black hair and rich brown skin. By comparison, Amanda's hair was stringy and dirty blond, her face spattered with freckles that she wished she could scrub away. No matter how many balloons she swallowed, she was still jealous of the new girl. Jealous and worried that Leandro might find her more suitable because Lucía was Colombian while Amanda was just poor white American trash. That's what Zapata called her despite Leandro's scolding the old woman.

When Amanda had first met her, she thought Zapata was Leandro's mother. But there was something so cold about the old woman that Amanda didn't think she was capable of being a mother. Not like Amanda had much to go on. Her own mother had thrown her out of the house, told her never to come back. All because she couldn't keep her own boyfriend off her daughter. Her mother had caught the asshole slam-dancing Amanda against their kitchen counter.

Instead of asking if Amanda was okay, instead of kicking the asshole out, she made Amanda leave.

It ended up for the better. She needed to get out of that house. And she would never have met Leandro if she hadn't left home. He treated her so much better. He appreciated her. And maybe after today, Zapata would also realize that Amanda was worthy of her respect.

At least today Zapata was screeching at Lucía. More Spanish, but Amanda didn't need to understand it to know that the old woman had become impatient with the new girl. Franco had come to tell them he had the van out front, and the others were already grabbing their backpacks, heading for the door.

Except for Lucía. She was crying even harder now, her arms wrapped tight around her stomach. Her face was streaked with sweat, not just tears. She looked as if she were in pain.

Amanda shuffled toward the door, watching and waiting, wanting to sit next to Leandro in the van. But his attention was focused on Lucía.

And then suddenly the girl collapsed, falling to the

floor. Her head slammed against the heavy wooden table leg.

Amanda couldn't believe it. Was she faking it?

Zapata was shaking her head and saying something to Leandro, only the old woman's voice was eerily calm and quiet. And it was Leandro who was cursing under his breath.

Amanda couldn't take her eyes off Lucía. She couldn't look away. She was waiting for the girl to move, but Lucía didn't flinch when Leandro shoved her. There was nothing gentle about his touch now. When Lucía didn't respond, it only made him angrier, and Zapata grabbed his arm before he could shove at Lucía again.

'She's done,' Zapata said. 'Get it out.'

Then she noticed Amanda. Her eyes widened, and Amanda thought she saw a flash of panic before the cold black eyes returned to their usual hard stare. Zapata walked toward Amanda, gesturing for her to leave, but Amanda couldn't stop watching Lucía and Leandro standing over her.

'We must go,' Zapata told her in a calm, steady voice as she took Amanda by the elbow. 'We can't miss our flight.'

The old woman squeezed and pulled at Amanda's arm to turn her toward the door, but not before Amanda saw Leandro pull a knife from his boot. He was still muttering to himself or cursing Lucía. Amanda didn't know which. She had never seen him like this. He didn't seem to notice that she was still in the room. He started cutting Lucía's clothing with the knife, ripping at it with urgency and anger. Was he helping her? Could he save her? Maybe it wasn't too late.

'What's he doing?' Amanda asked.

'It is none of your concern,' Zapata said as her fingernails dug into Amanda's arm and she dragged her along.

The old woman pushed her out the doorway, but not before Amanda saw Leandro plunge the knife again. This time into Lucía. And now Amanda knew what happened if a balloon ruptured inside her stomach.

2

The Coast Guard helicopter pitched to one side, sending Ryder Creed sliding. He tightened his grip on Grace. His other hand white-knuckled the leather strap that kept him anchored to the inside wall. Grace was tethered to him, one end of the nylon restraint secured to her vest and the other end wrapped around Creed's waist. Despite never having flown in a helicopter before, she didn't appear stressed at all.

Creed, however, didn't have a good feeling about this trip. In fact, he was beginning to regret taking the assignment. None of his dogs had ever been in a helicopter before. He couldn't help thinking the sixteen-pound Jack Russell terrier felt even smaller cradled next to him.

But Grace was taking it in her stride, already used to the thumping of the rotors and treating the roller-coaster ride as if it were just a part of the adventure. She watched and sniffed at the unfamiliar surroundings, anxious to get to work, because as soon as her vest went on, she knew they were headed for a job, and this girl loved her work. That was what made her such an excellent air-scent dog. She possessed a natural curiosity. The tougher the puzzle, the more excited she became.

'She's not exactly what I expected' was the first thing Commander Wilson had said when he met Grace and Creed on the helipad before takeoff.

While Wilson handed Creed his own 'mustang' – the aircrew's term of endearment for the orange flight suits they wore – he stared at Grace as though perhaps Creed might have brought the wrong dog. Even the rest of the crew – copilot Tommy Ellis, flight mechanic Pete Kesnick, and rescue swimmer Liz Bailey – looked at the terrier as if they weren't sure what to do with her.

But it was actually Grace whom the Coast Guard had requested. Last week she'd made the national news when she managed to sniff out two kilos of cocaine at Hartsfield's international terminal in Atlanta. A Colombian woman had creatively found a way to make chocolate bars with cocaine centers. She had made it through customs and was headed out of the area when Grace pulled Creed off the line they were working and raced after the woman.

Two weeks before, Grace had stopped a duffel bag filled with a case of peanut butter. It was coming down the conveyor belt out of the cargo hold of an American Airlines flight from Iquitos, Peru. They had already spent a morning going over checked luggage from incoming international flights when Grace alerted Creed to the red-and-black duffel that looked brand-new. Sure enough, in the gooey middle of each jar was a triple-bagged stash of cocaine. Each sixteen-ounce jar of extra-crunchy contained almost a kilo. Creed was told that the twelve-pack carton had a street value of nearly a million dollars.

Suddenly they were becoming celebrities. Just two days ago, Creed and Grace had traveled to prerecord an appearance on *The View* that was scheduled to air this week. Creed's partner, Hannah, was fielding calls for more appearances, on *Good Morning America* and *Fox & Friends*. Grace, of course, was taking the attention the same way she reacted to everything else – as if it were just another part of her daily adventure.

Creed not so much.

He'd worked hard to carve out a mostly private life for himself despite building a nationally known K9 business. At first he bristled at the media attention, until Hannah convinced him it could be a way for his sister, Brodie, to *find* him.

'Rye,' Hannah told him when he groaned at another photo of him and Grace, this time on the front page of *USA Today*. 'What if Brodie is still alive? She might see you. She'll recognize the name, if not the face. Maybe all this is a blessing.'

That was Hannah, always finding a positive spin, seeing blessings where Creed saw only chaos. That's how she had saved him in the first place. Seven years ago she'd seen promise in the drunk and belligerent marine who had taken on three guys in a bar fight. It happened at the end of her shift at Walter's Canteen on Pensacola Beach.

In all his life, Creed had never had to deal with an

angry black woman, especially one whose anger came in a calm and measured sermon that had sobered him more than any drill sergeant ever had. Somehow he ended up with a mop in his hands, cleaning up broken glass and sticky beer, instead of in an alley with a busted skull or broken ribs.

It was Hannah who'd convinced Creed to use the skills he'd learned as a K9 handler in his marine unit to start his own business. And since that night she'd managed to become his business partner, his confidante, his counselor, his family. She was usually right, even about the things he didn't want to admit. And maybe she'd be right about this.

Fifteen years ago his sister, Brodie, had disappeared, taken from an interstate rest stop. She was only eleven. Creed was fourteen. Brodie's body had never been found. It ripped apart his parents and forced Creed to grow up too soon, haunted and forever burdened by that autumn day when suddenly Brodie wasn't in the restroom anymore. She wasn't anywhere to be found.

His search for her inspired Creed to start K9 CrimeScents. The company had grown into a multi-million-dollar operation with a dozen employees, a training facility on fifty acres, with a waiting list for their services as well as for the dogs Creed trained.

Every cadaver search got his hopes up, because even though Brodie had disappeared as a little girl, there was always the possibility that she had lived on for any part of the fifteen years she'd been missing. So every time Creed's searches discovered a body – whether it was that of a child, a teenager, or a young woman – there was always a chance, always the slightest possibility, that it could be Brodie. And each time the body was identified as someone else, Creed felt the same overwhelming mixture of relief and misery. Relief that maybe, just maybe, his sister could still be alive. And misery, because if she was, what kind of a life was it?

Initially, when the despair from searching for dead bodies almost did him in, Hannah insisted Creed start training some of their dogs for search and rescue, and then she added bombs and drugs to the list. That was why she had him doing drug searches these past several weeks. When she found him passed out in his loft apartment or saw too many women coming and going, she knew he needed a break from tracking dead bodies. Otherwise the stench of death and the false hopes would suck the life right out of him.

So Creed told Hannah that he'd tolerate the media attention as long as it didn't bother Grace. And he would do a few more drug searches. But this helicopter ride was bringing back other memories that Creed had not expected, and now he wished he'd said no to Hannah and to this assignment.

Grace licked his hand. She was staring at him. An intense stare was supposed to be her cue to him that she had found what they were searching for. Grace was one of his few multitask dogs. All Creed had to do was put a different vest or harness on her and Grace knew what he wanted her to sniff out. But this stare was different. Dogs could detect their handlers' emotions, too, and Grace knew that something was wrong. She was an amazing little dog. He had found her half-starved and hiding underneath one of the double-wide trailers he kept for hired help. Hard to believe that someone had discarded her like trash. But then that was how Creed had gotten most of his dogs.

Hannah shook her head at him when he brought in another stray.

'Folks just taking advantage of your soft heart,' she'd tell Creed.

What no one understood, not even Hannah, was

that the dogs he rescued – those abandoned mutts that were worthless to someone else – had flourished into some of his best search dogs. There was a loyalty, a bond between Creed and the dogs. He'd given them a purpose, a second chance. In a sense it was exactly what they'd given him.

But now, for Grace's sake, he needed to shove aside those memories that had jolted him with the simple smell of diesel and the sound of the rotors. It was Grace's first helicopter ride, but it was hardly Creed's. Almost as soon as he'd boarded, the vibration had drummed out a rhythm that threatened to swallow his heartbeat. Without warning, his chest felt as if it might explode. He craned his neck so he could look out and down at the emerald-green water below. He took deep breaths and calmed his nerves. He tried to remind himself that it was the Gulf of Mexico under his feet and not the suffocating dust and rock of Afghanistan.

Times like this, it surprised him how much he could still feel that place. And yet, he had no one to blame but himself.

His mistake.

He'd been looking for an escape from his life and thought the marines would take him far away from his troubles, but instead he discovered that there were worse versions of hell than the one inside you.

'We're almost there.' Commander Wilson's voice blasted through Creed's helmet, startling him a bit.

Creed scratched behind Grace's ears – their signal that everything was okay. Finally she put her head down on his leg, but her ears were still pitched forward, letting him know that he wasn't fooling her.

3

ON BOARD THE COAST GUARD CUTTER
SCOUT WMEC-630

The water churned around them and the winds had picked up. Creed was impressed with the smooth landing that Commander Wilson had managed onto the deck of the Coast Guard cutter. Its crew had already halted the boat in question. The commercial fishing vessel, named *Blue Mist*, was a beaut. A seventy-foot long-liner that Creed guessed could keep at least eighty thousand pounds of fish in its hold. But the Coast Guard had reason to believe there might be something extra under that day's catch.

Commander Wilson had explained earlier to Creed

that the Coast Guard had been watching the *Blue Mist* for a couple of weeks now. It usually long-lined for mahi-mahi in the Gulf, following the fish's migratory path. But recently the boat had started going down into the Caribbean Sea as far as the coast of Colombia. That in itself wasn't unusual, except that the Coast Guard tracker watched the fishing boat pass by several mile-long stretches of sargassum. The brownish sea-weed floats on the ocean surface, and mahi-mahi traditionally feed on the creatures attracted to it.

Now on board the *Blue Mist*, Creed looked down into the hold. He was struck by how beautiful the fish were, even piled up on top of one another. Their sides glittered gold, blue, and iridescent green, their bellies white and yellow. They were bigger than he expected, three to four feet long. The heads varied in size and shape, and he suspected that the difference was linked to whether they were male or female. Most of them had rounded heads, a few protruding above the body line.

'Mahi-mahi used to be bycatch fish,' Wilson said, and only then did Creed realize that the commander had followed and come up beside him. On the deck across from them, two guardsmen were getting an earful from a barrel-chested man in a ball cap, baggy trousers, and a white T-shirt, most likely the *Blue Mist*'s captain.

'Fishermen thought they were a pain because they'd end up on their longlines when they were trying to catch tuna and swordfish,' Commander Wilson continued without any encouragement from Creed. 'Now restaurants are going crazy over mahi-mahi – including the European market.'

'Could be their hold was already full when they passed by the sargassum,' Creed said while he took out the items he needed from his backpack.

'True. But if that were the case, why continue south?' Wilson asked.

Thankfully, it wasn't Creed's job to have an answer. He pulled rubber waders up over his hiking boots and slipped a mesh pouch with a nylon strap over his head and shoulder. He had no idea why people did half the things they did. One of the reasons he preferred the company of dogs.

He did know, without Wilson giving him any more details, that there was a new Colombian drug cartel trying to establish itself. Choque Azul – 'Blue Shock' – had been busy in the last six to eight months reclaiming old drug routes up through the Gulf. The routes had been abandoned in the 1990s, when it became easier to cross the Mexican border into Texas and Arizona than it was to chance bringing their product up the Gulf.

But these days the brutal wars among the Mexican cartels – the Zetas and the Sinaloas – had sent the Colombians looking for new and creative ways to do business. Chocolate bars and peanut butter jars were small snatches, innovative and quirky tests. But home-made submersibles and commercial fishing boats were for the serious hauls. If the Coast Guard was correct about this vessel, then it was possible there was cocaine somewhere on board. Most likely underneath the piles of mahi-mahi.

Creed had never done a search of a fishing vessel before, and now, as he adjusted Grace's vest, he realized this wouldn't be easy. Wilson must have seen Creed's indecision.

'Bet you're wishing you'd brought a bigger dog,' Wilson said as he watched.

Grace was wagging and panting and anxious for Creed's command so she could dive down into the hold and get to work.

'Bigger isn't always better,' Creed told him.

Then, with Grace's eyes focused on him, Creed patted his right palm to his chest. Grace jumped up into his arms. He tucked her under his elbow and into the mesh pouch that hung from his shoulder. He attached her harness to clasps inside the pouch and let it drop to his side. This way Grace would travel comfortably above the fray while Creed waded through the piles of slippery fish. All she had to do was sniff, when he cued her to what she was to search for. Ironically, the cue word he used for drugs was 'fish.'

'Go find fish,' he told the dog as he felt her getting excited and wiggling in the carrier. But as Creed headed down into the pungent smell, he wondered if this might be too overwhelming a task for any air-scent dog.

They worked a grid for almost thirty minutes. The fishing vessel's captain was still yelling at the guardsmen about his 'dorados spoiling in the sun.' Grace's nose moved back and forth. Twice she went into rapid breathing, but still no alerts. Not even for secondary residue. Creed tried to shove aside the glittering fish to see the bottom of the hold, but he was knee-deep and it was like trying to dig a hole in sand. The fish slipped quickly back into the hole he tried to create. He never saw the bottom.

Without warning, Grace started squirming. Her nose lifted higher and began twitching. Her breaths came fast, with hardly a break in between. Creed slowed his pace, listening and watching, treating the small dog as if she were a live Geiger counter.

Suddenly he felt Grace's body go rigid. He stopped. Her eyes came up to his and she stared at him. It was their signal, her alert. But then she did something she'd never done before: she started whining, a low, soft cry that made the hair at the back of Creed's neck stand up.

'We've got something here,' he yelled to the guardsmen above.

They stared down at him. Even the *Blue Mist*'s captain had gone silent.

In minutes four men in rubber waders made their way down to the hold. They carried what looked like snow shovels, the blades three feet tall and just as wide. The shovels were able to push aside the fish and keep them from slipping back into the space the men cleared.

Creed kept his eyes on Grace. He'd pulled her close to him and stuck his hand into the mesh pouch so he could pet her. She'd quieted her whine but she was trembling now. Creed had sweat running down his back and forehead from the sun and heat, but Grace was shivering.

He didn't like this. He'd never seen her do this before.

The men cleared a ten-by-ten space all the way down to the bottom of the hold, hitting wood. And although Grace stared at the empty spot, she didn't stop shaking.

'There's nothing here,' one of the men said, and looked at Creed. Then the man craned his neck to look up at Commander Wilson, who had stayed on deck above them. 'We've got nothing.'

'Maybe your dog isn't so lucky this time,' Wilson called down.

'Under the floorboards,' Creed said without having a clue as to whether Grace had been thrown off by the overpowering smell of fish. There might be nothing at all under the boards either.

The men looked to Wilson, but before he could respond, one of them yelled, 'There's a plank loose!'

And suddenly the others were pulling crowbars from a canvas bag that Creed hadn't even noticed until now.

'Careful,' the one in charge told the men.

The wood creaked and snapped. Grace began to whine again, and it seemed to make the men go slower, but with a new sense of urgency. Nails screeched loose. Two boards popped away. Only then did Creed realize that Grace had stopped whining, but he still heard a low hum, almost a cry, that wasn't coming from Grace. It was coming from under the floorboards.

He heard more wood crack, and then suddenly one of the men said, 'Holy crap. There's someone down here.'

4

They were kids. Creed guessed the oldest was maybe thirteen, fourteen at the most. Three girls. Two boys. One boy looked younger than ten. Each of them crawled slowly out of the hold like a timid animal, needing assistance, then jerking and blinking at the sunlight. Wild eyes darted all around, looking for permission as much as trying to anticipate what came next in this terrifying journey.

They were filthy. Hair matted and tangled in clumps. Faces dirty and feet bare and bruised. Despite the stink of fish, Creed could smell the sweat and urine and feces that soiled their clothes. But through the smears of dirt and grime, one thing was obvious.

These weren't Colombian kids. They weren't being trafficked from their South American homes to the United States.

Now, in the sunlight, even the dirt and grime couldn't hide the obvious. Smears revealed blond hair and streaks of white skin as pale as the fish bellies that surrounded them.

These kids looked like they were from the United States.

Creed remembered what Commander Wilson had said about this vessel bypassing feeding grounds for mahi-mahi, its hold filled but continuing south, out of the Gulf of Mexico and closer to the coast of Colombia. Usually traffickers smuggled people *into* the United States. When did it start to go both ways? Were they delivering this cargo to South America?

Everyone on board had gone silent, even the guardsmen as they helped the kids up. They'd been looking for smuggled cocaine. Not human cargo. And certainly not kids.

The wind had calmed, almost as if it, also, were gasping at their revelation. In the silence Creed could hear the lapping of waves against the boat. A few gulls dared to hover closer to inspect the load of fish. But there was still a faint humming, a sad whimper like that of a scared or wounded animal. The same sound Creed had heard before the floorboards were yanked away. Grace had heard it first, and she still cocked her head, listening. Creed saw that her eyes were staring at the source, and he followed her gaze.

The sound was coming from the littlest boy.

He was small, with bony shoulders and stick legs. Creed caught a glimpse of his eyes. Fear had been replaced with the vacant look that often accompanies an overload of shock. His skinny arms were wrapped tight across his body. His chin tucked into his chest. He didn't look scared or upset. He simply didn't look like he was there anymore, an empty shell. Except for the whimper that came from inside him. It came without him opening his mouth or even moving his lips.

The other kids didn't seem to notice. Their own eyes were just as vacant.

And their rescuers? The guardsmen glanced at one another, and Creed thought they looked lost and uncomfortable. They were used to dealing with the criminals who did this sort of thing. They rescued victims from capsized boats and ministered to those brought out of the water. Usually their victims were glad to see them. But these kids cowered as if they still weren't sure who was friend or foe. And the guardsmen responded by keeping a safe distance, not wanting to treat them like cornered animals, refraining from any attempt to touch or comfort. Afraid it might spook the kids even more.

It was Liz Bailey, the Coast Guard rescue swimmer – and the only woman on board – who broke the silence. Suddenly she was there, having waded down through the mahi-mahi. She still wore her flight suit, and instead of its bright orange fabric scaring the children, they all looked at her as if they were bedazzled. Creed had to admit that, with her short, spiky hair and aviator sunglasses, she did look like a superhero.

'Let's get you something to drink,' she said to them while she pulled bottles of water and sports drinks from her shoulder pack.

Creed was closest to Bailey, and he moved in to help distribute her offerings. That's when he noticed that the rescue swimmer's hands were trembling.

'We need to get you hydrated.' Her voice was friendly and soothing but had the authority of a mother at summer camp, and it did not reveal an iota of the tremor or her uncertainty.

But the kids still didn't move.

Bailey gave the drinks to Creed to hold. She dug into her bag again.

'I have protein bars, too,' she told them.

The kids didn't budge. Instead, they huddled even closer together. The oldest girl just stared at Bailey as if she knew there could be nothing in that pack that would make this right.

'We're gonna get you back home,' one of the guardsmen finally said. But he stayed back behind his oversized shovel that kept the fish from sliding into the small reception area they had created.

Still, the kids just stared. None of them made a move toward Bailey's offerings or responded in any way to the guardsman's attempt at reassurance.

Creed felt Grace wiggling against him, restless in the mesh carrier under his arm. Bailey's taking treats out of her pack must have reminded Grace that she'd found what they were looking for, and yet she had not been rewarded. But it wasn't treats that Grace was interested in, though some of Creed's dogs did prefer treats. Grace insisted on her pink squeaky elephant, and she knew that Creed had it somewhere on him.

She poked her nose under his elbow. He put his

hand inside the carrier to calm her, but Grace wasn't satisfied. She pushed her head and shoulders forward and swatted at him with one paw.

That's when the little boy noticed her, and his eyes grew wide. The empty shell that up until now had only stared and whimpered, suddenly pointed and shouted, 'There's a puppy dog!'

All the children's heads bobbed up, following the boy's finger. For the first time, they were wide-eyed and alert. Creed took a step back, not wanting to add yet another object to fear. He started to gently push Grace farther into the mesh carrier when one of the girls asked, 'Can we pet her?'

Before he could answer, the other little boy asked, 'What's her name?'

'Does she bite?' It was the same little girl who wanted to pet Grace, but the question seemed instinctive, from years of parental instruction, as if it were something she was always supposed to ask before approaching a dog she didn't know.

'Is she your dog?'

'How old is she?'

Finally Creed smiled and put up a hand to ward off more questions. 'She's my dog,' he told them. 'Her name is Grace. I'm not sure how old she is because I found her when she was already grown up.'

'Where did you find her?'

'She was hiding under a trailer on my property. Someone had taken her from her home and dumped her. She was hurt and hungry.'

He watched their faces and realized what they were thinking. Grace wasn't much different from them.

Then the oldest girl said, 'I bet she was scared, too.'

Creed nodded. 'Yup, she was very scared. She wasn't sure who to trust. But she's not scared now. You all can pet her if you go slow and if you're gentle.'

He stood in place, waiting for the kids to decide on their own to come to him.

The littlest boy, who had noticed Grace first, came forward slowly and offered his dirty hand for Grace to sniff. She immediately licked his fingers and the boy giggled.

'That tickles.'

Suddenly Creed and Grace were surrounded, all five children taking turns, remembering to be gentle and letting Grace sniff, then lick. Smiles and giggles, even a laugh.

Creed looked over at Bailey and the guardsmen.

They still kept their distance and continued to stare at the macabre scene, all of them in awe as one Jack Russell terrier transported these scared and bruised victims back to being kids.

5

ATLANTA, GEORGIA

Amanda stared at the television screen as she clutched her stomach. Another luxury hotel. A gorgeous room on the fifteenth floor. Who needed a television in the bathroom? This room was larger than her bedroom at home. It was pristine white, the tiled floor wonderfully cool to the touch. Moments ago she had laid her curled body – fetal-position tight – on the smooth surface, her hot and sweaty cheek flat against the floor. She wished she could stay there forever, but again, the cramps jolted her. That, and Zapata pulling at her, insisting she get up and use the toilet.

'It is time,' the old woman coaxed Amanda, a

whispered calm so uncharacteristic that Amanda could hear the strain in Zapata's voice even as she tried to hide her impatience.

'I hurt so bad,' Amanda said, while her eyes stayed on the television screen and yet another guest was introduced on *The View*. 'It didn't hurt like this the last time.'

She didn't want to ask, didn't want to say it out loud, but Amanda worried that one of the balloons had burst inside her. What had happened to Lucía ... what if it was happening to her, too? Would Leandro slice open her belly before she was even dead? She couldn't stop seeing the girl slumped on the floor. She couldn't stop thinking about the knife in Leandro's hand. There had been no hesitation. *And all that blood*. Amanda had never seen anything like it.

'She was a weak girl,' Zapata said suddenly, as if she could hear Amanda's thoughts. 'You must not think about her. You are strong. Much stronger.'

The unexpected compliment pulled Amanda's attention away from the television to find the old woman's eyes. They were black stones – cold and hard, which reminded Amanda of the tiled floor, but unlike the tiles, there was absolutely nothing soothing or comforting in Zapata's eyes.

The old woman held out the drinking glass in her hand, offering it to Amanda as though it were a gift. Amanda had already drunk half a glass of the chalky liquid that she knew was a laxative.

She shook her head. 'I'll puke if I drink any more of that crap.'

Then she saw the flash of anger in the old woman's eyes – brief and electric, but shockingly powerful – before Zapata realized her mistake and stashed the anger back behind the cold stones.

'Where's Leandro?' Amanda wanted to know.

The last time, he had been there with her, stroking her back, caressing her sweat-drenched hair away from her face. His whispers had been gentle and sincere as he encouraged and praised her.

'He has other matters to attend to.'

Like getting rid of Lucía's slashed body.

But again, Amanda didn't say it out loud. Instead, she bit her lower lip and wrapped her arms tighter around her body as the pain continued to twist her insides into a knot.

'He said he would always be here with me.' She avoided Zapata's eyes. Actually, Leandro had never said such a thing, but Amanda took comfort in the small lie. She and Leandro had spent many hours alone together. How would the old woman know what had been said?

Zapata turned to leave as she muttered to herself, 'Dice muchas cosas.'

Amanda didn't understand, but from the way the old woman said it, she knew that Leandro would not be coming this time.

She wanted to return to the cold tiled floor. Her eyes found the television screen again. As she slid her body down and curled up against the pain, she watched the handsome man with the little dog take his seat in the middle of the talk-show hosts. The caption at the bottom of the screen identified them as RYDER CREED AND HIS DRUG-DETECTION DOG, GRACE.

The dog sat down at the man's feet, leaning against him, its tail thumping against the floor. It looked up at the man, almost smiling and definitely happy to be with the man.

Amanda laid her cheek on the cold floor. She closed her eyes as another wave of pain sliced through her stomach, and she thought, *That's all I am, one of Leandro's dogs.*

6

PENSACOLA BEACH

Back on land, Creed watched tourists enjoying the crowded beach even as the sun began to sink. Kids raced each other and skipped in and out of the surf with squeals of delight. The sounds and play of happy children. It made the scene on the fishing boat seem even more horrific.

He wanted to pack up his gear and head on home, but he had accepted an invitation from the flight crew to get a drink and an early dinner. Considering what they had just witnessed, the thought of food probably sounded odd to some. But for those who did this sort of thing for a living, Creed understood it was an integral coping mechanism.

It didn't bother him. Years ago he had learned to disassociate his stomach and hunger from emotion. The habit started when he was a marine and became more important when working with his search-and-rescue dogs. When they were on a cadaver search, it could take hours and be in the middle of nowhere, surrounded by miles of woods or wetlands. The dogs had to eat for energy, even if they had just found a decomposed body or body parts. The dogs didn't care if the air was filled with the stench of rotting flesh and the buzz of blowflies, so Creed had to learn not to care. Usually Hannah packed sandwiches for him along with the dogs' meals. When his dogs ate, Creed ate. And Grace was ready to eat.

He saw that Liz Bailey and Pete Kesnick had found a table on the busy patio that overlooked the Gulf. He was relieved to see just the two of them. Having peeled off his own flight suit and boots, he could still smell fish and wondered if everyone around him could smell it, too. But no one, other than Bailey and Kesnick, paid any attention to him.

In the shadow of the new and contemporary

Margaritaville Hotel, Walter's Canteen looked like a ramshackle leftover. The place had survived hurricanes Ivan and Dennis, and though it enjoyed some of the hotel's overrun, it was more popular with the locals than the tourists, many of whom came to dinner by boat and parked in a slip at the marina across the road. Some of them were also fishermen. Creed may not have noticed, but Grace did as they squeezed through the crowded tables.

'It's pretty busy,' Kesnick told him. 'So we got you a beer.'

'Thanks.'

'And a bucket of shrimp,' Bailey added, shoving aside the plate with a pile of shells from what they had already peeled and eaten.

Creed also noticed both of their bottles were almost empty, while the condensation had barely started to slide down the side of his. It'd take a lot more than a couple of beers to forget the sight of those kids lying like sardines under the floor planks.

He off-loaded his backpack and sat down, pulling Grace in close, but she was distracted by Bailey's out-stretched hand. Normally, he'd rein her in. Make her sit beside his feet. But after the day she'd had, she deserved some extra scratches. He loosened up on her leash, and Grace pranced over to Bailey.

He took a sip of the beer. It felt good going down, and the bottle made his hand slick with cold. Despite the setting sun, it was still hot. He could smell the shrimp and wondered how long it'd take to get rid of the fish smell from his nostrils.

'What happens to them now?' he asked, and could see that both Bailey and Kesnick knew what he was asking without further explanation.

It was Kesnick who attempted an answer, though he prefaced it with a shrug. 'I guess they find their families and notify them.'

'Can you let me know what you hear?'

'Sure,' Bailey told him.

Before they could continue, a waiter came scurrying over to their table.

'Sir, we can't allow you here with that dog.'

'We're outside,' Kesnick said. 'And she's a service dog.'

'Doesn't matter. There're people eating.' The guy was tall, with buffed arms and sun-streaked hair.

'It's okay,' Creed told them. He didn't have the energy to argue with a surfer probably pumped up on

Red Bull and taking his table patrol seriously. 'We'll do this another time.'

But as he started to stand, Bailey grabbed his arm.

'No, it's not okay. This dog rescued five kids today.'

'Sorry, but I don't make the rules.'

'No, you don't. Send over the owner,' she told him.

'Owner's not here tonight.'

'Yes, he is. You must be new. He's seated in the lounge. Martini. Gin, not vodka. Last bar stool by the window.'

Creed saw the waiter's face pale despite his tan skin. A vein bulged at his temple. He shot a look at the window in question. Then, without a response, he turned and made his way through the crowded tables to the lounge door.

'I don't want to get you two in trouble,' Creed said, but he could see how much Bailey and Kesnick were already enjoying this showdown. 'I almost got kicked out of this place once before.'

'Really? Because of Grace?'

'No, it was years ago. I was drunk and started a fight.'

Bailey stared at him, waiting for more. Kesnick, however, smiled and lifted his bottle of beer in salute.

The waiter was back at the lounge door, towering over a gray-haired man in a tan jumpsuit. The waiter was pointing at them, and the owner lifted his hand to shield his eyes from the sun. He said something to the waiter and sent him back inside, then he hobbled his way toward them with a scowl on his face.

'Seriously,' Creed said, 'I don't want to get you two thrown out, too.'

He was used to people treating him differently whenever he had the dogs with him, telling him where he could or couldn't park at rest areas. Warning him to keep his dogs quiet when they weren't even barking, or to keep them away from their children. But most kids liked dogs. Without parental interference, they were drawn to dogs. Their first impulse was to touch them, just like the kids on the fishing boat. Apparently it was an impulse so strong that it overrode other basic survival instincts.

'Hello, Mr Kesnick.' The gray-haired man put a hand on the flight mechanic's shoulder as he squeezed back behind his chair and scooted over to Bailey, all the while keeping his eyes on Creed. 'Hello, darling,' he greeted her as he bent down and kissed her cheek.

'Hi, Daddy.'

Creed raised an eyebrow at her and she smiled as she introduced them.

'Daddy, this is Ryder Creed and Grace. Creed, this is Walter Bailey, the owner of Walter's Canteen. He's also my father.'

'Part owner,' Walter corrected her as he shook Creed's hand from across the table. Then he took his hand and offered it to Grace to sniff. 'Sorry about the misunderstanding. Hey there, Grace.' Then to Creed, he said, 'She's a gorgeous little girl. We had a Jack Russell years ago.'

'Not that I remember,' Bailey said.

'Must have been before you were born. Addie, we called her. She was a bundle of energy. Need some water for her?'

'No, thanks,' Creed told him, and patted the backpack now on the wood-planked floor. 'I've got everything she needs. Do you mind if she eats here under the table while we do?'

'Not at all. In fact, I have the new boy bringing you all some appetizers. On the house.'

'You don't have to do that, sir.' Kesnick beat Creed in declining the offer.

'No, I insist. It's not every day I get to treat a

celebrity.' He wagged a finger at Grace then Creed. 'Two of 'em. I read the article about you in *USA Today*.'

'Daddy reads three newspapers every morning.'

'Those drug busts up in Atlanta. That was you two, right?'

'Yes, sir.'

He looked back at his daughter, concern suddenly furrowing his brow. 'You doing something with drugs out on the Gulf?'

'Don't worry. We're already back, safe and sound.'

Creed waited for her to tell him about the kids, but Walter simply nodded, accustomed to not getting to hear about his daughter's adventures until and unless she shared.

'Join us,' Kesnick offered.

'I'd like to but I'm chatting with some navy boys from Philly. Howard took them deep-sea fishing this afternoon. I'll stop back to make sure the boy-genius is taking care of you.'

He bent down to peck his daughter's cheek, again, then he pointed at Creed, his finger crooked with arthritis, his blue eyes serious. 'Those drug cartels are mean sons of bitches, excuse my French. You watch your back.'

They watched him squeeze and shuffle around the crowded tables, none of them saying a word even after he disappeared through the lounge door.

'Don't pay attention to him,' Bailey said. 'He reads a lot of thriller novels, too.' But she wasn't smiling.

7

Thunder rattled the glass. Creed rolled over to watch the lightning fork through the sky, illuminating the night outside the open window. A breeze brought in the smell of rain. He needed to shut the window before the downpour started, but he closed his eyes instead and he stayed put. Sleep didn't come easy for him. On the rare occasions when it came at all, it knocked him out completely.

He could hear a dog barking, but his eyelids were too heavy. Nearby an engine rumbled to life. The smell of diesel stung his nostrils. Another flash. His eyelids fluttered, caught a glimpse of blurred headlights, then closed again.

In the back of his mind he remembered how crowded the rest area was. Trucks hummed in back, in their own parking lot, separated from the cars and SUVs. Rain turned the wet, greasy asphalt into streaks of neon red and yellow and orange that danced and moved, the reflection of taillights and running lights coming to life. Creed's sister, Brodie, had been fascinated with the slimy smears. Leave it to Brodie, she could always see rainbows where the rest of the family saw only dirty pools of diesel. Creed remembered how she pranced from puddle to puddle, making sure she splashed in as many as possible as she ran the short distance from their car to the brick building that housed the restrooms. And although he couldn't hear her, he knew she was humming or singing the entire way. So happy, so good-natured – traits you'd never guess would be hazards.

'Her feet will be soaking wet,' Creed's father had grumbled from behind the steering wheel as he watched her.

The game was on the radio. Fourth quarter, only five minutes left, and his team was behind by three.

'Can't you shut that dog up,' he yelled over the backseat.

That was why Creed hadn't been able to escort Brodie. He had been told to take care of and shut up their family dog so his dad could at least hear 'the frickin' game.' It was bad enough that they would be driving all night and he would have to listen instead of watch. He was already mad that Creed's mom had to stay behind for a few extra days to take care of Creed's grandmother.

Ironically, years later, when Creed would find him with a bullet hole in his temple, Creed would wonder if the football game playing on the big screen in his father's living room had offered condolence or inspired madness.

But that night at the rest area, in the car with the pitter-patter of rain against the roof and the soft blue glow of the interior lights, there seemed to be nothing wrong with staying in the car while Brodie went all by herself to use the rest area's bathroom.

Now Creed heard the barking again. From the edge of consciousness he knew he needed to wake up before the dream gained traction. Before it grabbed hold and started to play in slow motion. Before it began to flicker and wrap around his mind while it slowly ripped at his heart.

He felt his body twitch. But his eyes only fluttered, lead shutters refusing to disengage. He knew what came next. *What always came next.* The dog was warning them. He could hear it barking louder now. Why hadn't they listened to the dog?

A clap of thunder jolted him awake. Creed sprung up as though someone had connected battery cables to his chest. In fact, his heart throbbed so hard that he rubbed his breastbone, half expecting to find electrodes left behind. There was nothing, not even a shirt.

It took him a minute to realize he wasn't at a rest area. He wasn't even in his Jeep. Instead, he was safe and sound in his bed, the flash of lightning revealing pieces of his loft apartment. He looked over at the alarm clock on his nightstand. The digital display had gone dark. The storm had knocked out the electricity again. There was enough tinge of light on the horizon just below the storm clouds to suggest sunrise. Unless he had fallen asleep hard and it was the next night's sunset. That had happened a few times, when exhaustion took him over so completely that it literally wiped him out for days.

From the foot of his bed Grace glanced up at him.

'I'm okay,' he told her, and the dog plopped her head back down, too exhausted to disagree with him.

He leaned over the edge and saw that Rufus hadn't budged. The old Lab was hard of hearing but had long ago earned his spot at the side of Creed's bed. Neither dog stirred as the thunder continued. Which reminded Creed, and he held his breath to listen.

The generator had kicked on. Living in the Florida Panhandle meant dealing with year-round lightning storms. That was the engine hum and the diesel smell he had mistaken for eighteen-wheelers. But there was no dog barking. As real as it seemed, it was only a part of his dream.

The breeze brought in a mist from the open window. Creed pushed himself out of bed to cross the short distance, but instead of closing the window, he let the rain spray his sweat-drenched body as he stared out over the property.

Woods bordered two sides of the fifty-plus acreage that he and Hannah had transformed into an impressive canine training facility. From this angle, even through the trees he could see the main house. It had been a dilapidated two-story colonial when Hannah convinced him they could restore it. All the other buildings on the property had to be bulldozed. Then, one by one, they built what they needed, revising and designing their plan as the business catapulted them into rapid success.

In the beginning it made perfect sense for Hannah and her boys to take the main house, while they used part of the lower level for offices. Creed insisted on a loft apartment above the dog kennels for himself. He told Hannah that he wanted to be close by to protect and care for their most valuable commodity.

Truth was, the dogs were his one constant and reliable comfort in life. And although a loft apartment above the dog kennels sounded odd, Creed had spared no expense. The open floor plan included a high-beamed cathedral ceiling, lots of windows, cherrywood floors, a wall of built-in bookcases, and a gourmet kitchen. Because he was on the road so much of the time, he had tried to create a retreat as much as a home for himself.

Still at the window, Creed noticed that the spray of rain had stopped as the wind decreased. He could see the storm clouds rolling away, the bolts of lightning reduced to flickers. The smudge of daybreak glowed orange. Now he could see the main house lights come on, one by one, while his loft remained dark.

He glanced back at the digital alarm clock, which

remained unlit. The good news was that it wasn't a widespread power outage. The bad news was that the lightning must have zapped the kennels and his loft apartment, again. This was the third time in two months.

Time to call an electrician.

Just as Creed reached for his jeans, he noticed headlights at the end of the long driveway. The vehicle had turned in, but slowed down and then stopped. The driveway was almost a quarter of a mile long, but Creed could see the entire length of it from his perch. He'd purposely made it long to keep them as far off the main road as possible. Sometimes people got lost and used it to turn around. Maybe someone had gotten lost in the storm.

He was about to shrug it off. But the vehicle didn't move. And then the headlights went out. For some reason the words of Liz Bailey's father came back to Creed: *Watch your back.*

8

During the ten minutes that it took Creed to pull on clothes and make it to the main house, the vehicle at the end of the driveway had not moved. He knocked before he opened the back door that led into the kitchen. The scent of cinnamon, baked bread, bacon, and coffee stopped him in his tracks. It wasn't until Hannah looked up and scowled at the shotgun in his hands that he remembered why he had been concerned.

'You going hunting?' she asked him as she wiped her hands and glided her large frame effortlessly from one task to another. 'Otherwise, I don't appreciate a gun in my kitchen.'

He glanced around before he remembered her boys were at Hannah's grandparents' farm for their annual two-week summer adventure. Finally he told her, 'There's a vehicle stopped at the end of the driveway.'

'Probably just someone waiting out the storm.'

'It pulled in after the rain stopped.'

'So you're gonna go shoot 'em?' She said it with a straight face, all matter-of-fact, with not a hint of sarcasm or humor. Hannah always had a way of defusing his paranoia and making what he believed was a perfectly reasonable decision sound ridiculous.

'No, of course not. Maybe scare them a little.'

He set the shotgun aside and squatted down to pet Lady, a black-and-white border collie. She greeted him with a head-butt to his thigh, making him smile and realize that she redefined the term 'lady,' but then so did Hannah, who had chosen the name for her.

Creed had found the dog along Highway 98. She'd been the victim of a hit-and-run. Her pelvis had been crushed. No tags and no one claimed her. Bright-eyed and scared, she still allowed him to pick her up. She wasn't the first dog they had mended back together. Lady, however, had failed miserably as a scent dog. She was always more interested in rounding up everyone than searching out any of the surrounding smells. Her natural instinct did make her the perfect companion for Hannah's two boys, as she watched over them and herded them away from danger.

And now Creed wondered if perhaps he was simply being overprotective. Had the incident on the boat spooked him into thinking a drug cartel would bother to come after him? Hannah was right. It was ridiculous. If they did send a hit squad, they wouldn't be so obvious as to park at the end of his driveway.

When he looked up he noticed Hannah had stopped her morning routine and was staring at him, hands on her hips, those brown eyes inspecting and examining him. He'd never been able to hide anything from her.

'Something happen yesterday? You didn't stop at the house last night.'

He stood and rubbed at his bristled jaw, but he felt it go tight despite his effort to stop it. 'We found five kids.'

'I thought you were searching for drugs on a fishing boat.'

'We were. A seventy-foot long-liner with about

eighty thousand pounds of mahi-mahi. Coast Guard had been tracking it. It had its hold full and was headed south to leave the Gulf.'

'Doing a pickup out in the middle of the water?'

'That was the suspicion, but there wasn't any cocaine. Grace found five kids. Hidden under the floorboards.'

'Good Lord! Stowaways?'

'No.' He shook his head, and his eyes left the kitchen, looking out the window as the sun crested through the trees. 'Not stowaways.' He realized how much he didn't want to think about it anymore. Didn't want to even talk about it. The incident on the boat was probably what had brought on his nightmare about Brodie.

'They're trafficking kids now,' she said without waiting for an explanation.

She turned back to the stove, still shaking her head, but thankfully not expecting Creed to tell her more. At least not now.

'That's a lot of food.' He needed to focus on something else and already found his mouth watering from the combination of aromas. Breakfast foods were always his favorite comfort foods.

'Andy's taking everyone through basic drills this morning.'

'I'll be out at the kennels if anyone needs me. Electricity is out.'

'Again? Seems like every time we have lightning, it's knocking it out. You sure you don't have one too many gadgets that's tripping everything up?'

'The more self-reliant the dogs are, the less work around here.'

She rolled her eyes at him. It was an old argument, but the truth was, Creed wasn't completely comfortable using so much automation for this exact reason. What happens when the power is out? He liked using the most advanced technology available, as long as he could have a backup system if anything malfunctioned.

'I've got everything running on auxiliary for now. I think I might be able to mess with it and get it back running.'

'I'll check at Segway House and see if we have any electricians. Wouldn't hurt to have a professional take a look. You know I don't like you messin' with hot wires. Believe me, you would not look good with curly hair.'

'Very funny.'

That's when Creed saw the headlights coming up the driveway. 'Looks like our stalker decided to be sociable after all.'

Hannah glanced out the window.

'Oh mercy, I forgot to tell you. I hired a new worker.' She started shutting off burners, putting on lids, and setting aside utensils. 'Figures he'd be early.'

'So early that he had to sit and wait at the end of our driveway?' He slipped back into his anger.

'Now be nice, Rye. This guy's had a tough time. He reminds me a little bit of you.'

Creed shook his head and smiled. He was the one who brought home discarded and damaged dogs, while Hannah did the same with people.

By the time the man parked and was getting out of his car, Creed was marching ahead of Hannah, the shotgun barrel down and relaxed in his right hand. He'd set this guy straight on appropriate etiquette. Being early for work was a good thing, but hanging out at the end of his driveway was bordering on creepy.

'Rye, just hold up there a minute or two.'

Hannah was trying to keep pace with him and she

sounded a little too nervous about their introduction. She volunteered at a halfway house. That's where she met runaways, recovering drug addicts, and abused wives. But Creed trusted her judgment when she brought one of them home. He was beginning to think she wasn't too sure about this guy.

At first glance the man looked young. Creed guessed he wasn't even twenty. Hannah had said the guy reminded her of him, but Creed didn't see any resemblance. The man was four or five inches shorter than Creed. He was clean-shaven and wore his hair close-cropped. He wasn't smiling when he met Creed's eyes. There was something there – something hard and dark. Distrust, maybe a little anger. He didn't flinch when he noticed the shotgun.

He came around the side of his vehicle and that's when Creed saw that the right sleeve of his denim shirt hung loose from the elbow down. He watched with those intense eyes as Creed noticed, almost as if he was daring Creed to dismiss him or say something inappropriate.

'Jason, this is my partner, Ryder Creed,' Hannah said, coming around to stand in between the two of them as if she might have to referee. 'Jason's been home from Afghanistan for a few months. Looking for work. You know how hard it is to find a job these days.'

'Unless you think there's a problem with me working here,' Jason said.

And there it was. Creed could hear the challenge in the young man's voice, even as he lifted his chin. Lady had followed them out of the house. She joined Crockett, a retired rottweiler who could still be intimidating if he wanted to be. The pair began sniffing Jason's boots.

'Hiring is up to Hannah,' Creed said, and pretended not to notice as the young man slowly opened his left hand for the dogs to sniff while still trying to maintain his rigid tough-guy stance. In that small gesture he could see that Jason was comfortable with them. He didn't flinch, didn't step back. Instead, he had silently opened up for them to check him out.

'I trust her judgment,' Creed added. 'Besides, the dogs don't care whether you have one hand or three. Just don't park and sit at the end of my driveway, okay?' He nodded at Hannah and turned to leave.

'Park? What are you talking about?' Jason asked.

Creed looked back at the man and met his eyes.

There wasn't a hint of embarrassment, guilt, or anything that looked like a lie. Only confusion. Creed glanced at Hannah, and for the first time that morning, he saw a flicker of concern.

9

COLOMBIA

Amanda could smell him before she heard him come into the room — a combination of sweat and that greasy hair gel he liked to use. She was still angry with him ... and maybe a bit scared of him. Right now she'd hang on to the anger. That was easier to deal with, so she kept her eyes closed, pretending to be asleep, though she was far from it. Back in the hot, humid room that she called home, she hugged a sweat-drenched pillow and tried not to think of the cool tiled floor and the luxury hotel that she'd left behind.

It had been a tough trip back. The nausea continued, despite getting all the balloons to pass. She had checked each one herself, pushing Zapata away. She had touched each one, rolling and feeling to make certain none of the rubber had broken or the ties had come undone. Amanda had counted and counted again until the old woman started looking at her as if she had gone mad.

And maybe she had. Maybe a little bit, because Amanda could swear that something felt ripped inside her.

Coming back through the airport, the customs officer had scrutinized her passport for a beat too long. Adding to Amanda's discomfort. No one had prepared her for what she should do if they detained her. There had only been warnings, no instructions.

'You just came into the country,' the man said, his eyes narrowing as he ran them up and down Amanda's body. 'What's the rush to leave?'

Before she could answer, Zapata had laughed. A sound Amanda had never heard coming from the old woman's mouth. It sounded so real, so genuine, so much like real laughter.

'Parents with too much money,' Zapata told the officer, as if there might be a secret bond between the two of them. 'They want what they want. I just follow their instructions.'

It made Amanda glance up at the man. Her eyes caught his and she looked away. It was enough for her to see that the man might be of Hispanic origin, brown skin and dark eyes. When he spoke again, she could hear a subtle accent, thicker now, as though Zapata had given him permission. He nodded like he understood the type, while he kept examining Amanda.

That was when it hit her. As Amanda watched his eyes take in her designer jeans, the makeup Zapata had insisted she put on, the fancy jewelry Leandro had given her, and the leather handbag, Amanda realized that all of it was part of her disguise.

She had thought Leandro had given her these things as gifts because he was grateful, because he cared about her. Instead, they were only part of a costume to make her look the role she was playing – the spoiled, rich American kid whose parents could afford to have her go back and forth from their Colombian vacation hacienda to their Atlanta home.

Now she heard Leandro whisper her name in the dark. He didn't reach for the lamp. As he made his way to her bed, she watched him through the veil of her eyelashes, not daring to move a muscle.

She felt his weight on the edge of the bed as he sat down, and she squeezed her eyes shut. Only then did she realize she had been holding her breath. He'd know for sure that she was pretending. Why hadn't she thought to fake her breathing?

'Amanda,' he whispered again, as though he were playing along.

She felt his fingers touch her cheek. So gentle. And suddenly he was stroking her hair.

'I do not want you to think about Lucía and what you saw.'

The knot twisted in her stomach as his words immediately brought back the image of the knife in his hand. Of it plunging into the girl.

'She was not strong like you.' He kept his voice low and quiet and soft. It was the same tone he had used with her before, when he gave her the gifts and when he praised her.

'Lucía was weak,' he continued, and so did his fingers. 'It is her father's fault that she is dead. It was his debt. Instead of paying it, he sent his daughter to do what he himself would never do. That was his decision to give up his own flesh and blood. He is a small, stupid man.'

His hand moved from her hair to her shoulder, gentle caresses.

'You know how he mourned the news of his daughter's death? A real man would put himself in place to pay off his debt. But no. You know what he did instead?'

But Amanda knew he wasn't waiting for her answer as his fingers slid down her arm.

'He sent me yet another one of his daughters. This one is even younger than Lucía. I am told the bastard has three more at home. He is willing to run through daughters before he is willing to pay back his debt like a real man. You see what I have to deal with, Amanda? How difficult my job is?'

He shifted his weight on the bed, and now she could feel his breath on her neck. His fingers continued their familiar path, still so gentle and caressing.

'But you, Amanda. You are strong. Things will only get easier for you, I promise.' His lips grazed her ear, and despite her anger and fear, her body was betraying her, yielding to him as he whispered, 'I am so proud of you.'

No one had ever said they were proud of her before, and so she let Leandro show her just how proud he was.

ONE WEEK LATER
MONDAY

10

THE EDGE OF THE POTOMAC RIVER

WASHINGTON, DC.

FBI agent Maggie O'Dell watched from the riverbank and wondered when she had started associating dead bodies with political fallout. Actually, that was a step up. Floaters used to be a reminder of her divorce. Years ago she'd lost her wedding ring while helping to pull a body from the Charles River. It had been cold that day, the water frigid. Debris ripped apart her latex gloves. Her hands were too numb to care or feel the cuts and scratches from the sharp branches and piercing vines.

It wasn't until hours later, after she had warmed and cleaned her hands – pouring rubbing alcohol over them – that she noticed the ring was gone. The worst part – she didn't remember feeling sadness or even regret, but rather, a calm acceptance. The lost ring seemed to only symbolize what she had avoided acknowledging. Her marriage had been lost long before the ring slipped off her finger and disappeared into the cold, dark waters of the Charles River.

O'Dell wiped sweat off her forehead. Today was the opposite of that day, with heat and humidity at the other end of the spectrum. It made it challenging for the forensic recovery team, but they were being careful. Not an easy task. Even from fifty feet out she could see that the floater was swollen and bloated. That meant eight to ten days in the water.

That many days in the water, along with the summer heat, made the recovery even more difficult. The skin would be loose. Tissue and organs would be fragile and susceptible to damage with the gentlest of knocks and jolts. The skin of hands and feet tended to separate from the bone.

'I can't figure out why you're here,' Stan Wenhoff said to her.

The question could have been taken as an insult, but O'Dell knew the District's medical examiner well enough not to take offense, or at least not to take it personally.

He stood next to O'Dell on the muddy riverbank. They were shoulder to shoulder. Neither of them took their eyes off the action in the water. Stan Wenhoff had been the District's medical examiner for almost twenty years. Over the last decade O'Dell had worked with him on dozens of cases, ever since she was a forensic fellow at Quantico.

She and Stan had a tempered relationship, but as a rule Stan didn't much like anyone in law enforcement. He didn't like having them stand over his shoulder during autopsies, second-guessing or questioning him. And he had no patience for newbies making inappropriate jokes, or worse – getting wobbly in the knees or freaking out about maggots. Nothing personal. It had taken O'Dell a few years and a whole lot of maggots – which she truly hated but had not once freaked out over – to understand how Stan worked.

As for his comment, she didn't take offense. She had no idea why she was here either. Lately her boss, FBI Assistant Director Raymond Kunze, had been sending her on all kinds of wild-goose chases. Several of them involved some form of payback or political cover-up.

It was a price he seemed willing to pay in order to stay in the good graces of certain senators and congressmen, along with a handful of presidential advisers.

'Any chance the body's been dismembered in some way?' she asked Stan in response to why she might be here.

'Don't know. Could be.'

'Well, there you go.' She said it matter-of-factly. No sarcasm intended, and Stan didn't question or comment further.

A part of her hated that she'd become a de facto expert on dismembered bodies. In her career as a profiler, she'd seen body parts stuffed into take-out containers, fishing coolers, Mason jars, and even wrapped in butcher paper inside a freezer. But standing in the midsummer heat and anticipating the insects, as well as the smell, she'd almost rather deal with a few body parts than a floater.

Bodies tended to sink in water. It was one of those things movies and TV shows rarely got right. It wasn't until days later, when gases started to form and collect, that the body began to float. From the apparent buoyance of this one, O'Dell suspected the gases were in full force.

'So what are *you* doing here?' she asked Stan, suspicious of why he had taken this assignment instead of sending one of his assistants. For as much as he hated law enforcement, Stan did enjoy the media. If there was even a whiff of a high-profile case, Stan tended to keep it for himself.

'What do you mean?' he asked halfheartedly.

Still, neither glanced at the other. The recovery team was making progress toward them.

'Why would you choose to be here in this heat? I'm guessing there must be something that piqued your interest.'

Out of the corner of her eye she saw Stan shrug and knew this was the most admission she'd get from the man. He surprised her when he said, 'The call that came in said there was "a package in the Potomac."'

'A package? That's creative.'

'But that's not even the interesting part,' Stan said, and finally he glanced over at her. 'The caller promised that this was only the first.'

'Oh, wonderful.' O'Dell restrained a groan. Now she understood why she had been sent here. It was just another frickin' serial killer case to add to her collection.

11

'The body's been in the water at least a week.' Stan offered what O'Dell already knew.

The recovery team had splayed the floater on a tarp spread out on the muddy riverbank. They wouldn't even attempt to fit the victim inside a body bag. Instead, they'd wrap the tarp as gently as possible around the bloated flesh, sealing up the ends for transport to the morgue. In the meantime, the team backed away and let Stan and O'Dell take a look before one of them started taking a series of photographs.

The body was male. That was about all that O'Dell could determine. But that alone was unusual. More than seventy per cent of serial killers' victims were female. Being in the water for a week would suggest the body would be washed clean, but debris dangled from the man's hair, long and wet slimy weeds that made it look like snakes were coiling around his head and into his face. Pieces of his flesh had already been compromised, scavengers in the water – fish or insects – teasing and tasting to see if this foreign object was something they could feed on.

O'Dell watched as Stan's short, stubby fingers took temperature readings. Slow and methodical, he began his on-site checklist. She stood over the body, but kept out of the medical examiner's way, even making sure that she didn't cast a shadow over him. But while he worked, she continued her own visual examination.

She had chased her share of serial killers in the past decade. It wasn't something that she chose to do. It wasn't as if when she was a little girl, she'd said, 'When I grow up I want to be an FBI profiler.' Just like her reputation for being an expert on dismembered bodies, hunting down killers had also developed into an accidental specialty.

O'Dell had an eye for details that others missed. She recognized patterns and suspected rituals while her colleagues thought she must be crazy. The strangest statistics and the most absurd facts stayed planted in her brain. She could easily become obsessed with a killer's MO, learning and gleaning psychological tells that the killer never intended to share. And once in a while – to O'Dell's detriment – a killer became obsessed with her, too.

Stan had said the caller who tipped off authorities about this victim had called it 'a package.' It wouldn't be the first time a serial killer had made up a clever reference for his victim. Nor would it be the first time that one called and alerted authorities, anxious to display his work. But so far, O'Dell couldn't see anything that made this floater stand out as a homicide, let alone as the victim of a serial murderer.

She noticed marks around the man's wrists and ankles, indents into the now bloated flesh that could have been made from ligatures. She wanted to take a closer look but stopped herself. She waited until Stan noticed them, but the medical examiner seemed to be focused on something underneath the corpse.

'What is it?' O'Dell asked.

Stan waved her off while at the same time motioning for the forensic team, calling them over.

'Can we roll him over? At least onto his side?'

O'Dell squatted down beside Stan, not waiting for an invitation. She could see the tiny welts on the inside of the man's legs that had gotten the medical examiner's attention. They looked like insect bites. That didn't seem unusual considering how long the body had been in the water.

They gently lifted and rolled the swollen corpse onto the left side and exposed the backside.

'Holy crap,' one of the CSU techs said. 'What the hell is that?'

The entire back of the man's body was covered in tiny welts, large patches of what looked like a rash on his calves, buttocks, and shoulders. What attracted O'Dell's focus was the tattoo that spread over the entire left shoulder blade. It looked like the Grim Reaper, only there was something very different about it, despite being marred by the skin welts. It was distinctly female, clad in an elaborate robe and holding a scythe along with other items that were lost in the eruptions.

The others dismissed the tattoo. Stan poked and pressed the patches with a gloved index finger. One of the CSU techs began taking photos. O'Dell stood up and pulled out her cell phone. She zoomed her camera in on the tattoo and took several shots.

Taking a step back, she noticed that the worst areas – the most densely rashed – were those that would be in contact – unavoidable contact – with the ground or a surface, if the man had been restrained on his back. Maybe tied down. She pulled her eyes away to glance at the wrists and ankles. This close, she could see that ligatures – which were gone now – had cut deep into the skin.

'Was it something in the water?' another of the CSU techs asked.

But Stan was already shaking his head.

'I can't say for sure until I take some samples, but I think this happened pre-mortem.'

'I've never seen anything like it.'

'I have,' Stan said as he pressed his latex-covered index finger against a particularly nasty area on the victim's shoulder. 'One other time. Not this bad. Nothing like this.'

'They're insect bites,' O'Dell guessed.

On closer inspection, the tiny welts looked like pus-filled blisters. And Stan was right – the skin wouldn't continue to produce pus and blister like this after the heart had stopped.

'They're not just any insect bite.' He looked over at

O'Dell and waited for her eyes. 'They're fire ants. And nobody just falls onto a gigantic mound of fire ants and lies there.'

'Not unless they're tied down.' She pointed to the wrists and ankles, which were bloated over the telltale markings.

'If I'm correct about these being fire ants, then this didn't happen to him anywhere near this river,' Stan told her.

'How can you be certain about that?'

'Fire ants can't survive in areas that freeze during the winter.' He said it without a doubt.

'So the killer tortured him somewhere else.'

'Not just somewhere else. It'd have to be at least five or six hundred miles south of here.'

'Oh great. So the original crime scene could be anywhere.' She pointed to the victim's shoulder. 'Any of you recognize the tattoo?' she asked.

The tech with the camera hunched over it and clicked off a couple of close-ups. Then he shrugged and said, 'Not sure.'

O'Dell crossed her arms over her chest and stared out at the water of the Potomac. So delivering the 'package' here must also serve some twisted purpose in the killer's MO. You didn't have to go far along this river to see monuments and historical landmarks from the water's edge. And once again, she couldn't help wondering if her boss had sent her out on yet another political goose chase.

12

Falco stared at his boots. It was better than watching the spiders. He hated spiders. So he kept his eyes on his boots. Mud globbed into the seams where the leather met the sole. The toes were smeared, the heels caked, leaving no signs of the high-polished condition he obsessed over. He had other boots but these were his favorites. These made him walk like a cowboy, and he liked that. They had cost him more than his poor mother made in a month.

Falco had grown up watching American Westerns, old black-and-white movies that made the actors look tough, the landscape unforgiving, and the women more vulnerable. He liked to wear white button-down shirts with short sleeves and black jeans. Black and white had become his signature. Sometimes Falco even dreamed in black and white. It made the blood look like black motor oil. Cocaine was already white. Lately his dreams seemed to be covered in blood and cocaine ... fire ants and spiders.

Falco's obsession with black and white made it clear – perhaps it was a sign that even his Catholic mother couldn't dismiss – that he was meant to be an apprentice under the Iceman. That code name brought with it a reputation, and at just its mention, Falco had seen the toughest men show fear, as though an injection of ice had been driven into their veins.

Few had ever seen the Iceman or met him. Those who bragged about getting a glimpse usually didn't live long enough to verify their description. He knew that would be his destiny if he were ever to betray his new mentor. Now Falco realized that no one would believe him anyway, even if he gave an accurate description. The man's features were bland, ordinary, and unremarkable. Easy to forget.

Choosing to be called 'the Iceman,' although clever, wouldn't give away the man's real identity. After all, an assassin 'iced' people for a living. Of course, Falco understood there were other reasons, deeper meanings for this nickname. It wasn't much of a trick, but no one questioned it and neither would Falco dare to.

'They're hungry today.' The Iceman's voice brought Falco's attention to the tabletop, where he had been trying to avoid looking.

He didn't want to watch inside the Plexiglas box as the spiders fed on the carcasses he had helped collect for this very purpose. Their long spindly legs worked like tweezers, dissecting, pulling, yanking. The Iceman was teasing them with food, only to swipe it away. But these buggers were fast ... and aggressive. Faster than Falco had ever seen.

The Iceman said they were 'special ones ... deadly ones,' and Falco found himself grateful. He wouldn't be asked to handle them with bare skin like the others. These required gloves and a delicate touch, and thankfully, the Iceman didn't believe Falco was ready or skilled enough, so Falco might luck out and not have to handle them at all.

'They're Brazilian wandering spiders,' the Iceman continued, and Falco knew there was a lesson coming. He didn't mind. He actually liked that the assassin considered him worthy. 'Their genus is *Phoneutria*. It's

Greek for "murderess," which is quite appropriate because they are the world's most venomous. One sting is more powerful than a rattlesnake bite.'

He glanced back and Falco knew it was to check his reaction. Satisfied, the Iceman nodded. He poked a long stick through a carefully drilled hole in the side of the spider case. Falco watched as several of the spiders attacked the stick, rearing up on their hind legs. They were fast . . . so incredibly fast. Two raced up the stick until they ran into the Plexiglas wall.

'See how they defend themselves? Instead of running away, they attack. They're very aggressive that way. They have to be because they don't make or stay in webs. Their habit is to wander around in search of prey at night. Then they seek shelter in dark places during the day – log piles, boxes, shoes, and in bunches of bananas. That's usually where they'll leave their hatchlings, attached to the peel. It looks like nothing more than a puff of cotton.'

The Iceman pulled the stick out and the spiders continued advancing up it until the stick disappeared out the small hole and they were forced to drop down or cling to the inside wall of the box.

'Do you remember what I told you the last time?' he

asked, but now he remained bent over his spiders, his eyes not leaving them, his back to Falco.

Thankfully, he couldn't see Falco's eyes dart from side to side, trying to think what it was the man wanted him to remember about the last time. Immediately his mind conjured up the image of how the ants had covered the man's naked body so quickly, red-black streams of them racing and pouring over the skin like water. And just then a trickle of sweat broke free and slid down his back. It took effort to keep from shuddering at the thought of those ants crawling and biting.

'Find what matters to a man,' Falco said, as if, of course, that was the first thing that entered his head. It had to be what the Iceman wanted.

'What else?'

'Find out what matters most to him, then crush it. Discover his worst fears and make them come true.'

The Iceman nodded. 'If you're successful, he'll beg you to kill him just to put him out of his misery.'

Falco knew that was the Iceman's signature and why so many feared him. Other cartels sent hit men and death squads to cut the heads off their enemies and dismember their bodies, leaving them in the streets or hanging from bridges as a warning. The Iceman could find you no matter where you tried to hide, and he would destroy your life and your mind, as well as your body.

'Their venom includes a neurotoxin that acts on the nervous system and muscles. The initial bite causes intense pain that spreads through the body and shocks the muscles. It's said that men who are bitten can experience painful, long-lasting erections. What an interesting fate for our Casanova, yes?'

Falco felt a shiver slide down his back. He knew the Iceman didn't expect him to answer, and he remained quiet.

'Bring him in,' the Iceman told him, suddenly jerking his head in the direction of the doorway. He said it loud enough to be heard in the next room. 'They're ready for him.'

Falco's boot heels clicked on the cheap linoleum, even with the mud that had started to dry. He liked the sound – a click then a clack – a stride that announced confidence. Before he crossed the threshold he could hear the man in the other room already whimpering. No matter how much Falco hated spiders, he knew that by the end of the day this guy was going to hate them even more. And that made Falco smile.

13

Maggie O'Dell sat at a corner table in the cafeteria. The window looked down at the beginning of the forest. From her perch she could see the unmarked trailhead. It was overgrown and easy to miss unless you were looking for it. O'Dell was one of the few who used this path into the pine forest and onto the running trails that forked and wound through the trees.

Right now she wished she had her running gear on and she could escape. Even the heat and humidity would be a welcome relief. She'd already retreated from her cramped office down in the Behavioral

Science Unit, six floors below ground. Lately she found herself needing a window, to see the outside and the sky. Sometimes even the elevator trip down made her feel like she might suffocate from the walls of earth surrounding her.

She knew her claustrophobia was progressing but she didn't dare tell anyone. Assistant Director Kunze would find a way to use it against her. She'd learned years ago to hide any vulnerabilities and discovered early on that it was best not to remind her male colleagues that she was different. She wore form-hiding suits: navy or black, sometimes brown or copper. No jewelry, other than a watch, nothing that could get pulled or caught or grabbed. No spiked heels, only leather flats had become a part of her uniform. And never, ever anything pink.

She had the cafeteria to herself, if you didn't count the sounds coming from back in the kitchen. O'Dell hadn't been seated for five minutes when Helen – who had been a reliable and constant force in the cafeteria for longer than any agent could remember – brought out two coveted chocolate-frosted cake doughnuts on a plate and set them on the table in front of O'Dell.

'You're getting too skinny,' she told the agent,

pursing her lips to confine her smile, obviously pleased with herself for remembering how much O'Dell loved doughnuts, and that chocolate-frosted ones were her favorite. As quickly as Helen put the plate down, she pivoted on her tiny feet and scurried back toward the kitchen.

'Thank you,' O'Dell shouted, but the woman didn't take time to turn, instead she raised her bird-like hand to wave her acknowledgment.

A run would have been better at calming her, but she bit into the soft cake doughnut and decided this was a well-deserved treat for putting up with Kunze's floater assignment.

She had brought her laptop, a notebook, pen, and a color printout of the photo she had snapped of the victim's tattoo. It hadn't taken her long to find similar images, despite the red pustules that marred this victim's skin. Her first impression had been wrong, but not by much. The tattoo wasn't a version of the Grim Reaper but rather a female skeleton referred to as Santa Muerte, the saint of death.

Turns out people prayed to Santa Muerte for 'otherworldly help' for a variety of things, such as landing better jobs or stopping a lover from cheating. O'Dell had been raised Catholic, but the idea of praying to some mediator other than God had always seemed like a waste of time and effort. Her mother, however, prayed to Saint Anthony when she couldn't find something and invoked Saint Christopher before she stepped from the Jetway onto an airplane. Of course, the prayers to her favorite saints were usually fortified with her earthly companions, Jim Beam and Johnnie Walker.

Having tracked serial killers, mass murderers, and terrorists, O'Dell had grown weary of and impatient with those who used religious icons and ideology simply to promote and validate their predilections. So she wasn't surprised when she discovered that some prayed to Santa Muerte for fending off wrongdoing and carrying out vengeance. Nor was she surprised to learn that Mexican and Colombian drug runners often sought out Santa Muerte's protection to ward off law enforcement. Safe houses set up shrines with miniature altars. Smugglers placed small statues of the saint on the dashboards of their vehicles, even as they drove across the border.

The more O'Dell read, the more she believed the victim from the river probably didn't tattoo his left shoulder blade with the saint so he could find a better job. Chances are it was to protect him from the job he already had. And O'Dell had made up her mind about the man before her cell phone started vibrating on the tabletop.

She glanced at the caller ID as she grabbed the phone. It was an extension she recognized from the ME's office.

'This is Agent O'Dell.'

'I'm confirming fire ants,' Stan Wenhoff said without an introduction. 'The blisters contain a toxic alkaloid venom called solenopsin. It's from the class of piperidines. The liquid is both insecticidal and antibiotic. Odd combination, I know.'

'So fire ants inject this when they bite?'

'Fire ants bite only to get a grip. They actually sting and inject from their abdomen.'

'Impressive little buggers. Can this stuff cause death?'

'This many stings could certainly have sent him into anaphylaxis. He'd have difficulty breathing, rapid heart rate. His throat would swell. Certainly may have contributed to his death. His lungs and heart tissue showed signs of congestion, consistent with undue pressure. Probable cause of death was suffocation. I need to wait for blood analysis results, but I suspect a high concentration of cocaine will have also contributed to his demise.'

'What about the ligature marks?'

'Definitely restrained. Both the wrists and ankles. I can't estimate for how long, but there was a good amount of struggle.'

'I'm looking at similar images of the tattoo,' O'Dell told him.

Before she could go on, Stan interrupted. 'And you're discovering it might be linked to the drug trade.'

'So you recognize it?'

'No, can't say that I do. But I'm guessing a man who puts a tattoo of a female skeleton that looks like the Grim Reaper on his back, a man who may have died of a drug overdose and who was most likely tortured by being tied down on top of a massive mound of fire ants ... well, it wouldn't take a stretch of the imagination to guess this is drug-related.'

'Dumping the body in the river could be a warning, but why in the Potomac? You said you believe he died somewhere down South. Do you still believe that?'

'You're free to double-check, but my recollection is

that fire ants don't exist in areas that periodically have temperatures below freezing. Messes up their whole colonization thing. Besides, I'm guessing he probably died closer to his home.'

'And you know where that is?'

'Yes. I can even tell you his name.'

The offer surprised O'Dell enough that she hesitated before asking, 'How are you magically able to do that?'

'Actually, no magic at all. I found a driver's license shoved halfway down his throat. And despite the fact that he is currently a bit bloated, the resemblance is enough that I'm quite certain it's his.'

14

O'Dell stopped in her office to collect copies from her printer. She used it as a detour to dilute her frustration before she confronted her boss. Everything about 'the package in the Potomac' – from the tattoo to the driver's license shoved down the victim's throat to the dumping of the body in a public place – was adding up to be some kind of drug-related hit.

Why had she been sent? She specialized in profiling killers, tracking them, and stopping them before they killed again. But if this was a drug-cartel hit, it should be investigated by the DEA.

And that's exactly what she intended to ask AD Kunze when she showed him a copy of Trevor Bagley's driver's license. She had obtained a printout from the Alabama Department of Motor Vehicles, but she included the copy Stan Wenhoff had emailed her of the crumpled, bloody original that he had removed from the man's throat.

The creases in the laminated card made it difficult to identify Bagley. The bloodstains that had seeped behind the lamination suggested that the victim was still bleeding when his killer forced it down his throat. But Stan had confirmed the card alone would not have caused a suffocation that led to the man's death. That, he still maintained, was due to the cocaine and the fire ants.

Still, O'Dell wanted AD Kunze to see the mess and had even used the color option on her printer to make a copy of the driver's license, along with a photo of the bloated corpse and the shot she had of the tattoo.

She marched down the hallway, through the lobby, and headed for the assistant director's closed door.

'He's with someone,' his secretary told her. When she realized O'Dell wasn't going to stop, she jumped out of her chair and shouted, 'Someone is in there with him.'

O'Dell knocked, two short taps. Ignoring the secretary coming up quickly behind her, she pushed the door open before Kunze could respond. He looked up from behind his desk, surprise registering on his face before he scowled, first at O'Dell, then at his secretary, who had stayed back in the doorway. Across the desk from Kunze was, indeed, a visitor. And when the woman turned to look over her shoulder at the intruders, it was O'Dell's turn to be surprised.

'Senator Delanor-Ramos?'

O'Dell saw the woman flinch and realized she should have left off the Ramos. The senator had been doing everything possible to disassociate herself from her ex-husband, and with good reason.

'Call me Ellie,' Senator Delanor said, standing and meeting O'Dell with an outstretched hand. 'It's good to see you again, Agent O'Dell.'

Less than a year ago the senator had used her political connections, including Assistant Director Kunze, when she was concerned about her then husband, George Ramos, and her two children. They had gone out in their houseboat on the Gulf of Mexico and gotten caught in a night of brutal thunderstorms.

But Ramos had fooled everyone: the authorities, his friends, his family, even his wife. He was using his kids and the storm as a cover to make a drug pickup in the middle of the Gulf. O'Dell and her partner, R. J. Tully, had been sent to rescue Ramos and his kids. Instead, they ended up arresting him.

'I didn't mean to interrupt,' O'Dell said.

'Yes, you did.' AD Kunze glared at her. 'Or you wouldn't have barged into my office.'

'I'm so sorry, sir,' his secretary said. 'I did tell her—'

'That's fine, Ms Holloway. I'm sure it must be something terribly important.' He continued to glare at O'Dell before he shifted his attention back to the senator. 'I'm sorry for the interruption, Ellie.'

'No, not at all. I should let you all get to your work,' Senator Delanor said. 'Raymond, perhaps you can call me later.'

He nodded, and O'Dell could swear she saw a look exchange between the two, one that seemed more intimate than professional. Nevertheless, Senator Delanor headed for the door, brisk, confident steps in three-inch heels. O'Dell couldn't help thinking that the junior senator from Florida looked like a model, which probably caused some to underestimate her. The woman carried herself like a CEO for a Fortune 500 company, but she was still a politician, and O'Dell didn't trust politicians.

Self-preservation seemed to trump everything else

with them. O'Dell had stuck her neck out for this one's family, and the senator's presence here today only made O'Dell more suspicious of Kunze's motives for sending her to oversee the retrieval of the package in the Potomac. Was he using her again to repay some political favor?

Raymond Kunze had been O'Dell's boss for less than two years. He would never be able to fill the previous assistant director's shoes. Kyle Cunningham had been an icon at Quantico. To O'Dell, he had been a mentor and, in some cases, even a father figure. His death had left the entire department feeling his absence. Perhaps Kunze came into the position with a chip on his shoulder, knowing he could never replace Cunningham.

Whatever the reason, he appeared to take it out on O'Dell over and over again, as if making her prove her worth. He had sent her into the eye of a hurricane to investigate a cooler full of body parts. Last fall he had her 'stop off' in the Nebraska Sandhills to check on cow carcasses that had been mysteriously ravaged. And then there was the storm on the Gulf that he sent her into to retrieve Senator Delanor's husband and children. Each and every time, O'Dell stumbled onto something murkier, uncovering secrets and even con-spiracies – and in Senator Delanor's husband's case, illegal dealings. She no longer trusted her boss's motives.

The door had barely closed and O'Dell continued her march to Kunze's desk. Instead of slapping the sheets of paper down in front of him, she placed them respectfully on the desktop, her compensation for barging in and interrupting.

He glanced at the papers and shook his head. 'So what is it that has you all hot under the collar?'

She bit her lower lip to stop a comeback. Every time she thought she had made some headway with this man, he erased it with another degrading comment like this.

'Why don't you just tell me what you know and save me a bunch of time?'

'What are you talking about?'

'The package in the Potomac.' She pointed for him to take a closer look. 'It's a drug hit, isn't it?'

He rubbed his square jaw and took a deep breath, glancing at the top copy of the mangled driver's license. In another life, Raymond Kunze could have been an NFL defensive back. Probably where he got his witty repartee. Usually he wore blazers that fit him a size too small, emphasizing his massive shoulders and tight abs. But the colors he chose – today's was a shiny emerald green – made him look more like a cheap bouncer at a nightclub.

'What makes you think it's a drug hit?'

She pulled out the photo of the victim's left shoulder blade and set it on top.

'A tattoo? That's your proof?'

She pulled out the photocopy of the crumpled, bloody driver's license and laid it next to the tattoo, as if they were cards in a deck and she was presenting him with a blackjack.

'A driver's license? Why are you wasting my time with this, Agent O'Dell? It looks like you have plenty of pieces to the puzzle, so you might be able to do what I sent you to do – *investigate*.'

She stood still, watching him and trying to determine whether or not he already knew any of this. Had she jumped to conclusions?

'You're making a serious judgment on poor' – he sorted through the pages again to find the man's name – 'Trevor Bagley.'

'Are you saying this isn't a hit by a drug cartel?'

'I have no idea, Agent O'Dell.' But he didn't look up at her. There was something he still wasn't telling her. 'I suggest you go do your job and find out.'

'Stan Wenhoff believes Bagley was restrained ... tied down. There are ligature marks on his wrists and ankles. He thinks he spent some time lying on a mound of fire ants. His entire back' – she pointed out the photocopy – 'is covered in tiny pustules.'

Kunze winced. 'And why don't you think this is the work of a serial killer?'

She shifted her weight from one foot to the other. Crossed her arms over her chest.

'I don't know that for sure.'

'That's right, you don't. I suggest you get back to work, Agent O'Dell.'

When she didn't move he looked up at her and pointed to the door.

'Please shut it on your way out.' He pulled a file from his stack, shoving aside the pages she had placed on his desk and dismissing her with an exaggerated sigh of frustration.

She turned and left.

15

Ryder Creed never thought he'd actually be anxious to go back to searching for dead bodies. He was, however, certain he was finished with drugs. Hannah had promised this would be the last day, at least for a while.

They had been at it for hours. He'd refused to let Grace work on the tarmac today because of the heat. So instead of inspecting checked luggage before it made its way to baggage claim, they were inside the international terminal. They had been walking up and down Concourse F as hundreds of passengers arrived and were processed.

Creed kept Grace moving through the federal inspection station, along the carousels where the assortment of suitcases, duffel bags, backpacks, and boxes rode conveyor belts. He and Grace weaved through and circled around them and the security checkpoint, then they started the same route all over again.

His badge and Grace's vest gave them access to anywhere they chose to go with barely a nod or a glance from the US Customs and Border Protection officers. By now, Creed and Grace were well known. Even Grace recognized some of her favorite CBP officers, especially those who had given her treats or stopped to pet her. Both were things Creed did not appreciate people doing with his dogs while they were working, but Grace was an exception. The high-energy Jack Russell needed more interaction to keep her from getting bored.

In assignments like this, a dog handler's top priority was to keep the dog engaged and motivated. A dog that tired from being in the same place and only ran through the motions would be antsy to leave and might miss an alert. The dog should never consider it work. It was supposed to be fun and interesting.

Creed remembered his marine unit sergeant drilling it into him: 'Make the search more exciting than pee on a tree.' Whatever the dog wants and needs, the dog gets.

The marines even gave their canine comrades a military rank one notch above their handlers to reinforce that the dogs receive and deserve respect. It was something that Creed kept in the forefront of his mind, and something he made sure the handlers who he trained did, as well.

It was almost time for a break when he noticed Grace start to sniff the air. She pulled him along, toenails clicking on the floor as she went into what Creed called her scamper-mode. He tried not to rein her in as they quickened their pace through a new crowd of passengers that had been waiting for their baggage to come down the carousel. Grace seemed to ignore the squawking beeps on the machines that alerted the passengers that their bags were ready and would be coming down the conveyor belt. She'd been hearing those beeps for hours and they no longer were interesting. But something or someone on the other side of baggage claim was drawing her attention.

A CBP officer waved Creed over. He had stopped a

man on crutches. A cast covered much of the man's left leg, starting at the knee and running all the way down to his ankle. It wouldn't be the first time someone tried to smuggle drugs in a cast. But as Creed and Grace continued across the baggage claim area, Creed suddenly realized Grace wasn't leading him to the man in the leg cast. Grace was taking him to someone else, and her nose was twitching.

16

Amanda tried not to grip her stomach. Zapata had already stared darts at her as she led the way through the baggage claim area. Today Amanda's stomach hurt even worse. Leandro had promised that this would be the last time, if only she followed his strict instructions.

The only thing Amanda could think about was that one of the balloons had certainly burst open. It had to have. There was no other explanation for the pain in her stomach. Something was ripping away inside her. And once again, Leandro wasn't here. Nowhere in sight. He had left her to Zapata's care, and Zapata's patience had obviously been used up on the last trip.

She waited by the restroom door while the old

woman weaved her way through the crowd, attempting to retrieve their luggage. The designer suitcase was packed with belongings that Amanda rarely needed or used. It was all just another part of the disguise, because passengers traveling without luggage drew attention. It didn't matter if the suitcase continued to look brand-new and never got unpacked.

Amanda sat on a bench against the wall. Sweat dripped from her bangs. She had pulled back her stringy hair but her bangs needed trimming and were constantly falling into her eyes. They didn't fall now. Instead, they were plastered to her forehead.

She tried to get her mind off the nausea. She used to enjoy watching strangers in airports, making up stories about them, guessing where they were going or where they'd been. Now she saw only faces staring at her, faces that pretended to look away when she caught them. She knew Leandro had spies everywhere. He'd told her so.

Alongside the bench she noticed a newspaper machine. Lately she'd gotten into the habit of reading them through the glass to check the date. Too many hours and days spent in hotel rooms made her lose track of time. But she didn't even look at the date in the corner. Instead, her eyes fixed on the front-page photo. She recognized the man and his dog from the television talk show: Ryder Creed and Grace. His name sounded like a movie star's name.

She was reading the article when out of the corner of her eye she saw something running toward her. At first, Amanda thought her stomach pain might be making her hallucinate. How else could she explain the little dog coming her way with the man from the newspaper following close behind?

Her heart started thumping in her ears. Her eyes darted in the direction that Zapata had gone. The old woman was at the conveyor, waiting for the suitcase and glancing over her shoulder to check on Amanda. She hadn't noticed the man and the dog. They were zigzagging around people and luggage, but somehow Amanda knew the dog was headed straight for her.

She stood on wobbly knees and braced one hand against the bench to steady herself. The man wasn't dressed in a uniform. Instead he wore blue jeans, a T-shirt, and a long-sleeved shirt with the sleeves rolled up, the tails out, and the buttons undone. His jaw was bristled and his hair tousled. He looked nothing like an airport officer – too young, too casual, way too hot.

He hadn't noticed her and was still looking around, trying to figure out where his dog was leading him. He hadn't realized yet that Amanda was the dog's target.

Drugs, Amanda remembered from the talk show and the few lines she had just read.

Holy crap!

Now she remembered from the TV show. The dog sniffed out drugs. It was headed directly toward her. Could it smell the drugs inside her?

Was that even possible?

She took a few steps and felt dizzy. Glanced back toward Zapata and saw that the old woman had turned and was watching her.

Amanda looked around while the baggage claim area tilted and the floor started to move. Not far away a security officer questioned a man with a cast on his leg. People stepped around them, hurrying to gather their belongings. Everyone seemed in such a rush.

The dog was closer. Less than twenty feet away. Zapata had started back, stopping for a stream of people going by, and Amanda could see the old woman didn't even have the suitcase. One last look and she could see the anger on Zapata's face. That's when Amanda waited for the man with the dog to meet her eyes, and when he did, Amanda willed her feet to move – one in front of the other.

Hurry, she told herself.

The path cleared and she called out, 'Uncle Ryder,' as she rushed past the dog and practically fell into the man's arms. Her heart was pounding against her rib cage as she threw her arms tight around his neck and held on.

'Please save me,' she whispered in his ear.

17

The girl smelled of sweat and French milled soap, the kind that hotels had in little fancy wrappers. As far as Creed could tell, she had no luggage except for a leather bag around her shoulder. Even as she strangled his neck and whispered her pleas, Creed could see Grace sitting very still and staring up directly into his eyes. The dog was alerting. She was telling him that this girl was her target and there were drugs somewhere on her.

He hadn't realized until almost the last seconds that it was the girl and not the man with the leg cast that Grace had been racing toward. Grace's intent stare told him there was no doubt. Was this display some kind of ploy to get the drugs in her handbag past security? The girl could have recognized him and Grace. They'd been all over the news, and she'd have seen or heard their names. But how did she know they'd be at the airport today?

He tried to untangle her long, thin arms from his neck, trying to be gentle and not dismantle her act, while his eyes started to search around them.

'She's there,' the girl whispered. 'Don't let her take me, please. She's right behind me.'

And sure enough, the woman had cautiously approached them. She looked as if she needed to capture a wild animal without spooking it or alarming everyone around them. She was maybe forty, dressed casually in slacks and a matching blouse, a designer handbag on her shoulder, dark eyes, and dark hair swept up in a matriarch style that made her look older.

'Amanda, dear,' she said in perfect English, but Creed could hear the Spanish accent. And no matter how much the woman pretended, she had not been able to fake the least bit of sincerity. It was enough for Creed to realize that the girl might not just be high or playing a game. That she might actually fear this woman.

'It's my uncle Ryder,' the girl named Amanda said,

without looking back at the woman. 'I didn't realize he was working here today.'

The girl stood back now, and Creed held her shoulders. He felt her body sway as though she would fall backward if he released his hold on her.

'You remember me telling you about my uncle Ryder,' Amanda said, and she squatted down to tap Grace on the head, like someone who had never petted a dog before in her entire life. 'And this is his dog, Grace.'

The dog allowed the pats but she didn't take her eyes off Creed, telling him in her own way that this was what he wanted her to find. He hadn't released her yet, so she continued to alert, patient, but her hind end wiggled.

'Where are your parents, Amanda?' Creed decided to play along.

'Oh, they're still at the vacation villa in Colombia.' She looked up at him, meeting his eyes, and now he had dog and girl staring at him, each wanting something from him. 'I'm sure they wouldn't mind if you just took me home.'

'No, they would not like that,' the woman said, barely containing her anger.

'Everything okay here, Mr Creed?' One of the CBP officers had wandered over.

Both women and Grace now stared Creed down, as though their eyes could make him say and do exactly what they wanted, what they needed.

He took a better look at the girl. Her face was flushed with perspiration, her cheeks almost gaunt, as though she hadn't eaten for days. She was tall with long limbs, like a gawky teenager who hadn't grown into her body yet. Although she wore pencil-tight jeans, her blouse billowed out and over her thin frame. He stared into her eyes. They were bright blue and anxious but the pupils weren't dilated. Her face was painted with too much makeup to make her look older, but Creed guessed she couldn't be more than fifteen or sixteen.

'Need me to call someone?' the CBP officer asked.

'No, that's okay, Officer Salazar,' Creed said, glancing at the man's name tag and noticing that his right hand rested on his gun belt. 'I'm just surprised to run into my niece. I didn't realize she'd be here today.'

Creed watched the woman's face and could see the spark of anger before she tucked it away. She lifted her chin and shook her head, defiant, as if she wasn't used to being treated this way. He felt her eyes scan the length of him, settling on the badge hanging from the lanyard around his neck. She was trying to figure out what authority, if any, he had here. He wasn't dressed in a uniform, and he knew she was contemplating how she could dismiss him, especially now, in front of the CBP officer.

'I've been taking very good care of her for her parents,' she told Officer Salazar, as if imploring him to intercede. 'Her uncle barely knows her. He has not bothered to keep in touch with the family.'

She had just made a mistake. A big mistake. Whatever game the girl was playing, Creed decided he disliked even more the one her keeper was playing. A teenager he could forgive for making up stories and games, but this woman's insistence on lying was making him suspicious and starting to piss him off.

'All the more reason for us to catch up,' Creed said, and smiled as he offered a hand to Amanda. 'I was just going to take a break. How about I walk you to your ride?' And with only a glance at the woman, he added, 'I'm sure Officer Salazar won't mind helping you process your luggage.'

'Not a problem. I can do that. Anything for you, Mr Creed. We certainly appreciate all your help.'

Creed shook the man's hand, thanking him. Officer Salazar's back was turned to the woman and he wasn't able to see her eyes flash daggers into Creed.

'Amanda and I'll meet you out front.'

He took the girl's arm as he pulled the pink squeaky elephant out of his shoulder pack and tossed it to Grace. She caught her reward in midair. At least he was able to get one of the three females to stop staring at him.

18

'You have exactly three minutes to tell me what the hell's going on,' Creed told the girl as he tightened his grip on her arm and led her through the crowds in baggage claim.

With a glance over his shoulder, he saw the girl's keeper still watching them, even as CBP Officer Salazar stood beside her at Carousel #3, waiting for her luggage to come around on the conveyor belt.

Grace scampered beside them, squeaking her pink elephant in her mouth. At least one of them was happy with their day's findings.

'She's a bad woman,' Amanda said, noticing him look back.

'Less than three minutes now.'

'She's made me do terrible things.'

'Like carrying drugs?'

'What? No! That's crazy.'

But he could feel her body almost melt.

'Bad decision to lie to me. I know you have drugs somewhere on you. Are they in your handbag?'

She shook her head.

'Because I've seen it all. Candy bars with cocaine middles. Peanut butter jars.'

Grace and her squeaking managed to clear a path as people stepped out of their way to see what was making the unusual sound, despite the clamor of so many other noises.

Creed pulled the girl across to the other side of the concourse and toward the Ground Transportation exit.

'Please, don't let her take me,' the girl whispered when she saw where they were headed. 'They'll kill me this time.'

'Where are the drugs?' he asked.

'There are no drugs.'

'Grace says there are, and she's never wrong. One last chance, where are the drugs?'

'You'll turn me in. I'll be arrested. Please, they'll kill me.'

'I know most of these officers. They won't hurt you.'

'They have people who'll get to me. They'll kill me.'

She was shaking now, and her skin was slick with sweat. If this was part of some game, she was very good at it.

And then she said something that made Creed's insides twist into knots.

'I'm only fourteen and my stomach hurts so bad because they made me swallow forty-two balloons.'

'Holy crap,' he said under his breath.

He felt her eyes searching his reaction. He slowed his pace, took some deep breaths. He looked back toward Carousel #3, trying to see through the crowds. The woman and Salazar were gone. Luggage retrieved. Salazar would make sure it was processed quickly. A car was probably waiting out front. If not the car itself, then certainly the driver. If the girl was telling the truth, the driver would most likely be armed. And there could be others watching.

Creed reversed course. Immediately Amanda thought he was taking her back to the CBP officer, or worse, back to her keeper. She started to cry. She was too weak to pull away from him, and now he understood that she was in pain. That's why she was shaking and sweating.

'Settle down,' he told her.

Instead of continuing back into baggage claim, he took a right and led her toward a door that warned NO EXIT. One of the benefits afforded him and Grace was a parking slot just outside the terminal. Creed pulled his ID badge off his neck and slid the card through the slot beside the door. The flashing red light clicked and started flashing green.

He pushed the door and held it open for Amanda to go through. When she hesitated, Grace nudged her leg, then went around her and marched across the threshold as if she were showing her what to do, even standing on the other side as far as her leash allowed. She waited and wagged, a bit impatient with this new part of the game.

He saw the girl turn to look back. She was clearly debating her choices.

'You came to me,' Creed reminded her. 'If you want my help, you're gonna need to trust me.'

He watched her face – pain, fear, anxiety – she couldn't hide it anymore. He almost wished she'd choose to stay. He still had time to fetch Officer Salazar and let him take care of her. That was CBP's job. Creed and Grace's job was simply to search and find. Maybe if he didn't still remember those girls and boys from the fishing boat – the looks on their faces forever embedded in his memory – maybe he'd have let Salazar take care of it from the very first lie. Because he knew as soon as this girl walked out this exit with him, his life would never be the same again.

She looked up at him, eyes watery, nose running, and nodded. 'I guess I have nothing to lose,' she mumbled, so quietly he figured she was telling herself instead of him.

And she squeezed past him through the doorway and into the hall that would take them directly to his Jeep.

He let the heavy door shut behind him and waited for the lock to click. All the while, in his mind, he kept thinking that he had absolutely everything to lose.

19

Creed watched the rearview mirror. His security clearance parking meant he didn't have to deal with any of the airport checkpoints. Whoever was waiting to pick up this girl and her keeper would never get a glimpse of his Jeep Grand Cherokee leaving.

Maybe if he was lucky – God willing – it would take them a while to figure out who he was. But because of his and Grace's unwanted celebrity, they certainly would figure it out quickly. And when they did, they would know exactly where to find him. Right now Creed wasn't sure what would be worse – the drug thugs finding him or having to tell Hannah that he was bringing home one of their mules.

Hannah had brought home quite a few unsavory characters from Segway House: drug addicts, runaways, wounded soldiers like Jason. But this was different. None of them had targets on their backs. Nor did they have thousands of dollars' worth of cocaine in their gut that belonged to someone else.

He glanced at the girl and wondered if her name was even Amanda. She had curled herself tight into the passenger seat, buckling up only on his insistence. Still, she managed to hike her feet up and hug her knees to her chest. He'd covered her with a jacket when she mumbled that she was cold. She kept the jacket in place, though she turned down his request to flip the seat warmer on. It had to be almost ninety degrees outside. He kept the temperature on her side of the Jeep at seventy-three.

She no longer trembled but her face still glistened with sweat. She was still in pain. She'd taken a bottle of water that he'd offered earlier but it remained in the cup holder on her side, unopened.

Creed had never dealt with drug mules before, but he knew enough to realize that if a balloon with cocaine had burst inside her stomach, she'd already be dead. But there was nothing to stop it from still happening. A few times he had to look hard to make sure she hadn't died on him. He kept thinking she had fallen asleep because she was so quiet, but each time he glanced over, he noticed that her eyes stayed open. Her head pressed against the seat's headrest. She stared out the window, almost as if she were expecting to recognize some of the scenery.

She didn't ask any more questions and neither did Creed. He didn't want to hear anything else, not right now. There would be plenty of time to decipher her lies. Hannah would help him figure out what to do with her. She'd be madder than hell with him, but she'd still help.

It was about a four-hour drive from the Atlanta airport to his home in the panhandle of Florida. Usually he took Interstate 65, but outside Montgomery, Alabama, he exited and traveled a two-lane until he was convinced that no one had followed him.

Every time he glanced in the rearview mirror to check on Grace, she was staring at him from her perch. The backseat of the SUV lay flat with Grace's bed in the middle and their equipment squeezed into the far corner. She had her pink elephant beside her but she caught his eyes in the mirror every time he looked at her. Then she'd turn her head and glance in Amanda's direction.

Under other circumstances he'd probably laugh at her persistence. She didn't understand why he'd brought the 'fish' with them. He'd never brought it inside the car before. In all of her training and in all of her past experiences, he would ask her to 'go find fish.' People in a crowded airport looked at Creed funny when he used the word 'fish,' but if he used the word 'drugs' for the cue, they might scatter and run.

Grace could search for bodies dead or alive as well as particular things, like drugs. But she needed different cues to know what she should search for. As well as the different harnesses or vests Creed put on her for certain tasks, he also used different words for what she was supposed to search out.

So Grace was confused. Today she had completed her task successfully. She had searched out and found what he had asked for. For which she'd been rewarded with her pink elephant. But unlike ever before, her master had brought the 'fish' with them, and poor Grace had no idea what she was supposed to do with it. She was looking to him to help her figure it out.

'It's okay,' he told the dog. 'Just lie down, Grace. All done.'

She laid her head down on her front paws but her eyes stayed on Creed. He'd feel them there for the entire trip back home.

20

WASHINGTON, DC.

O'Dell could see Benjamin Platt waiting for her in the far corner booth of Old Ebbitt Grill. He was looking at a menu and hadn't seen her yet. A half-empty pilsner reminded her how late she was. Still, she took an extra few seconds to stand back and take a good look at him.

Despite the restaurant's dim light, she knew she would automatically peg him for a military officer – ramrod-straight back, clean-shaven, handsome face, short-cut hair, and the long, steady fingers of a surgeon. The serious set of his jaw remained, whether examining test tubes of level 4 viruses or simply making a decision between cheddar or American cheese for his burger. Sometimes she wished he wasn't always so serious. He had a wickedly dry sense of humor and a kind and gentle manner, but his position demanded a tougher façade. O'Dell was one of the few people who saw the other side of Benjamin Platt. His serious manner was, of course, an understandable occupational hazard of his chosen profession.

As an infectious-disease officer (actually, director of USAMRIID, pronounced U-Sam-rid – United States Army Medical Research Institute of Infectious Diseases), his choices had to be careful and measured. The habit seeped into his personal life. Even his choice of seating was a well-thought-out process, taking the side of the booth that put his back to the corner wall so he'd be able to see everyone approach or pass by the table.

Maybe it didn't bother her because her own career had ingrained similar habits in her that she had allowed to invade her personal life. Only recently had she realized how much of a personal life she *did not* have. When you chased killers for a living, you tended not to trust anyone except yourself. It was easier to keep people out.

She'd learned to compartmentalize the horrible crime scenes she'd witnessed over the years, and along with those images she'd stashed into separate compartments, she added the emotions of anger and fear. She'd gotten so good at it that she didn't even realize she did the same thing with her personal life, bordering off her feelings and keeping people at arm's length.

Then one day she realized she no longer even had much of a personal life. Why had she been surprised? You couldn't shut people out just because you didn't want to risk feeling too deeply or possibly getting hurt. Especially when she worked so hard to put up all those barricades in the first place.

In her experience, the hurt always came. It was just a matter of time. And that was the one thing she and Ben shared. They were so much alike that it was easy to be together. Like they had an unstated understanding of what to expect from each other. But perhaps that wasn't enough to build a relationship on.

He saw her. Smiled. Like an officer and a gentleman, he stood up from the booth to greet her.

'Sorry I'm late,' she said as he leaned over and kissed her cheek. He smelled good, like he'd just gotten out of the shower. And only now did she realize that his hair was still damp, his face smooth from a second shave of the day. His khakis looked freshly pressed and his polo shirt was neatly tucked in. Had he primped just for her? Like a date? She searched his eyes for an answer, but he was already looking for the waiter.

'You're always worth the wait,' he said with a glance as he continued to politely wait for her to sit down before he slid back into his place. He waved at a waiter, finally getting one's attention. He pointed at his own pilsner and held up two fingers.

Maggie smiled and wondered when they had become so predictable with each other. Maybe it was simply that they had become comfortable with each other. Nothing wrong with that. Theirs had been a crazy dance. They had become friends – very good friends – then almost lovers. 'Almost' because of Ben's deliberate and measured choices, as though taking that next step was something that needed to be analyzed and calculated.

Recently he had made the mistake of confessing that he wanted children. O'Dell shouldn't have been surprised, knowing he had lost his only daughter at the age of five. But when he announced it as though it were a requirement before they proceeded – that request, that admission, had been like a cold shower, putting the skids on whatever physical attraction had been there. So they had decided that they would be friends only. And just when they decided that was best, things started to heat up again. They were in the middle of heating up again over the last month or so, and neither of them seemed to want to admit it and rewrite the rules all over again. So they resorted to flirting, exchanging long, meaningful glances like a couple of goofy teenagers. Yes, a crazy dance.

They ordered burgers, fried calamari, and house salads off the late-night menu. Ben asked for blue cheese on his burger, raising O'Dell's eyebrow and making him grin, as if to say, 'See, I'm not so predictable after all.' So he had known exactly what she had been thinking.

As soon as the waiter left, Ben asked, 'How's Gwen doing?'

Gwen Patterson was O'Dell's closest friend. No, she was more than that. Fifteen years O'Dell's senior, Gwen was also a mentor as much as confidante. Three months ago, she'd been diagnosed with stage II breast cancer. O'Dell knew that Gwen was still trying to wrap her mind around that fact. As she told Ben about

Gwen's latest consult for yet another opinion, O'Dell couldn't hide how worried she was that putting off the inevitable surgery would only make matters worse. All she could do was continue to nag Gwen, but her friend was already avoiding seeing or talking to her because of it.

By the time the calamari arrived, O'Dell realized she needed to change the subject. She asked Ben, 'Can you take Jake and Harvey for a couple of days?'

Ben had become her dog sitter for her overnight assignments. Even their dogs got along great, and Ben had a huge backyard to accommodate them. It was as though they already shared custody.

'Sure. Digger will love having them. Where is Kunze sending you this time?'

She told him about the floater they'd pulled from the Potomac. Sharing her suspicions of it being a drug hit, and even how she had found Senator Delanor-Ramos in Kunze's office. Any details she shared she knew Ben would keep to himself. His position at USAMRIID had conditioned him to keeping classified information classified, and therefore, made him the perfect confidant.

'You think it has something to do with the senator's husband?' Ben knew where she was headed.

'His trial is coming up.' George Ramos was being held without bond in a federal prison in Florida.

'She's on the Senate's Homeland Security Committee. Maybe she was just going over Senate business.'

'Since when do senators come to Quantico for meetings?' O'Dell gave him a look, and he shrugged as if he already knew it was lame.

'Still, you don't know that her visit had anything to do with this victim.'

'A package in the Potomac,' she said. 'Stan thinks the guy was probably killed hundreds of miles south of here. Someone delivers a body, calls it a package, and deposits it within view of Washington, DC – do you really believe it's not politically connected?'

'Could be a coincidence.'

'I don't believe in coincidences.'

They sat back as the waiter brought their burgers and salads.

'Two more?' He pointed to their glasses but spoke directly to Ben. And Ben looked to and waited for O'Dell.

'Sure,' she said, knowing full well she wouldn't allow herself a second. She'd take a few sips, and Ben wouldn't notice, or at least he politely wouldn't acknowledge it.

When the waiter left, Ben leaned across the table. 'So I'm guessing Kunze *isn't* sending you someplace? Where is it that you're headed?'

'Andalusia, Alabama.'

'How exotic. Probably not a vacation destination.' He stared at her, elbows planted on either side of his food, hands clasped with no intention of beginning his meal until she explained.

'Kunze wants me to investigate,' she said as she picked up her fork and stabbed at her salad, trying to diffuse the concern in his eyes. 'In order to do that, I need to find the original crime scene.'

'In Alabama?'

'That's the address on the victim's driver's license. Seems like a good place to start. Besides, I'm guessing there are probably a lot of fire ants somewhere around there.'

21

The first thing that went through Amanda's mind was that she had traded an angry, skinny, old woman for an angry, large, black woman. Both of them seemed like they would rather kill her than deal with her.

She couldn't believe Ryder Creed had chosen to put her fate in the hands of this woman. He looked like such a nice guy. She hadn't seen anger when she looked into his face. His eyes were a deep sky blue, like on a warm, sunny day when there isn't a single cloud. She hadn't seen a hint of anger in them – frustration, suspicion, impatience, but not anger.

Those eyes had convinced Amanda that he could be trusted. She was second-guessing that decision now. All of this simply reinforced what she already believed – that she couldn't trust anyone but herself, even when she was sick and hurting.

'You need to take her to a hospital emergency room,' the woman, named Hannah, said while her eyes lasered up and down Amanda's cramped body. 'That's my best advice.'

'They'll kill me,' Amanda muttered. She had already said this three times to Ryder Creed, and she made sure her eyes remained focused on him and him alone. Did she really need to guilt him into rescuing her a second time? She didn't have the energy to do that.

'Maybe you should have thought of that before you swallowed their product.'

'Hannah, she's just a kid.'

It was still too soft for a scold but Amanda was relieved that Ryder Creed had finally said something, anything, that sounded like he might defend her.

'She's only fourteen,' he added.

'That what she told you?' And the black woman rolled her eyes. She didn't believe a word of it.

'It's true.' Amanda shouted it, surprising herself. She had lied about her age for so long, always trying to look and sound older, and here she was telling the truth and this woman only raised her eyebrows at her.

She grabbed her stomach. The pain hadn't gotten any worse but she didn't want them to know that. Instead, she needed to keep reminding them that she was hurting ... bad. Right now, it was her only salvation.

'I think one of the balloons might have ruptured,' she told Ryder Creed, mustering up some tears.

'None of them ruptured, missy,' Hannah told her with a bite on the title 'missy.' In fact, the indifference on her face hadn't changed in the least, even the risk of a ruptured balloon didn't seem to alarm her. 'If one of them had ruptured, you wouldn't be here telling us about it. You'd be dead. But I don't suppose they told you that, did they?'

'It just hurts so bad.'

'Did your boyfriend use latex condoms?'

'My boyfriend?' How could she know about Leandro?

'The man who talked you into doing this. I bet he talked real sweet to you, didn't he?'

Amanda felt her face go red. She was already hot and sweaty. Maybe they wouldn't notice.

'The balloons ... they're condoms, isn't that right?' the woman asked. 'Did he use latex ones?'

Amanda only shrugged. Leandro had said he used the best, the strongest. He tied them so carefully. But she didn't know what condoms were made of.

'I don't know,' Amanda finally said.

'You might be allergic to latex,' Hannah said.

The woman crossed her arms over her chest and glanced at Ryder Creed. For the first time, Amanda thought she saw a hint of sympathy in the woman's face.

'It didn't hurt this bad the last time.'

And then immediately she realized her mistake, even before Hannah scowled at her. Any hint of sympathy disappeared. She could hear the disdain in the woman's voice.

'Just how many times you done this?'

'Hannah, come on. You know they made her do this.'

'They put a gun to your head?'

'Hannah—'

'I just want them out of me!'

'The ER will know what—'

'No! They'll kill me. Don't you understand that?'

Amanda curled herself into the corner of the sofa, pulling her knees to her chest. She watched them out of the corner of her eye, from underneath sweaty bangs and long hair that she'd let fall into her face to hide behind. She felt tears stream down her cheeks, but she muffled her sobs. She could see them staring at each other and they seemed to do it for the longest time, as if neither one wanted to give in to the other.

'Upstairs bathroom,' Hannah finally told Ryder. 'Get me the laxative from the top shelf in the medicine cabinet.'

'Laxative?'

'How else you think they're coming out?'

He glanced at Amanda in the same way someone looks at a wounded animal, but then without saying a word, he headed out of the room.

'And you,' Hannah said to Amanda, 'get ready to start counting. I hope to God for your own sake that you remember how many you swallowed.'

22

NEWBURGH HEIGHTS, VIRGINIA

Maggie O'Dell curled into the sofa, bare feet tucked underneath her and her head swirling from the nightcap she had convinced herself she deserved, since she hadn't finished her second beer at Old Ebbitt's. Now she wished she had invited Ben to come back to her house.

She had recently rebuilt and remodeled much of the two-story Tudor after a fire had destroyed the front section of the house. The process had been painstaking, but amazingly, she could no longer smell soot or ash or any hint of what had happened. Still, the place felt different.

She knew the fire had destroyed more than the plaster and beams and furniture. It had taken a chunk of O'Dell's sense of security. The house sat on a wooded acre, isolated by a creek and a natural preserve behind the property. Ironically, she had bought the place with a trust her father had left her – her father, who as a firefighter had died in the line of duty when O'Dell was just twelve. She thought she had created a sanctuary with its high-tech security system and the natural barriers of the high-banked creek that ran along the back of the property. Even the stately pines that bordered the sides reminded her of sentries standing guard, shoulder to shoulder.

She also had two canine bodyguards: one she'd rescued and the other had rescued her. Harvey, a white Labrador retriever, lay on the sofa beside her, his head against her thigh. Jake stayed at her feet, the German shepherd constantly on alert. The dogs put up with her late nights, many of which were spent here in the living room instead of her upstairs master bedroom. She couldn't remember the last time she had slept more than three or four hours at a time. She accepted the insomnia as if it were just another occupational hazard. However, the nightcap was beginning to do its job.

Just as she decided to call it quits for the night, she noticed a new email. The icon flashed in the corner of her laptop's screen. She'd come up empty-handed after putting through several searches in the databases she had access to. ViCAP hadn't come back with any matches close to an MO of fire ants being used as torture. Not that she expected any. What was more remarkable was that none of the floater's info seemed to ring any bells.

O'Dell was used to looking closely at a victim's lifestyle, habits, whereabouts, connections – anything that might lead her to the killer. Some victims were at higher risk than others, even if they were chosen randomly by a killer. Driving late at night in an unfamiliar area, accepting a ride from a stranger, drinking at an establishment of ill repute, buying drugs, engaging in prostitution put a person at higher risk. Yes, it might sound like blaming the victim, but it was an unfortunate fact that some homicide victims – like, perhaps, a drug dealer – put themselves at more risk than the ordinary person. And knowing how and where and under what circumstances the victim met his or her killer could oftentimes beat a path to the killer's identity.

However, Trevor Bagley had no outstanding warrants, no arrests, no fines – not even an unpaid parking ticket. All taxes – property and income – were up-to-date. According to the Alabama real estate tax assessor, Bagley owned a house on ten acres. His mortgage had no late-payment fees.

His 2012 Dodge Ram pickup had been paid off. As was a brand-new Land Rover that was also registered in his wife Regina's name. Bagley's driver's license was current. He was self-employed and so was his wife. In the last year he had been an independent contractor working for a commercial fisherman.

There was no record of drug use or abuse for either Bagley or his wife. No debt or liens against them or their property. Just two respectable taxpayers minding their own business.

The only thing O'Dell could find about Trevor Bagley that possibly sent up a red flag was his discharge from the military. She wasn't given access to see why and suspected it might have been a dishonorable discharge. She'd need to investigate that more closely.

Now, as she scanned the email that had just come in, she saw no new information. Nothing to even suggest drug dealing. How could she have been so wrong?

Had she let a tattoo of Santa Muerte judge this poor man? Was it possible he was the random victim of a sadistic killer?

She typed Bagley's home address into the Google Maps search. Just as she suspected, the ten acres were in a remote part of southern Alabama. Few roads showed up. The Conecuh River ran on the left side of the property. Not far to the south was the Conecuh National Forest. Before she clicked on the satellite view, she found herself wondering if it was possible Bagley was tortured in his own backyard.

Maybe Regina Bagley could help shed light on how her husband could have met a fate like this. Unfortunately, the woman wasn't answering her phone. O'Dell had already reserved a morning flight but she wasn't looking forward to it. Never mind that she hated flying, she hated even more to have to break such news to a family member. How exactly was she supposed to tell Mrs Bagley that her husband had been tortured and his body dumped nine hundred miles away in the Potomac River?

23

As far as assignments went, the one that the Iceman had just given Falco would be his most challenging. Little did it help that he hated dogs. No, that wasn't exactly true. If it were, this would be easy. He didn't hate dogs – he was frightened of them. But never in a thousand years would he admit that to anyone, least of all, the Iceman.

He didn't even have a good reason to fear them. He wished he could point to some vicious attack or at least a scar from a dog bite. But there was nothing like that.

Several years ago, in his hometown of Mosquera – a suburb of Bogotá, Colombia – it seemed that stray dogs had taken over the city. More than thirty thousand dirty mutts roamed the streets. You could see them lounging under trees during the day and prowling the alleys for food at night. You couldn't walk the city sidewalks without stepping in their crap. It was disgusting.

One by itself might have been a pathetic sight. But they traveled in packs. They looked like savages, desperate and hungry, with long legs, protruding ribs, scruffs of fur, glassy eyes, and frothing mouths. Maybe not frothing. Panting and flashing yellowed fangs. It was what he remembered. He was still just a boy at the time.

It didn't help matters that his mother had told him that a pack of wild dogs had attacked and eaten a five-year-old boy who had wandered away from the safety of his backyard. Never mind that it was probably a story that mothers told to misbehaving young boys in order to instill enough fear in them to straighten up and do right.

It had given Falco nightmares. Sometimes he still dreamed of being chased by a pack of rabid dogs. He could hear them thundering closer and closer until he could feel their razor-sharp fangs snapping at his heels. Usually he woke up just as they started to drag him down.

A thumping sound made Falco jump and almost swerve off the road. As he checked the rearview mirror he was already embarrassed by his reaction. In the back of the Land Rover the bundle twitched and jerked.

How the hell could the bastard still be alive?

He glanced at the vehicle's navigation system. He still had forty-seven miles to go. Falco adjusted the rearview mirror to take a better look. He'd rolled the guy up in a plastic tarp and wrapped a sturdy cable around him, tying it securely.

How was the son of bitch able to breathe?

No way he'd manage to get out, even in forty-seven more miles, but Falco didn't want any blood in the back of the Land Rover. It was bad enough that he had to keep all those burlap bags back there. He'd grown quite fond of this vehicle. Earlier, he worried that the Iceman would make him dump it.

'You haven't gotten rid of the Land Rover yet?'

'It has a V8 engine,' Falco had told him with a grin.

The Iceman didn't smile.

'Besides, I changed out the license plates like you told me.'

'Where?'

'That strip club on Davis Highway. Figured some drunk horny guy's not gonna report it, even if he ever knew what his license plate number was.'

If he wasn't mistaken, he thought the Iceman almost smiled. Almost. He did nod and that, alone, was praise from the man.

'Still, I'll tell them to get you a decent ride. Have they, at least, been paying you on time? You let me know if they don't.'

That wasn't a problem. The money was good. Falco didn't know what to do with it all. Really, he didn't know what to do with it. They paid him in cash. It wasn't like he could walk into a bank and open an account.

He had started wrapping stacks in aluminum foil about the size of a meat loaf, then labeling them 'meat loaf' or 'pot roast' on the outside with a black marker. But his freezer didn't have room for many more. He'd gotten the idea from an old black-and-white movie. He figured if someone found them, they'd just feel sorry for him that all he had to eat was meat loaf and pot roast.

A freezer full of anything was certainly more than his mother had when she was raising him. Sometimes he wished she could see him. She'd love this Land Rover. The seats were made of smooth leather, softer than anything he imagined she'd ever sat on. Maybe in a month or so he'd try to find a way to send her some money.

Falco glanced in the mirror again at the bundle twisting and thumping. Of course, his mother would want to know about his job. Maybe he'd tell her he was a deliveryman.

He smiled at that and turned on the radio, blasting the volume until he couldn't hear the thumping anymore.

24

Creed ignored the sweat dripping down his back and the buzz of mosquitoes. Bastards would eat him alive if given half a chance. He'd drenched a kerchief in Hannah's special elixir and tied it around his neck. Then he rubbed some of the liquid over exposed parts of his body: face, neck, hands, and ankles. The rest of the stuff he sprayed on Bolo and raked through his short coat. Must be working. The big dog was snoring, sprawled out in the knee-high grass alongside him.

His snores made Creed wonder if this could all be a waste of time. Maybe he was being overly paranoid once again. Were the drugs inside Amanda worth it?

Was she worth it? Seems like it would be easier to cut their losses and consider her collateral damage.

He had taken up a patrol post in his neighbor's field across the road from his own property. Nestled inside the tall grass at the edge of the pine forest, he had a perfect view, not only of the entrance to his own driveway, but the entire stretch along the road. Anyone who dared to come onto his property would have to somehow manage it from this side. Otherwise they'd need to cross a river and hack their way through the thicket and forest.

Creed couldn't imagine a bunch of arrogant drug-cartel goons going through the trouble, especially in the pitch-black of night with only a sliver of moonlight. No way could they stumble around in the dark in an area they didn't know without bringing flashlights.

But then, what did he know about drug-cartel hit men?

He did know a thing or two about staging a security post – watching and looking out for the enemy. Unfortunately, stuff like that from his Afghanistan tours stuck with him. Of course, there was a big difference waiting for the enemy with only a shotgun and a dog, instead of an AK-47. But then, Bolo wasn't any dog.

Named for the law enforcement acronym BOLO, Be

On The Lookout, the dog had lived up to his name on more than several occasions. As far as Creed could tell, he was a mixture of Labrador retriever, with his webbed paws and lopsided grin along with Rhodesian ridgeback, sporting the breed's telltale ridge of hair that ran the length of his spine in the opposite direction of his coat. He had a nose on him that made him one of Creed's best air-scent dogs, yet Creed used a lot of discretion before taking Bolo on a job.

Ridgebacks were developed in South Africa and nicknamed African lion hounds because they could keep a lion at bay until their master was able to make the kill. They were known for strength and intelligence. Large and muscular, they had an imposing, almost daunting presence, but they weren't usually aggressive dogs. More mischievous than anything else. They could, however, be loyal to a fault and dangerously overprotective of their master.

On one of their last outings, a sheriff's deputy had yelled at Creed. Without warning and in only a matter of seconds, Bolo had flattened the rather large man. Ninety pounds of dog had to be removed from the man's chest, though Bolo hadn't bitten him or grabbed any limbs.

It wasn't the first time the dog had attacked someone he thought was a threat to his master. It was one of the reasons Creed had to be careful what assignments he took Bolo on. It was also the reason he had him along tonight. Though not specifically trained as an apprehension dog, he was the closest thing Creed had to one. He figured the dog could probably take down an intruder faster and better than Creed could with the shotgun. But he was in no hurry to find out.

He had brought a sleeping bag, though he didn't expect to sleep. The rolled-up bag cushioned his back from the tree bark. He'd be stiff and sore by morning from sitting all night in the damp, but it was nothing some laps in the pool wouldn't smooth away. Just as he started to readjust his long legs, Bolo's head shot up.

'It's okay, buddy, it's just me.'

But it wasn't just him. And now Creed could hear the approaching engine. He put a hand on the dog's back to keep him by his side. In the dark Creed tried to see the vehicle, but even as the sound grew louder he couldn't see it. Then he realized why, as he spotted movement about a half-mile up the road.

The vehicle didn't have its headlights on.

25

The SUV had slowed to a crawl. Probably trying to avoid the slightest tap on the brakes that would flash the red backlights. By the time it came to a stop it was less than twenty feet from the entrance to the driveway. Creed and Bolo crouched in the ditch, already within striking distance.

The big dog knew to be quiet, but Creed could smell his sweaty coat and feel his anxiousness. He held firm the strap on the back of Bolo's harness, just in case the dog decided to bolt and play hero.

As far as Creed could see there was only one person inside the cab. Though the vehicle had stopped, the driver had not killed the engine. So

Creed was surprised when the driver's door creaked open.

He felt Bolo tense and go rigid. Thankfully, he didn't lunge. Instead, the dog cocked his head to the side. Both dog and master waited, Bolo sniffing the air and Creed squinting to see through the tall grass.

In the forefront of his mind he kept thinking, *What the hell does a drug-cartel's hit man look like?* Anything he imagined certainly didn't match up with the small man who leaned out and took jerky glances all around him. He seemed jittery and nervous, even knocking his head on the door frame as he jumped down.

The man moved around to the back. His hands swung free at his sides. No weapon. When he popped the liftgate and opened it, Creed could see a large bag with bulges, slick and black, almost like a body bag. But the man wasn't messing with it. Instead, he started yanking and pulling at another shadow that was up against the inside of the vehicle. Creed heard a yelp and knew it was a dog even before the man dragged it out and dropped it to the ground. The dog fell on its side, and as it tried to get to its feet the man kicked it.

He could feel Bolo pulling and struggling against the

leash. Before the man could lift his leg for a second kick, Creed let go of the leash.

Bolo hit him full force, slamming the man to the ground. He started to scream, but Bolo's front paws came down hard on his chest and Creed could hear the gasp as air literally got knocked out of him.

'Good boy, Bolo. Stay put.'

'Are you ... nuts?' the guy managed to stutter.

He ignored him and went to check on the dog – a skinny black Lab with a sagging belly that up until recently had been nursing puppies. Creed petted her and helped her to her feet. Told her she was a 'good girl' and asked her to sit in the grass.

Before he stood back up to look inside the open lift-gate, he knew what he'd find. His fingers couldn't untie the knot quick enough, so he ripped open the end of the black plastic bag. He expected them to be already dead, but one by one the puppies started wiggling up and out.

He didn't need to ask what this guy had intended to do. By now, Creed knew too well. People had gotten into the bad habit of dumping their unwanted dogs at the end of his driveway. It was how he had acquired many of his dogs, including Grace.

But so as not to take too much advantage, this guy was going to leave only the adult dog. The puppies he had gathered up into a trash bag. He probably would have dumped them in the river after he left Creed's place.

'What's your name, mister?' Creed asked, without leaving the puppies and without giving Bolo a command.

'Can you get your dog off of me?'

'Even if you don't tell me, I have your license plate number.'

'We couldn't afford one dog, let alone six.'

Creed counted the puppies, making sure all of them were still alive.

'Can you get your dog off of me? I can't breathe,' the man complained.

'Yeah, that feels pretty bad, doesn't it? To not be able to breathe.'

'Damn! You're crazier than people say.'

'Oh, you don't know the half of it, mister. Because if I so much as hear that you get another dog or even think about getting a dog, I'll come find you. Do you understand that?'

The man went silent.

'Bolo, stay.'

Creed gathered all the puppies back into the bag, using it to hold them in his arms but letting all five little heads poke up and out. The mother dog saw that he was taking them, and he didn't need to ask her to follow. She was already at his heels.

'You can't leave me here with this dog!'

He ignored the guy again and kept walking. When he got back to the house, he'd whistle for Bolo to come home.

TUESDAY

26

ALABAMA

Early morning thunderstorms had delayed O'Dell's flight from Washington, DC, to Atlanta. Instead of taking a second roller-coaster flight on to Mobile, she rented a car in Atlanta, deciding she'd rather drive the four hours. Her trip turned into five hours. In the pouring rain. With lightning strikes that threatened to slice the compact rental in two.

She had chugged down a couple of Diet Pepsis as her breakfast and now acid churned in her stomach. By the time she drove into Andalusia, her nerves were raw from tight-fisting the steering wheel. Her eyes were blurred from the constant dance of windshield wipers trying to slice through the battering rain.

The café was several more miles outside of town, very much off the beaten path. But it was where the Covington County sheriff had suggested they meet, adding that the Bagleys' acreage was only about ten minutes away.

She'd left him a voice message earlier when she realized her delay. She wouldn't have been surprised if he had decided not to wait, but his black-and-white SUV was in the parking lot next to the elongated building. The large sign out front advertised HUNTING, FISHING, CAMPING right under BLUE LAKE CAFÉ. Maybe that explained its remote location and all the pickup-truck-driving clientele.

The sky had already started to clear, puddles now the only evidence of the storms she had just driven through. O'Dell stepped out of the air-conditioned car and immediately felt the heat and humidity hit her in the face, fogging up her sunglasses. She kept the glasses on. Figured she needed them. They were the only thing she wore that made her look like she might have the authority of an FBI agent. Of course, she wanted the authority but without looking like a fed. So she had dressed appropriately.

Her oversized chambray shirt was buttoned properly,

despite the T-shirt underneath, with room to conceal her Glock, in case she needed it, tucked into the waistband of her threadbare jeans. Her shirtsleeves were rolled up haphazardly, and she wore lightweight ankle-high hiking boots that looked weathered. Still, when she walked in the door, every head turned in her direction. She may have succeeded in not being pegged as a federal agent, but what caught everyone's attention was the one thing she had not been able to conceal. She still looked like an outsider. There was no disguising that.

A middle-aged man in the corner with bristled steel-gray hair waved at her. His white shirt with a gold badge on his chest gave him away. The chair scraped the floor as he pushed it out, standing to greet her. He was tall, broad-shouldered, and barrel-chested. His bulk matched his deep voice. But when he took her offered hand, he squeezed gently, instead of shaking it like a man who isn't used to female colleagues.

'So you ran into those thunderstorms?' he said in place of a greeting, waiting for her to sit down.

Of course, he already knew she had driven through the downpours from her voice message. That's what had caused her delay. Instead of getting impatient, she decided it was a good place to start. So she nodded and obliged him with the courtesy of some weather chitchat.

'I couldn't believe it just kept pouring.'

He laughed, a rich, deep-throated sound that seemed genuine. 'Welcome to the South in the good ole summertime.'

O'Dell hated the games of social politeness. It was a waste of time on a day already delayed. She didn't want to be pulling up to Trevor and Regina Bagley's house just as the sun was setting. However, she had dealt with small-town law enforcement enough to know that what happened in the cafés and coffee shops was just as important as what happened in the field or at the crime scene.

And to her advantage, she was already learning a few things about the sheriff, though not by his own admission. Sheriff Jackson Holt was recently divorced. His ring finger still bore the indent and faded skin. She caught him reaching for the absent ring to twist it in a habit that hadn't had time to be replaced.

The divorce, however, had not affected his meticulous appearance. His uniform shirt and T-shirt underneath were bright white, the sleeve patches like new, and the gold badge attached with careful consideration. All his attention to detail probably meant that he played by the rules – all of them, never deviating from them, which could be a disadvantage. O'Dell was hoping to find an excuse to take a look around the Bagley place, despite the fact that Regina Bagley wouldn't be in the mood for it. And despite the fact that they had no grounds for a warrant.

Winning over the local sheriff was one of the reasons she'd agreed to meet him for lunch – now a late lunch. And the amazing aromas from the kitchen reminded her that she hadn't eaten yet today. Over catfish and hush puppies that made her want to move in out back behind the café, she filled in Sheriff Holt with the limited details she had decided to share. Never did she mention drugs or even hint at the idea that Trevor Bagley's unfortunate death may have been related to dealing in drugs.

'They pretty much keep to themselves,' he told her when she asked about the couple. 'Their acreage backs up to the national forest, so it's kinda remote. I'm not sure what they do for a living. They don't bother anybody. No complaints, anyway. Bagley inherited the property from his daddy. Somebody mentioned that he might have done a tour in Afghanistan. Said they remembered him in a uniform at the funeral.'

O'Dell kept to herself the fact that Bagley had been discharged from military duty. Perhaps she was wrong about it being dishonorable if he was still wearing his uniform.

For the first time, she wondered if his military service had anything to do with his death.

27

Hannah would be glad to get out of the house. Didn't matter that the girl had been sleeping most of the time, especially after Hannah had given her a homemade pain remedy. Her throat and stomach would take some time to heal. Sleep would do her good.

Hannah had insisted they set her up in a guest bedroom on the main level, clear on the opposite end of the house, as far away as possible from Hannah and her two boys. Her boys were still with her grandparents, but if Amanda was still here when they returned, both of them already knew not to come over to this part of the house.

There were only two doors down this hallway. One

was the guest bedroom and the other door led to the basement. Actually, not a basement as much as a deep, windowless, cinder-block room that had been used as a storm cellar years ago.

Rye had taken out the steps in hopes of replacing them when he had time, but Hannah couldn't risk her boys snooping. They'd fall and break their necks. It had to be a fifteen-foot drop. She made Rye put on a heavy metal door with an electronic keypad lock that her boys would never be able to access. And then she still told the boys never to come down this hallway. It seemed the perfect place to send this girl. Not down to the storm cellar, but rather to the guest bedroom at the end of the hallway. Hannah wasn't sure why, but she didn't trust the girl. Rye obviously thought she was overreacting, but her instincts had never been wrong before.

Still, she brought the girl a bowl of homemade chicken noodle soup, fresh strawberries, and a grilled cheese sandwich. Amanda had stared at the tray with eyes wide and jaw dropped open. She looked like an eight-year-old being presented with an extravagant Christmas gift.

'Your momma never bring you a tray in bed before?'

'No one's *ever* brought me a tray of food.'

Just before Hannah could feel a bit sorry for her, the girl's eyes narrowed, as if she just remembered something, and then the snarky teenager showed up again in time to add, 'You're not trying to poison me, are you?'

'Good heavens! What kind of a world did you grow up in, child?'

'I'm not a child.'

It came out automatically, defensively, but without much conviction. Hannah noticed her sink into the bed pillows, adjusting herself with the tray on her lap, clamping onto it as if she were worried that Hannah would take it back if she fussed too much.

'You need anything, Mr Creed is out at the dog kennels.'

'You're leaving?'

Suddenly there was panic in her eyes. No, not just panic. Hannah could see the fear make the girl's whole body go rigid. And it reminded Hannah of the danger Rye had brought onto their property and into her home.

She gave a quick explanation of the house's security system, including a one-time guest code if Amanda decided to leave. God forgive her, but Hannah almost hoped the girl would decide to up and leave by the time she got back. No good could come from helping this drug mule.

Ryder didn't understand. Had said as much last night.

'How can you have more compassion for drug abusers at Segway House than you do for this girl?'

'They come because they want to stop abusing drugs.'

'She came to me, Hannah, asking for help. Isn't that the same thing?'

'Did she come to you or was she running away from them?'

'What difference does that make?'

At that point she had to admit she wasn't sure. There was something that nagged at her about this girl. She didn't seem quite as young and innocent as she pretended to be. Bottom line, Hannah didn't trust her. And she couldn't explain that, either.

'We don't know a thing about her, and she's sleeping in the same house my boys call home.'

'You brought Jason here, and how much do you really know about him?'

'I know he was wounded fighting for our country.'

'And that's enough for you?'

She didn't have an answer. Her boys' daddy came back from Iraq in a flag-draped coffin before their littlest boy could celebrate his first birthday. She knew her judgment might be clouded when it came to helping the young soldiers who found their way to Segway House. But she had also learned long ago to listen to her instincts, to trust her first impressions. She crossed her arms and watched Ryder do the same, as if they were standing off against each other. It wouldn't be the first time. But he surprised her with what he said next.

'The whole time I was driving back from Atlanta with her, I kept thinking, *Is this something that could have happened to Brodie?*' He wasn't expecting an answer. He avoided her eyes, stared at the wall across the room as if he could see something there that he hadn't noticed before. 'Those kids on that fishing boat . . . Kids disappear every day and they want us to think they're dead. That it's just a matter of time before we find their bodies.'

Then he looked at her, met her eyes. 'But what if they're not . . . What if Brodie's not . . . She could have been Amanda. She could still be Amanda. Waiting for the chance to run away. Or maybe she's given up on the chance of ever getting away.'

He didn't talk much about his sister, even though Hannah knew he thought about her with every search. She told him it wasn't healthy to consume his own life with one that might already be gone. But she knew from her own personal experience that losing someone before you're ready to say goodbye can leave you with little reason and a whole lot of empty.

Last night she had told him they needed a plan. The girl could stay for now, while her boys were gone. Anything longer was asking for trouble. But even as she watched him gather up the balloons of cocaine, she didn't ask what he intended to do with them. If it had been up to her, she would have flushed them down the toilet.

She told herself they'd both be thinking clearer in the morning. But morning hadn't even broken the horizon and Creed had brought her a whole other pack of trouble – puppies!

Neither of them had raised puppies in a long time. Most of their dogs came to them a bit older. When Creed explained the black garbage bag, she just shook her head. Then she insisted on keeping them in the house until he could make a separate place for them in the kennels.

Lady had helped the scrawny momma round up the puppies again and again. By the time they finally settled into the temporary pen Hannah had created for them, all were exhausted. Still, the half-starved mother dog had devoured the bowlful of warm chicken and rice that Hannah had prepared for her.

Now she stole a peek at them as she tiptoed toward the back door. Lady was the only one who looked up at her. The border collie was still standing guard outside the pen, watching over them.

'I'll be back in a few hours,' she told the dog.

Getting in her car, Hannah felt a prick of guilt, because all she could really think about was going to get her boys and driving far away.

28

SEGWAY HOUSE

PENSACOLA, FLORIDA

The guy was skinny and small. He looked like he might be fifteen. Jason had seen plenty of his type in the military. What they lacked in stature they tried to make up for with their mouths. Big talkers. Bullshit talkers.

He told them his name was Falco, as he grabbed a chair from the corner and asked, 'You mind if I join you fellows?'

Fellows? Not fellas. His English was good but too formal. And not good enough to hide the Spanish accent. Jason wondered why he bothered. Who cared?

'Suit yourself.' It was Tony who answered for them because it was Tony who Falco addressed.

Jason didn't blame the guy for singling out Tony. Even gathered around their poker table, they probably looked like a sorry bunch of rejects: Jason with his empty shirtsleeve dangling, Colfax with his glass eye and Frankenstein scars, and Benny with both legs sliced off above the kneecaps.

Tony was the only whole one. In another world, in another lifetime, he'd be holding down a good job with benefits as an electrical engineer for some big frickin' corporation. Unlike the other three, Tony was still in one piece. He had no scars, no missing limbs, no blown-off parts. Tony could have passed for one of the blond college boys down here on summer break, shooting the breeze until he took off to go catch some waves over on Pensacola Beach.

They joked about Tony having no scars – how fit and trim and good-looking he was, like a shiny copper penny – all the while knowing full well that he was about as worthless as a penny, as worthless as the rest of them.

Forget about scars. Tony had what he called brain fevers. Jason once saw Tony during a full-blown one.

All of them had some level of PTSD (post-traumatic stress disorder), but nothing like Tony's brain fevers. His were beyond any brain injury Jason had seen since he got back. Technically they called it TBI – traumatic brain injury. Like that made a difference. For Tony, it was as if his brain began to boil, the anger sparked by an electrical storm from within. You could almost smell it – sweat and spit and sometimes blood. You didn't want to be anywhere in the line of fire when it happened.

On days like today, when Tony's meds were working – or when he decided to take them – he was a good guy. He was witty and told great stories. In combat he would have been the guy who had your back – no matter what. On the outside, Tony was the only one of them who probably sounded normal and looked whole. So Jason could understand this guy named Falco thinking that Tony was the leader at their table.

'I'm looking to recruit a few good men,' Falco said with a wide-tooth grin.

No one said a word. Colfax shuffled the deck of cards and started dealing them out, purposely bypassing Falco.

'I know you're all ex-military.'

'Really?' Benny said. 'What gave us away? The spit-and-polish shine on our shoes?'

Jason smiled. Colfax snorted and finished out the deal. Falco glanced at Benny's wheelchair without a hint of humor or embarrassment, and definitely not a trace of apology. He was here to make his spiel.

'I know you guys have special skills, right? Ones you probably can't use anymore.'

'Oh, absolutely,' Tony said. 'We were all special ops. Highly classified, though. We can't even talk about it.' He winked at Falco, then picked up his cards and gave them his full attention.

Some of the most annoying things about having only one hand were also some of the stupidest. Jason had to put his cards down every time he wanted to scratch his nose or take a drink of his soda. Alcohol wasn't allowed on the premises. Most of the other guys drank Red Bull or coffee. He popped the soda can's tab and everyone at the table looked up at him as though he had fired a gun. Sudden loud noises were always a problem, but not usually a soda can. Jason realized that this guy Falco had actually succeeded in rattling his buddies.

Falco noticed, too. From out of nowhere he placed

a crisp one-hundred-dollar bill on the table. All eyes checked it out.

'We don't play with money,' Colfax told him.

'I don't play with money, either.'

The big-ass grin was gone. His eyes turned dark as they darted toward the door. He placed another bill on top, waited a beat, then placed another and another, as if he were showing a hand of cards. Only, he didn't stop until there were ten crisp Ben Franklins staring up from the tabletop and he had exactly what he wanted – everyone's attention.

'I know you guys must have some serious bills. You definitely don't have enough cash or you wouldn't be in a place like this,' Falco said. 'You guys served your country. Took a bullet.' He waved a finger at Benny. 'Or a frickin' bomb, right? And yet, here you all are.'

He put his hand over the bills to emphasize his point. 'There's a lot more for each of you,' Falco told them. 'This is just ... Let's call it a signing bonus.'

'Why don't you tell us what it is you want,' Colfax said.

'I need a little wet work done. Oh, and it'd probably help if you hate dogs.'

29

'Penelope, I don't train apprehension dogs,' Creed said.

As if on cue, the dog snarled at Creed through the vehicle window. Long and bright white glorious fangs in a massive and strong snout. German shepherds were usually the breed of choice for air-scent dogs, especially for police departments. Creed, however, didn't have a single one, only because he often took in and trained rescues. Many of them he'd gotten from the tall, lean woman who stood beside him, smiling at the dog in the car.

This dog looked powerful and sleek, with black markings on his brown coat that made him look regal.

'He's a beaut, though.'

'And you used to not train drug dogs or bomb dogs,' she countered.

Penelope Clemence had been calling and telling him about dogs for the last three or four years. She had an eye for those that were trainable, and Creed respected and appreciated her expertise. But every once in a while she talked him into a dog simply because the dog had pulled her heartstrings.

Creed had never asked what exactly her connection was to the Alpaloose Animal Shelter. He knew she was not a paid employee or listed as a member of their staff. Hannah had told him that Penelope donated much more than time to the shelter. Evidently it was enough money that she got away with some avant-garde tactics.

It surprised Creed that the woman had money because she drove a beat-up Jeep Wrangler with a chunk of the grille missing and huge, thick tires that made her look like an off-roader. Her short hair was the color of honey in what Hannah called a 'chic cut.' She wore her fingernails long and they were always manicured and polished, but her jeans were thread-bare, worn through at the knees, and her hiking boots had seen better days. Maybe that look was chic, too. Creed paid little attention to such things. All he knew was that Penelope Clemence didn't look rich and certainly was not what he expected a philanthropic matron to look like. Truth was, Creed had no idea about her life outside the animal shelter. He never asked, and she never offered additional information.

Although Penelope had called Creed about many dogs that he ended up adopting from the shelter, she had never brought one out to his facility. Today he was distracted. He wanted to tell her about the puppies he'd just acquired last night. But he knew it wouldn't matter. He already guessed this shepherd was another heartstring dog for her, and he owed her a listen.

Despite how gorgeous this guy obviously was, there was no way he could have such an aggressive dog in his kennels. Already ropes of saliva dangled from the dog's mouth as he bounced around the backseat of Penelope's SUV, trying to get at Creed.

'Why do you think I'd want a dog that obviously hates me?'

'Oh, sweetie, he doesn't hate you,' she said in her wonderful southern drawl. 'It has nothing to do with you. He hates all men.'

'Oh good, that makes me feel so much better.'

'He's wonderful with other dogs. Very loving.'

That didn't surprise Creed. Still, he couldn't train a dog that wanted to attack him.

'He's crazy smart and only two years old.'

Before Creed could respond, Penelope clapped her hands three times and the dog sat down.

'Good boy, Chance!' She buzzed down the car window enough to toss him a dog treat. He caught it, chomped and swallowed. It was a pathetically small treat for such a huge mouth, but he stayed put, hoping for more.

'You named him Chance, expecting me to give him another?' Creed whispered so the dog wouldn't get excited at hearing his name.

'His previous owner likes playing the slots in Biloxi. Thought he'd bring her good luck. Turns out her new boyfriend doesn't much like the dog. Especially when he's hitting on his girlfriend and the dog attacks.'

'That's what she said?'

'In her police record. Then she changed her mind. Recanted. Said the dog attacked her boyfriend for no reason at all.'

'Damn, that's cold.'

'Boyfriend or the dog. She chose the boyfriend. Dog's gotta go.'

'And because he attacked someone—'

'That's right. He's on the docket for elimination this week. Actually, tomorrow.'

Creed let out a long sigh. He tucked his fists into his jean pockets.

'Can't you get in a lot of trouble for this?' he asked her.

'What are they going to do? They can't fire me. I think they need my annual donation and volunteer services more than they care about one dog.'

Creed forgot and leaned against the vehicle. Chance jumped up, banging front paws against the inside of the door. He snarled and was trying to bite through the three inches of open window.

When Creed glanced over at Penelope, he caught her with eyes wide and mouth open, as if she wanted to give another command but realized it might be too late for that.

'Does anyone know you brought him here?'

'Brought who?'

He smiled and shook his head. She was good.

'Let me go get Andy,' he said. 'She'll need to settle him down. Most likely she'll need to be the one to train him, too.'

30

SEGWAY HOUSE

'Are you sure that's her real name?'

Hannah looked up from the stack of papers and nodded at Claudia Reed.

'I got it from her passport.' Then before Claudia could ask the next obvious question, Hannah added, 'Yes, it's a valid passport.'

Hannah had been volunteering at Segway House since the day she helped open its doors. She hated, however, that the anniversary of her service reminded her of her husband's death. Ironically, if it hadn't been for Marcus getting killed in Iraq, Hannah probably never would have become involved in such a place.

She also never would have met, let alone become friends with, the petite blonde sitting behind the computer. They came from two entirely different worlds. Claudia's childhood had been filled with beautiful things and privileges that generations of wealth and influence afforded her, while Hannah grew up on her grandparents' farm, working from dawn till dusk and scratching for every dollar she earned. But war was the great leveler, and this one had taken both their husbands without asking for pedigree or résumé.

Claudia Reed and Hannah had started Segway House with three other military wives who had also lost their husbands, in either Iraq or Afghanistan. Claudia was the only one who could afford to work full-time as the director without taking a salary.

Their fund-raising efforts were always tough. People were tired of a decade of war and wanted to forget about it. The problem was, the number of veterans who needed help only continued to grow while their government also grew tired and cash-strapped.

Hannah had just started to go through the stack of requests Claudia had handed her when she walked through the door. Last week they had approved and written checks for thirty-four grants, a total of

$47,810. This week looked to equal that challenge. At a glance, she had seen requests to finance a ramp to be built for a new amputee. Another veteran was asking for a quick loan to help to have his electricity turned on, so he could return to his home. He was still waiting for his first disability check. They didn't do loans. They called them grants and didn't accept payback, but many of these young men and women were fiercely proud and included the wording in their request if for nothing more than to feel better about asking for money.

Segway House wasn't limited to veterans. In the last year they had started taking in runaways, drug addicts, abused women and, sometimes, their children. They never had enough rooms to meet the demand. And there were always more needs than they could address.

At the same time, their clients and residents confided in them things that they didn't even share with family members, and because of this, Hannah knew that she could trust Claudia.

'She's not listed as a runaway.'

'Missing?' Hannah asked, but already knew that there was no one looking for Amanda.

Claudia shook her head and finally gave her fingers

a rest from the keyboard, swiveling her desk chair to focus on Hannah. 'Do you need anything?'

Hannah knew it would be the only question she would ask. Claudia wouldn't push her to reveal anything else. Nor would she give unsolicited advice.

'I fear she's one of those kids who done slipped through the cracks,' Hannah said, letting herself slide into slang in hopes of relieving some of the seriousness.

She wasn't sure what she expected when she asked Claudia to do a national search. All she knew was that she had a bad feeling about the girl. Whatever trouble she had gotten herself into had not stopped back at Hartsfield's international terminal just because Ryder had rescued her. And no matter what he wanted to believe, Hannah knew neither of them would be able to protect this girl if that drug cartel decided they wanted their property back.

'Do you know if we have any residents with electrical experience?' she asked, purposely changing the subject. 'I need someone to check out our breakers before Rye hooks up any more of his gadgets.'

31

The quiet was almost unnerving. O'Dell shut the cruiser door, and the echo it produced made her immediately notice. There were no sounds of traffic or jets overhead. No humming air conditioners or barking dogs.

During the entire trip – what Sheriff Holt claimed was ten minutes but seemed like twenty to O'Dell – they had met up with only one other vehicle on the winding back roads. Rows of huge live oaks flanked both sides of the Bagleys' long, graveled driveway, and the canopy of branches and leaves overhead made it feel like they were driving through a tunnel. Even the two-story house was tucked back into the woods that surrounded the property.

The quiet and isolation had O'Dell's mind already working. A man could be tortured on this property and no one would ever hear his screams for help or his cries of pain.

There was no response to the sheriff's knock on the front door. No shuffling of feet, no shift of curtains. O'Dell walked to the corner of the porch, keeping away from the only window, then turned to get a better look down the driveway. She wondered at what point someone inside would be able to see the black-and-white cruiser.

'Mrs Bagley,' the sheriff called. 'I'm the Covington County sheriff. Sheriff Holt. Just want to talk to you. Nobody's in trouble.' Then he glanced over his shoulder at O'Dell and shrugged. 'I guess she's not home.'

She did a quick visual search of the pickup that was parked alongside the house on the grass, instead of on the graveled patch in front of the house. She was close enough that she could see through the garage window and the space looked empty. According to the county property records, a Dodge Ram pickup and a Land Rover were registered to the Bagleys.

Sheriff Holt's cruiser had left tracks where the downpour had washed the gravel thin. But there were no other fresh tire tracks. No one had arrived or left, at least not during or after the thunderstorms.

The two other buildings on the property looked old and worn and unused. O'Dell swept her eyes over both structures, scanning the windows and scrutinizing the rooflines as well as the discarded equipment against the sides, looking for anything out of place or any movement.

She didn't see anything out of the ordinary, and yet something didn't feel right.

Sheriff Holt raised his fist to knock again but stopped in midair when he noticed O'Dell easing her Glock from the small of her back. His eyes went wide and his ruddy face went pale. She put an index finger to her lips as she came up beside him. He fumbled with his own gun, unsnapping the holster and making too much noise. It wouldn't matter. O'Dell knew if someone was inside waiting for them, he or she was already in position.

She leaned her shoulder against the frame just to the left of the windowless door and nodded for him to do the same on the other side. He squeezed his bulk awkwardly against the porch rail, giving himself plenty of distance away from the door now that he understood what threat might be waiting for them.

O'Dell listened, cocking her head. Still, there were no sounds coming from inside. She held her weapon in her right hand, and with her left, reached across the door and tried the knob. It turned with no resistance, and that's when her heart started to race. She glanced up at the sheriff, met his eyes, giving him a chance to tell her 'no.' After all, they had no warrant. No reason to enter. Nothing except O'Dell's gut instinct.

Slow and easy didn't play well if someone was waiting on the other side. It only gave them more time to aim. She took a deep breath and shoved the door open as she rolled back against the outside of the house and out of the line of fire. The door hit the inside wall, sounding like a gunshot and making Sheriff Holt jump. But nothing followed. They were greeted by more silence.

O'Dell eased around the doorjamb, letting her Glock lead the way inside.

More silence.

The large entrance included plenty of hiding places: an open staircase, a long, narrow hallway beside it, and too many archways leading to other rooms. Sheriff Holt raised his chin toward the staircase, then squeezed past her to start his slow climb. O'Dell noticed a set of keys on the desk in the entryway. Sunglasses, a wallet, and what looked like a grocery or errand list were also on the desk.

She moved slowly. Peeked into rooms, carefully opening doors and trying to keep her back to the wall as much as possible. The old house creaked with almost every step, and she could easily hear the sheriff above her. If someone was inside hiding, they should be able to hear any movement.

Even before she entered the kitchen she could smell bacon and burnt toast, but both were a bit stale in the air, not fresh. It looked as if breakfast had been interrupted and abandoned. On the stovetop a skillet was filled with bacon now congealed in grease. A plate with two slices of burnt toast was left on the countertop, alongside a container of melted butter. The table had two place settings: plates, silverware, water glasses filled to the brim. Coffee mugs waited by the coffeemaker, coffee made but not poured. A carton of cream left open beside it.

The coffeemaker was the closest. O'Dell took several steps and leaned over, but before she put her nose to the cream she could smell that it was spoiled. She took another look around the kitchen. How long ago?

She pulled a paper towel from the roll and used it to pick up the carton of cream. She swirled the contents from side to side and could feel the chunks swish inside. She had no idea how long it took for cream to curdle, but she guessed it might be days, not hours.

'What the hell?' Sheriff Holt came into the kitchen and stared at the macabre scene.

'Looks like they left in a hurry. I take it you didn't find anyone upstairs?'

'Nope, didn't find anybody, but I sure as hell found something stranger than this. You're gonna want to take a look for yourself.'

32

The statue in the middle of the makeshift altar stood almost two feet tall. The female skeleton dressed in a black robe held a scythe and looked very much like the Grim Reaper. Had O'Dell not seen the same image on the bloated corpse of Trevor Bagley, she might have been as taken aback as Sheriff Holt was.

'It's an altar,' she said.

'Damn straight. But what the hell for?'

'Santa Muerte. The saint of death.'

She ignored his dumbfounded stare and walked across the bedroom to get a closer look. The sheriff seemed surprised at her reaction. Maybe he was expecting her to be as alarmed as he apparently was.

She calmly slipped her weapon into her waistband at the small of her back and pulled her shirt over it.

'You've seen this sort of thing before?'

'Only on the internet.'

This one was quite elaborate, by the standards she had viewed. A bloodred cloth covered the entire length of the dresser top. A shorter white lace cloth lay on top. About a dozen small red and white votive candles, melted down from use, created a border around the edges. Other items were carefully placed around the statue: incense, a bowl of apples, rosary beads, small containers of oil, prayer cards, several plastic toy skulls and one rubber spider, a full pack of cigarettes, a bottle of Espolòn tequila and another of Patrón, with an empty glass in front. There were other items she didn't recognize, but she knew each had its own significance and purpose.

'Is it some kind of cult thing?'

O'Dell shook her head and looked around the room, examining the other contents.

'People set up altars and pray to Santa Muerte for a variety of reasons – good health, a new job, a faithful husband or wife, for protection, or for vengeance. Not really much different from Catholics setting up a shrine to the Virgin Mary.'

'Hey, I'm Catholic, and this isn't like anything I've seen. Tequila? Cigarettes?'

She didn't remind him about the practice of lighting candles, using incense, taking in food for an Easter blessing. Almost every religion had something that outsiders could view as strange. But she did have to admit, praying to the saint of death gave her pause, and she glanced back at the altar.

Something wasn't right.

The empty glass. The photos she had seen of other altars always included tequila poured and waiting in a glass or in several small shot glasses. She also didn't remember any spiders. Skulls, yes, but spiders?

'Don't touch anything.'

'Of course, I'm not gonna touch any of this freak show.'

'No, seriously. This house might be part of a crime scene.'

'Already thought of that.'

He shot her a look that verged on impatience. She had to admit that, outside of his initial panicked fumble to get his weapon out of its holster, Sheriff Holt had been careful and methodical.

'Sorry,' she said. 'Is this the master bedroom?'

'Far as I can tell. The other has a twin bed with boxes stacked on it. And a treadmill.'

On the opposite wall were framed family photos, and O'Dell stopped at one that showed the Bagleys. Regina Bagley was small and pretty, with long black hair. In the photo Trevor wore his red hair military short. His pale, freckled skin looked even lighter next to his wife's mocha-colored skin. The fact that Regina might be of Hispanic descent should not have tripped off any alarms, but O'Dell suddenly found herself wondering if Trevor's beautiful wife had shared his same fate, or if she had played a hand in his. Why wasn't she here?

From the upstairs bedroom window O'Dell had a better view of the grounds behind the house. It looked like acres of forest. Was it possible Mrs Bagley had gotten away? Or was she still out there?

O'Dell turned back to look at Sheriff Holt, waited for him to meet her eyes.

'There's something I didn't tell you.'

He put his hands on his waist, thumbs in his gun belt, and raised an eyebrow. Had it not been for the adrenaline rush, O'Dell thought he might be angry.

'Trevor Bagley was tortured before he was killed. I

think it might have happened somewhere close to here. Maybe on his own property.'

'Damn! That's a helluva way to go.'

'Do you have a dog handler you could call?'

He nodded. 'I'll see if I can get him over here tomorrow.'

Then he looked over her shoulder, out the window, and asked, 'So where the hell do you suppose Mrs Bagley is?'

O'Dell shrugged. 'Hopefully she's somewhere far away from here, hiding.'

WEDNESDAY

33

The gray sky made the Bagley property look more ominous. Even O'Dell's rental car flicked on its headlights automatically as she drove under the long stretch of canopy created by the massive live oak trees.

Sheriff Holt was already there, waiting with one of his deputies. Both were sipping from stainless steel travel mugs. It looked like they had a map spread out on the hood of the SUV. A paper bag anchored down one corner. Both men wore their uniforms – white shirts pressed, badges glistening, gun belts cinched tight. She wondered how they intended to search the property in such high-polished shoes.

Holt had told her earlier on the phone that he'd

managed to get a search warrant. She didn't ask for details. O'Dell didn't get too concerned about formalities, but she'd pegged him as a by-the-rules kind of guy. This was his county and she could hear the relief in his voice. She knew he'd want to cover his tracks. Now she wondered if he simply intended to sit back and direct the search while he and his deputy sipped coffee and ate doughnuts.

Holt was on his cell phone, and his deputy hurried over to meet her car.

'Agent O'Dell, I'm Deputy Jimmy Franklin,' he told her as soon as she opened her car door.

'Deputy Franklin.'

He seemed too anxious. He came at her with his hand outstretched, but not as a gesture to shake hands. Instead, it was almost as if he thought he should help her get out of the car.

Awkward.

'I'm fine, thanks,' she told him as she ignored his aid.

When he realized his mistake his face went crimson. O'Dell pretended not to notice, shut the door on her own, and went to the trunk. She popped it open and started to get her gear. Poor kid didn't look old enough to drink alcohol legally. Even his uniform seemed a size too large. The shoulder seams sagged and the gun belt was cinched at its tightest notch. His patrol hat came down too far on his head, making his ears stick out. Still, he was all spit and polish, looking official and shiny, just like his boss, while O'Dell had come dressed for mud and mosquitoes.

'I can help you with that, ma'am.' Evidently he hadn't been embarrassed enough because here he was by her side, reinforcing O'Dell's image of a Boy Scout.

'I've got it,' she told him without a glance, and trying not to wince at the 'ma'am.'

That's when she noticed that Holt had finished his phone call and was crossing the yard to meet a Jeep Grand Cherokee coming up the driveway. Deputy Jimmy followed.

O'Dell continued to stuff her daypack with a few necessities, including Deet, a black-light torch, some evidence bags, and finally a couple of protein bars – although she wouldn't mind snagging one of those doughnuts. She wasn't sure what she was expecting to find.

Stan Wenhoff had insisted that the insect bites on Trevor Bagley's corpse were caused by his body – his live body – lying on a mound of fire ants. She had no idea what the crime scene would look like. Would there still be stakes in the ground where his wrists and ankles were tied down? Would the grass be trampled? Would there be blood mixed in the mound of ants?

It was one of the reasons she had brought a portable black light. It resembled a flashlight, only with UV ultraviolet light. If they found an area in question, the black light might be able to indicate if there were any bodily fluids left behind. Almost an impossibility, considering the downpour of just the previous day. But she had been stunned in previous cases when a forensic team discovered pieces of flesh mixed in the soil of outdoor crime scenes. Some remnants were difficult to destroy. She was counting on that, especially if the dog and its handler were going to lead them to where Bagley may have died.

O'Dell slid the daypack over her shoulders to wear as a small backpack. When she slammed the car trunk shut, she saw that two men had arrived with the Jeep. The search dog was waiting patiently, just inside the open liftgate. The dog's handler had his back to her while he gathered up his gear. And then the dog noticed her and began wagging and wiggling impatiently. No, the dog hadn't just noticed her, *it recognized her.*

It was Grace! And O'Dell's stomach took a sudden slide, because not only did she recognize the dog, she also recognized her owner. He was tall – over six feet – with broad shoulders and a slender waist, and he filled his jeans quite nicely. He turned at that moment to see what had gotten his dog excited. It took only a few seconds, and Ryder Creed smiled.

For O'Dell, the flush came as a surprise. An annoying surprise that accompanied a flutter in her stomach.

34

Creed was glad to have Jason along, no matter if the kid had a chip on his shoulder and insisted on being incredibly antisocial. It gave him an excuse *not* to talk to Maggie O'Dell about anything other than this assignment.

He had already explained the process to Sheriff Holt. He and his deputy appeared relieved that they'd have to stay behind. Creed preferred as few people as possible. They only provided more distractions for his dogs. In this case there was no urgency. It wasn't like they were searching for a missing child or an injured victim. As best as Hannah had explained, they weren't even looking for a body. Only the crime scene.

Before he noticed her daypack, Creed knew O'Dell would insist on going along. He knew he'd never convince her to stay put with Holt and his deputy. But he also knew she would respect his guidelines. She wouldn't be a distraction for Grace. She would be a distraction for him. And he hated that that was true.

There was one rule he never broke, and he took pride in the fact that he did not mix business with pleasure. Many of the women he knew intimately didn't even know what he did for a living. Maggie O'Dell was the only woman who had made him come close to breaking that rule. That she didn't even bother to notice only made him a bit crazier.

They had worked a case together four months ago. Both their lives had been jeopardized. Things got a little heated – some sparks, electricity, not unlike right now. But it was only one kiss. No big deal. He hadn't heard from her since, but then she hadn't heard from him either. So why did it bother him?

'Tell me what exactly we're looking for.' He cut to the chase.

'I'm not sure.'

'Holt said something about a crime scene, but that the victim was recovered somewhere else?'

'Somewhere else being the Potomac River.'

'DC?'

'Yes.'

He watched her glance over her shoulder and couldn't help thinking it was just like the feds, holding back information from the local law enforcement. Not necessarily a bad idea. There was a reason for the practice, but as far as Creed knew, Sheriff Jackson Holt did a decent job of following the rules and keeping his mouth shut. But Creed wasn't here to defend anyone. He usually tried his best to stay far from the fray.

'You pulled him from the river?' he asked when it didn't look like she was going to offer more.

'Yes, but the medical examiner doesn't believe he died anywhere close to the District.'

Another glance, this time at Jason.

'We don't need to know all the details,' Creed told her. 'But I do need to know what you expect Grace to find. Or at least, what you're hoping she might find.'

'I'm not sure. I don't even know what to look for.'

There was more hesitation but not out of secrecy. She really did look like she did not know.

'There were insect bites,' she continued, 'all over the back of the body. Red blisters. Pustules. The ME said they contained a toxic alkaloid venom called solenopsin. Supposedly it's the same stuff fire ants inject.'

Creed saw Jason wince and shake his head as he asked, 'Someone killed this guy by putting fire ants all over him?'

'More likely they tied him down. There were ligature marks on his wrists and ankles.'

'Son of a bitch.' Jason shook his head.

'And you think they did this to him somewhere close by?' Creed asked.

'This is his property. Well, his and his wife's.'

'And what does she have to say about all this?'

'Looks like she may have left in a hurry. Sheriff Holt's been trying to locate her. Their Land Rover's missing. He has an APB out on it.'

Creed wiped a sleeve across his forehead and took another look around. Then to O'Dell he said, 'Do you know if there's blood?'

'The way this guy was bitten, it looks like it.'

'Insect bites? That's all we've got? My dogs don't have miracle noses.'

'The ligatures dug deep enough into the skin that his wrists and ankles most likely did bleed.' She was staring at him now, waiting as if for his assessment.

'How long ago?'

'Excuse me?'

'Does your ME know how long ago this happened?'

Her eyes darted away, and he could tell she knew this whole search was, indeed, a long shot.

'Maybe a week.'

'I can't make any guarantees.'

'I don't expect any. Look, I'm not even sure this is the right place.' O'Dell readjusted her ball cap, tucking in strands of hair. Then she put her sunglasses back on before she looked at Creed again. 'Truth is, this could be a waste of time, but my gut keeps telling me something happened here. Something bad.'

If this had been the first time Creed was meeting Agent O'Dell, he probably would have wanted to roll his eyes and chalk it up as a wasted trip. But in the other case they'd worked on together he'd seen her instincts prove dead-on.

'This is Jason's first search. If you don't mind, we'll treat it like a training exercise and see what Grace comes up with. But if after an hour she's not hitting on anything—' He glanced around. 'How many acres are we talking about?'

'Almost ten.' Before he could answer, O'Dell saw his skepticism and added, 'An hour sounds fair.'

Then she leaned down to pet Grace, and to the dog she said, 'It's so good to see you again, Grace.'

35

Creed snapped the leash off of Grace when he was satisfied the terrain was manageable. Still, he told her to stay on the footpath that weaved through the forested area. Otherwise he'd be risking the dog getting tangled in the shrub and thick underbrush. Despite his restrictions, Grace scampered off, nose in the air, pleased and excited.

He hadn't put on any of her special vests or harnesses as added guidance for what he wanted her to find. He didn't want to confuse her. Nor did he want to limit her.

He'd promised Hannah he'd give Jason a chance. For some reason she believed this sullen, brooding young man had the ambition to become a dog handler. Creed had yet to see even an ounce of ambition in this guy. He seemed too angry and self-conscious to notice anything other than his own misery. But Hannah was willing to trust Creed about Amanda. The least he could do was offer the same about Jason.

'I doubt we'll find anything,' he told Jason, though he was watching O'Dell's reaction out of the corner of his eye. 'But you can never let the dog know. She takes her leads from her handler.' Even as he said this, Grace looked back at him.

'As far as she's concerned,' he continued in a casual tone, purposely not using her name, 'I need to relay that I'm just as excited as she is. And that this search is going to be more interesting than piss on a fence post.'

He saw O'Dell smile. Jason's stoic expression didn't waver even a smidgen. With his ball cap low over his eyes, he tromped through the grass, picking up and dropping his feet as if they were cemented in concrete instead of in hiking boots. He didn't want to be here, and Creed wished he'd left him back at the kennels cleaning up dog crap.

The grass continued to get higher as the path started

to disappear. A light breeze kept the humidity bearable. It was blowing in their direction, an unexpected gift, bringing the scents toward Grace. The thick overhang of branches protected them from the heat. Still, he'd need to keep Grace to twenty-minute work intervals. A scent dog could easily hyperventilate.

'You have to be careful in this kind of weather,' Creed said. Although Jason didn't seem interested, Creed kicked himself into training mode. He'd never given instructions to someone who didn't care about learning. 'When a dog is working a scent, she isn't just breathing more quickly. She's actually pulling in more air and sending it around inside her nose in an attempt to identify it. She's breathing in about a hundred and fifty to two hundred times a minute, compared to the thirty times a minute when she's out for a leisurely walk.'

Just as he finished he noticed Grace was, indeed, sniffing more quickly, whiskers twitching, muzzle darting in all directions. Her small body had been zigzagging through the brush, clearing one area and dashing off to the next. With the path no longer visible, she had weaved farther into the trees and gotten ahead of them. But now she stopped. And so did Creed.

'Did she find something already?' Jason asked, keeping his voice low and standing as still as Creed. Maybe he *had* been paying attention.

'I don't know.'

Creed looked back. They had climbed a gradual incline, and he could see a roofline through the trees.

'I wouldn't expect there to be anything this close to the house.'

He looked to O'Dell.

'Grace won't step on the ants, will she?'

He was about to say that she wouldn't just as she started to paw the ground. She wasn't supposed to touch what she found. Sometimes dogs forgot in their excitement. But Grace never did. And sudden panic knotted in his gut. He signaled for O'Dell and Jason to stay put, and he hurried while trying not to disturb or alarm Grace. She stopped before he reached her. Turned around. Found his eyes and stared at him.

Creed slowed his pace. He took careful steps and held her gaze.

When he got closer, Grace glanced back at what she had discovered, as if pointing it out to him, telling him that it was right there in the tall grass. Then she started looking at his pockets and his daypack. She wanted her reward, and she knew where he kept the pink elephant. But she wouldn't leave her post until he gave the okay.

He couldn't reward her for a false alert. It was one of the golden rules. Only one time and it could ruin the best scent dog. If she had found a mound of fire ants, he'd need to see if there was blood or some decomp before he could reward her.

A couple more steps and he could see what she had unearthed. It wasn't a mound of fire ants. Not even close. The item was partially buried, but enough of it had broken free that he recognized it as an article of clothing. One sleeve poked up from under the ground.

Creed fumbled with the clasp on his daypack and shoved his hand inside to find Grace's toy. He didn't take his eyes off the item, even when he knew his fingers were trembling.

He tossed the pink elephant to Grace as he turned to O'Dell and Jason.

'It's not fire ants,' he told them. 'It looks like a T-shirt. A child's T-shirt.' He swallowed the bile that caught him off guard before adding, 'And it's covered in blood.'

36

This was not at all what O'Dell had expected.

Creed and Jason had left her. She could hear Grace squeaking her toy. They waited in a clearing about fifty feet behind her. She knew it was part of Creed's routine. He did it out of respect for the law enforcement officers he worked with. He and his dog provided a service – search and find or search and rescue. He wasn't trained for cadaver retrieval or evidence collection, and so he quietly left them. No questions asked. No sticking around to appease his curiosity. All he wanted to do was reward his dog and move out of their way.

But O'Dell had caught something in his eyes before

he retreated with Grace. There was surprise and sadness mixed with unease that this might not be the only thing buried here. That this was only the beginning of what they might find. And in that brief passing glance, she noticed one other thing before he stepped away ... she caught a glimpse of his dread.

Now, as she stood here alone, she shared that sentiment.

It was always tough when a child was involved. O'Dell had witnessed seasoned investigators tear up at the sight of a child's body. As much as they trained and hardened themselves, that was the one thing that could dismantle almost every tough guy's attitude. And she wasn't immune to it either.

She had already called Sheriff Holt and asked him to bring in a forensic team. They would need to include the house and the outbuildings in their search. She hesitated now, holding a paper evidence bag that she had stuffed into her daypack earlier. She was more than qualified to collect this. She had done it many times before. But something stopped her.

The T-shirt looked to be the size for a small boy, maybe five or six years old. The blue-and-yellow-striped sleeve poked up and out almost as if its owner had just wiggled out of it. The other sleeve and half the chest were still buried in the dirt. From what she could see, there were no puncture marks, rips, or tears. However, rust-colored splatters stained the fabric. Even with the cloud cover and the canopy of branches, it wasn't dark enough for her to use her black light. She didn't really need to. She knew it was blood.

Fire ants.

That's all she wanted to find here today. A possible crime scene where Trevor Bagley may have been tortured and, as a result, died. O'Dell had hoped to resolve whether or not Bagley was a drug dealer or a drug runner. All she wanted was to learn more about the victim, to understand his killer. But this ...

Was it possible that Mrs Bagley had taken the child and fled?

O'Dell tried to remember going through the house yesterday. There were no photos on display with any children. She was sure of that. The spare bedroom had not been decorated with the typical stuff that kids love. In fact, there had been a treadmill in the corner and storage boxes on the bed. She couldn't remember seeing any toys, no bicycle or video games – there was nothing to indicate a child lived there. Even the breakfast that had been interrupted was set up for only two people, not three. Two adults – coffee mugs, no juice or milk glasses.

She squatted and examined the T-shirt again, without touching it. She realized she was holding her breath. She could be wrong about the blood. Then she remembered the altar set up in the Bagleys' bedroom. She'd worked other cases involving all kinds of strange rituals. That someone had possibly tortured Trevor Bagley by tying him down over a massive amount of fire ants, that they had listened to him scream and writhe in pain – that alone was strange and cruel. But if a child was involved . . .

Her eyes made another careful scan around the immediate area. Except for where the T-shirt lay, the grass and dirt nearby didn't look disturbed or dug up. There appeared to be no signs of a grave. But even that brought little relief. It certainly didn't mean that a body was *not* buried close by, only that a killer may have been more precise.

More questions than answers. All the more reason they needed to continue looking.

O'Dell stood and folded the evidence bag back into her daypack. With her cell phone she snapped off several photos. Then she pulled out a bright orange ribbon and tied it to one of the branches at eye level and just above their discovery.

Finally she turned away, feet suddenly heavy, and walked toward Creed and Jason, stopping three times to tie additional ribbons to shrubs, marking a path for the forensic team. The underbrush was thick and it took effort not to get tangled. If it hadn't been for Grace, no one ever would have ventured this way. O'Dell couldn't shake the feeling that they had stumbled upon something that was never meant to be found.

When she looked up, the two men were watching her, waiting for her. Even Grace had stopped her play and had already relinquished her pink elephant. They were ready to continue.

37

There was something she wasn't telling him. It wouldn't be the first time law enforcement officers had held back information or important details from him, but for some reason Creed expected more from Maggie O'Dell. Yes, they had worked only one case together, but he thought it had been enough for her to know him, to know that she could trust him. And yet, she didn't trust him.

That was her problem, not his. It became his problem if it endangered his dog. Grace was fine. She was ready to start all over again. So why did he feel anxious, on the verge of anger?

'I don't get it,' Jason interrupted Creed's thoughts.

'Get what?'

'She didn't find what you wanted her to find but you rewarded her. How do you keep her from trailing off and finding some other discarded item?'

'It wasn't some discarded item. At least not to Grace. She thinks she did find what I asked her to search for because it has the same scent.'

'The same scent?'

Creed glanced over at Maggie. She wasn't anywhere near denying it.

'Blood. She smelled the blood. I try to reward her for anything she finds with blood on it, or remains. Human blood or remains, that is.'

He was surprised to see Jason's face pale. He thought he'd made it plain when they found the child's T-shirt that it had blood on it.

'She can tell human blood from animal blood? Son of a bitch,' he muttered, visibly shaken by the revelation. 'I guess I was thinking there was a chance it was just dirt. Or animal blood.'

This time Creed met Maggie's eyes. He wanted to ask what the hell was going on, but instead he focused his attention on Grace. She was in a hurry. She rushed from side to side, her nose held high, as if the scent she was trying to harvest floated up above.

She already sniffed deeply, quick breaths that in the humidity made Creed nervous. He kept track of the time, not allowing her to go over the twenty-minute work intervals. He made her stop for water, and she patiently obeyed but as soon as he gave the okay, she raced off.

She leaped over fallen branches and started bounding from tree to tree. Once in a while she hesitated at the base of a trunk and stared at the protruding roots. At one tree she pawed the ground, then stood on her hind legs and scratched at the bark. She inhaled and snorted.

Nothing there. And she took off again.

He wondered if finding the T-shirt had thrown her off. Was she expecting to find the new scent – the one she was obviously working – was she expecting it to be buried in the same way?

Creed tried not to react. She could be feeling his anxiety, his anticipation. He checked his tracking monitor. They had gone almost a mile from the house. It was going on two hours since they began. Grace was not the least bit exhausted. If anything, she was overly excited, not even concerned about her reward. She was definitely in a scent zone. They'd have to wait to find out whether it was part of the one they had just found.

He dreaded that it might be the child this time. As awful as it had been discovering those kids on that fishing boat, at least they were alive. It was nothing like finding the dead body of a child.

Oftentimes he'd lose track of the number of bodies – or parts of bodies – he and his dogs had helped find over the course of seven years, but he knew exactly how many of them were children: sixteen. He hoped today he wouldn't be adding number seventeen.

In the next clearing between trees Creed noticed that the grass looked trampled. Small shrubs were broken, their leaves already turning brown. He stopped at the edge and put up a hand to warn Maggie and Jason to stop, as well. Almost immediately he could smell it – something rancid, as if someone had dumped out a garbage can.

'Something definitely happened here,' Maggie said before he had a chance to point out the disruption in the landscape.

Off to the right, branches had been tossed onto a pile along with other debris. Without getting closer, he could decipher pieces of two-by-fours and a roll of wire mesh. It looked as if someone had been constructing something and left the scraps behind. Then he saw the shovel, its blade half-buried in the ground, the wooden handle teetering sideways. He felt his stomach clench. So here was the torture chamber they were looking for. Or perhaps a grave.

But none of this interested Grace.

Creed turned around to find her pawing at another tree. This time she stood on her hind legs, her front legs pedaling the air and her head thrown back, as if she were trying to see up into the branches. He'd never seen her work a scent like this. It looked like she was trying to capture it floating above her.

And then it occurred to him just as she finally sat back on her haunches and turned toward him, finding his eyes and giving her alert.

Maggie and Jason only now noticed as Creed walked the short distance to the trunk of the tree. He didn't see it until he was standing directly underneath. The woman's eyes stared down at him, her long black hair tangled in the branches. Her body was snagged in the upper V, hidden from view by the leaves and the mass of kudzu that engulfed the tree.

He felt Maggie and Jason come up beside him.

There were no gasps from either of them. Only a 'son of a bitch' from Jason and a resigned sigh from Maggie. The sigh almost sounded like regret, as though she was too late.

And then in a calm, casual voice, she said, 'I think we just found Mrs Bagley.'

38

O'Dell handed her cell phone to Creed. She had called Sheriff Holt and explained to him what they had found. After a long silence Holt had asked her to 'please repeat that.' He sounded out of breath.

The forensic team had arrived and had only just begun collecting evidence at the first site. There wouldn't be enough ribbons in her daypack to leave a trail this far, so she handed the phone to Creed. He could give the coordinates according to his GPS tracker and hopefully lead the forensic team here.

On Creed's instruction, Jason had taken Grace away from the area to enjoy her reward. Other than his first curses, the young man didn't look fazed by their discovery, but then O'Dell didn't expect him to be. A couple of things he had said earlier confirmed that he had not lost his arm below the elbow in some freakish industrial accident, but rather in combat, probably in Afghanistan. The vacant, brooding look on his face told her the loss was most likely recent – months, not years. So death was no stranger to him. Watching him with Grace, she caught him smiling at the dog's crazy antics. To Grace, it had been a good day – two major finds.

But neither was what O'Dell was looking for. Not even close. She was, however, convinced more than ever that Trevor Bagley had also died out here on his own property.

She glanced at Creed. He had wandered away, trying to get a better signal on her cell phone. Now she saw him explaining to Sheriff Holt as he held his tracking monitor up. The overcast sky had begun darkening. Somewhere in the distance she thought she heard the faint rumble of thunder. They had maybe another hour if they were lucky.

The pile of leftover construction rubble had to hold some answers to this puzzle. O'Dell walked toward it, her eyes picking out pieces she could identify. Some of the wooden planks looked rotted. Certainly not from a new or recent project. The grass and underbrush had grown up around it. Even to get there she'd have to wade through an area of knee-high scrub.

The roll of wire mesh intrigued her. It reminded her of something you'd use for a window screen. She had seen gardeners put this fine of a mesh over plants to keep out pests. Or maybe, in this case, it was to keep insects in? Could it trap fire ants and keep them in one confined area?

She was almost close enough to touch it when the ground fell out from under her. She plunged down into the earth. The surprise sucked the air from her lungs. Her hip slammed against something hard before she landed on her knees. Moist burlap had broken her fall, as well as the wire mesh and branches that had been concealing the hole.

The sudden darkness made it impossible to see. She tried to catch her breath. Needed to wait for her eyes to adjust. Stanch her immediate panic before the claustrophobia grabbed hold.

She tested her feet underneath her. Clawed her way to a standing position. Her right knee hurt like hell but it didn't collapse. With tentative fingers, she broke through the darkness. The dirt walls were wet and slick. About a foot on each side of her.

She looked up and her knees wobbled. The pit appeared to be twice as deep as she was tall. The overcast sky allowed very little light to filter down. She couldn't hear Creed or Grace's squeaky toy. Only muffled sounds, as if she had dropped out of existence.

'Creed. Jason,' she yelled. 'Grace.'

She remembered her flashlight – not a flashlight, a black light – but even the UV purple-blue light would break the darkness. She shoved her hand into her daypack and fumbled around inside until her fingers found the long cylinder.

'Grace!' she tried again. Surely the dog would hear her and come looking.

She flipped the black light on and was disappointed to see how little it helped. Still, she swung the stream of light around her. Burlap hung from the walls in strips. Some of the rotted planks were thrown into the corner. That must have been what she had slammed her hip into.

She felt dirt falling on her head and looked up to find Grace peering over the edge.

'Hi, Grace. What a good girl.'

Out of the corner of her eye O'Dell saw something flit across the dirt wall just inches away. She jerked back and shot the black light at the spot where she had seen the movement. And suddenly the entire wall came alive. Dozens – no, hundreds – of scurrying creatures glowing bright blue, fluorescing in the black light.

She gasped, almost screamed.

'Maggie, are you okay?'

She heard Creed's voice but didn't dare look up, not wanting to take her eyes away for even a second. She couldn't believe it. How was this possible? They had been searching for a torture chamber all day and she had literally stumbled into it. But there were no fire ants.

Oh God, if only there were fire ants.

'Maggie?'

She couldn't breathe, let alone speak. All she could do was stand paralyzed and watch as the walls started to crawl with hundreds of fluorescent scorpions.

39

The first sting surprised her even though she had been expecting it. It felt like a needle driving deep into her neck until it hit bone and was left there. The second sent a tingling down her spine. It wasn't until after the third – maybe the fourth – that she felt the burn begin.

She couldn't look up without her head spinning. Through a blur she could barely make out Creed yelling to her over the edge – and maybe Jason, or was she seeing double? Because suddenly there were two Jack Russell terriers, too. Then there were three and now four.

She closed her eyes and shook her head. She couldn't

hear Creed's voice. Grace's bark sounded muffled and miles away. A scorpion raced up her arm and she flung it off, only to see another on her shoulder. She could feel them in her hair, on her neck and back. She didn't dare scream and risk one crawling into her mouth. The stings hurt less through her clothing. It was difficult to breathe. Her chest hurt. Sweat dripped down her face and she wanted to throw up.

There was a flash of light around her, and it took her a minute to realize it came from above. The men were trying to figure out what to do, shining light down into the hellhole to make sense of her silence.

Dirt trickled down on her but she couldn't look up. It took all her effort to stand still. Her stomach cramped and a new panic raced through her when she realized she couldn't swallow. She watched scorpions move freely up and down her body, but now she didn't feel them.

More dirt rained on top of her and a shadow came over the opening. Someone was coming down. She stole a glance up and saw boots descending straight above her, avoiding contact with the walls. In no time Creed was in front of her, his shadow taking up the small space. She couldn't see his face. It was too dark.

And she couldn't hear him. Her ears were filled with the sounds of water rushing and her heart thumping.

She could feel him slipping something under her arms. A rope. He cinched it quickly. Suddenly she was being yanked up, a jerk and jolt at a time. She tried to hang on with hands that wouldn't obey and couldn't grip. Jason grabbed onto her and she worked her feet over the ledge of dirt. Her first instinct was to twist and pull the rope off herself. Somehow she managed, then flung it back down for Creed.

She rolled over, attempting to sit up, and felt something tapping at her. She swatted instinctively to find Grace's muzzle in her hair. The dog yelped and jumped back. That's when O'Dell realized she had brought some of the damned scorpions up with her.

Again, she tried to sit up. Her head began to spin. She closed her eyes. She needed to breathe. She needed to take in the fresh air, but her lungs and throat felt thick.

Someone was slapping her to keep her awake. No, they were slapping off the scorpions that were still attached. Rolling her this way and that. It was too much. She couldn't lift an arm – even a finger – to try to help. Nothing worked.

Her eyelids fluttered open only to see the leaves and clouds swirling above her. She was being swept up and she couldn't hold on. So she closed her eyes again and tried to think of a cool breeze and the feel of ocean waves washing over her body again and again until her mind was somewhere else, where panic and fear and pain didn't exist.

40

'She's going into shock,' Creed told Jason.

It was taking forever to get back to the house, back to his Jeep. He carried Maggie while Grace and Jason led the way. Jason held the GPS tracker.

Creed had punched in the coordinates and found a shortcut so they didn't have to wind all the way around and backtrack the ground they had covered in their search. But the shortcut included woods so thick he had to slow down just to maneuver between trees.

Every time he stopped to catch his breath he heard Jason stomp and mutter something too garbled for Creed to understand. But he could guess what the young soldier's frustration was about. He couldn't help carry Maggie with only one arm.

Before they started, Creed had taken a photo of one of the scorpions he'd smashed and kept. He'd texted the picture to Hannah with the instructions: 'Find out what kind this is ASAP. Need to know what to do. Multiple stings.'

Now he heard his phone ping, and Jason pulled it out of his pocket immediately.

'She needs to know if it's Grace or one of us.'

But before Creed could answer, the kid was poking in the answer quickly. He operated the phone while holding the tracker, both in his one hand and without slowing his pace.

'Hey, I can walk on my own,' Maggie said into Creed's shirt collar, but she didn't move her head from his shoulder.

'Maybe, but not fast enough.'

'Are they poisonous?' she asked.

'We're trying to find out.'

'She says you smashed it too hard,' Jason told him without looking up. 'She can't tell if there were stripes on its back.'

'I think there were stripes.'

Jason's thumb went back to work.

Creed still couldn't see the house or any of the out-buildings. To make matters worse, the sky continued to get darker. Grace kept looking back at him to make sure he was okay. He was relieved she hadn't gotten stung. A bigger dog might be able to handle a scorpion sting, but Grace was sixteen pounds. Speaking of pounds, he shifted Maggie and noticed that she was slipping in and out of consciousness.

Shock, definitely shock.

He wanted to yell for Hannah to hurry. *Come on, what the hell is it?* Was he carrying a dead woman?

'She says most scorpions in Alabama and Florida don't have venom that's lethal.'

'These might not be local,' Creed said. 'Tell her to send the photo to Dr Avelyn.'

'What do you mean they might not be local?' Jason stopped in his tracks to look back at Creed.

'Think about it. Have you ever seen that many scorpions all in one place?'

'Son of a bitch.' And he started tapping and walking again.

Grace began barking and bounded off to the right, trying to lead them through an even thicker underbrush.

Before Creed could tell her they weren't searching any-more, he could see the roofline. Finally!

'Good girl, Grace.' Creed followed. To Jason he said, 'Looks like Grace found a shorter cut.'

'She's better than a GPS.'

It was the first time Creed had seen the kid actually smile or at least come close, because almost immedi-ately he was frowning again and went back to staring at Creed's cell phone, not wanting to miss Hannah's next message.

Sheriff Holt and his deputy were waiting for them. They helped Creed fold Maggie into the passenger seat of his Jeep. Holt already had his SUV's engine running and the top bar lights flashing. Maggie was conscious again and trying to shove away their help until she realized she couldn't even buckle herself in. That's when Creed noticed the backs of her hands were swollen. So was her neck.

'Jason,' he yelled as he swung open the liftgate and helped Grace get in. 'What do you have for me? Anything?'

'Dr Avelyn wants to know how long since the last sting.'

Creed glanced at his wristwatch.

'Do you know?' he asked Jason, because he had lost all track of time.

Jason scrolled the screen on Creed's cell phone and said, 'It's been almost forty-five minutes since you texted the photo.' He scrolled back and punched in the answer.

Then both men waited. Sheriff Holt and his deputy were at their vehicle, ready to go.

'Pinchers are too big,' Jason read. 'The bigger the pinchers, the less likely they're lethal.'

'That's it?' Creed shoved his fingers through his hair in frustration and only now noticed the swollen sting marks on the backs of his own hands. 'That's what she expects us to bank on?'

'Wait. She said she has some antivenin just in case.' Jason looked up at him. 'Seriously? She has scorpion antivenin? Who the hell is Dr Avelyn Parker?'

Creed heaved a sigh of relief and couldn't stop from smiling. Then he finally said, 'She's my vet.'

41

Jason had offered to drive Agent O'Dell's rental car. Creed hadn't wanted to bother with it but O'Dell had been conscious enough to argue and put up a fuss. All of her belongings were in the trunk. After several attempts at retrieving the keys from her daypack and Creed telling her they didn't have time, Jason stepped over to her side of the Jeep and made the offer. Relief swept over her face and she struggled but handed him the pack through the window.

She looked bad, flush with fever and drenched in sweat, but he could see her shiver. Her eyes squinted, a bit unfocused, and Jason could tell she was fighting the pain. He had no idea what it felt like to be stung by a scorpion, let alone dozens of them. As a kid he'd found a wasps' nest and was so fascinated by the honeycomb that he picked it up to go show his mom. He was stung three times before his mom rescued him. To hear her tell the story, it might as well have been dozens of stings. But he could still remember that just those three hurt like hell. He had no memory of pain from his arm being blown off. In fact, he didn't even know it was gone until he woke up in a hospital bed.

Jason watched the sheriff's SUV and Creed's Jeep peel out, both kicking up mud and gravel. He waited for them to wind down the driveway out of sight before he wandered over to the rental. The Ford compact was wedged between a tree and the Montgomery County Crime Scene Unit van. None of the forensic team was anywhere to be seen, and he figured they were either on their way to recover the body from the tree or they were at the scene.

He stood in the middle of the yard and looked around and listened. It was so quiet, only a few birds calling to each other. There was no sign of the chaos that had taken place here. Nothing strewn around the lawn. No broken windows or splintered doorjambs.

No blood.

Maybe he was too used to seeing shelled-out buildings and ripped-up roadsides from IEDs. It would help
if explosions would quit invading his sleep. His mom –
that same brave woman who'd rescued him as a kid
from wasps – told him he needed to stop thinking
about all 'that stuff' so much and to 'think happy
thoughts' instead. Pretty hard to do when every morning he reached for his toothbrush and was reminded
that his frickin' hand was gone.

So it was difficult to imagine such chaos happening
without bombs exploding or people screaming.
Without any blood.

Probably no one would understand, but, ironically,
today he felt more alive than he had since he came
home from Afghanistan. Finding that woman's body in
the tree – that was nothing. Now, if the tree had been
filled with pieces of her – that would be more like what
he was used to seeing.

However, his adrenaline had really started pumping
when he helped Creed pull Agent O'Dell out of that pit.
Swatting away scorpions, tracking and finding the way
back through the brush – suddenly he had a purpose
again. He missed the urgency. He missed feeling a part
of something bigger and more important than himself.

Jason knew Ryder Creed didn't like him. He wasn't sure why, but he didn't give a rat's ass. He'd Googled Ryder Creed and couldn't believe the guy was only twenty-nine years old and had been in Afghanistan. He sure as hell acted like an old man. But Creed was a marine. Jason was a ranger. Maybe it was that simple. Damned marines thought they were something special.

Jason knew the only reason Creed had brought him along today was because of Hannah. He'd overheard them talking. At least Creed was honest. Jason couldn't figure out if Hannah just thought he was another lost soul at Segway House for her to save. He hated that – just the idea that someone would think he needed to be saved. Son of a bitch, he was the one who was supposed to be out saving people. He did not need saving.

He pointed the key fob at the rental car. He was going to hit the UNLOCK button when he noticed the door was already unlocked. He stopped in his tracks.

That didn't feel right. Agent O'Dell didn't seem like the type who would leave her vehicle's doors unlocked, even in the middle of Nowhere, Alabama. It would be an instinctive habit for someone like her, in her profession.

Jason dropped to his hand and knees. Keeping three

feet between himself and the car, he leaned down to look under the chassis. It was a habit from his own most recent profession. He leaned his shoulder into the mud as he scanned the entire length of the undercarriage for anything that might look like an explosive device.

Ordinarily he might consider this a bit over the top. He admitted he had some residual paranoia. Okay, a lot of paranoia. Hell, he couldn't sit in a bar or a restaurant without knowing where all the exits were. He didn't care about getting blown up again or some crazy asshole storming in and shooting up the joint. Dying didn't scare him. Living did, especially if it included having another piece of himself hacked off.

Getting blown up once should be reason enough for a healthy dose of paranoia. But given the day's events, what he was doing right now seemed totally appropriate. Even if there wasn't anything attached to the undercarriage of the vehicle. Appropriate or not, as he pushed himself back to his feet, he was glad there was no one around to see him.

Agent O'Dell probably just forgot to lock the car doors. Simple as that.

Still, when Jason opened the driver's door he did it slowly. He let the door click, and he pulled it open only an inch to make room for his fingers. Then with eagle eyes and trigger-sensitive fingertips – on the only hand he had left to blow off – he carefully caressed the rubber around the entire opening, searching for a thread of wire that didn't belong.

Again, he found nothing.

This time he cursed and told himself, 'Damn it, dude, you seriously need to lighten up.'

He shook his head and plucked his sunglasses from where they dangled on the neckline of his T-shirt. He shoved them back on, pulled the door open wide, and slid into the driver's seat. He was still berating himself as he adjusted the seat when he noticed the burlap sack dislodge from underneath. It plopped down on the floorboard between his boots. Before he could lift either foot he saw the snake poke out and raise itself up three inches.

Jason had grown up camping in this area and knew how to distinguish a coral snake from the other colorful, but less deadly, snakes. There was a clever saying, and it ran through his head as he kept his feet motionless and felt the sweat dripping down his back.

'Red touches black, venom lack. Red touches yellow, kill a fellow.'

The snake started waving back and forth, as if checking out its surroundings, but Jason thought it looked like the tail, not the head, coming dangerously close to whipping the side of his boot.

He tried to focus and examine the colors. The tip of the tail had rings of black and yellow with no red. That was good. Couldn't be a coral without red. But just when he thought he was in the clear, the snake pushed out several more inches. He could see a ring of red, thick with black spots, in the scales. Farther down, wiggling up out of the burlap, he saw a thick black ring and it was separated from the red by a thin yellow ring.

Red, yellow, black . . . His mind began to spin. What was the saying?

Without taking his eyes off the snake flitting its tail between his feet, he repeated the saying under his breath: 'Red touches yellow, kill a fellow. Son of a bitch, I'm screwed.'

42

Somehow Jason managed to slide his cell phone from his back pocket without moving his feet or legs. He caught himself holding his breath as he counted the phone rings. He thought he had used up all his adrenaline but he could feel it kick into full force.

'Come on, pick up,' he whispered as he watched the snake's tail go perfectly still, standing straight in the air. Could it hear his voice?

'This is Creed.'

Finally!

'What do you know about coral snakes?'

'You hardly ever see them. They pretty much keep to themselves.'

'There's one in Agent O'Dell's car.'

Silence.

'It's on the floorboard between my feet,' Jason continued, keeping his tone low and even, despite the panic jumping around in his gut.

'You know for sure it's a poisonous one?'

'Red touches yellow, kill a fellow.'

'Stay completely still.'

'Already doing that, man.'

'Coral snakes are usually shy and docile. That's why you don't see them much. They like to hide. They'll only strike if they're disturbed or feel threatened.'

'I'd say being stuffed into a burlap sack and shoved under the car seat might have disturbed this one.'

'Can you see its head?'

'No, I think it's still in the sack. Its tail's sticking out, waving around.'

'That's good. They do that sometimes. It's trying to fake you out.'

'Fake *me* out?' Jason had to swallow a laugh and keep still. His nerves were wound tight. 'Can you call the forensic team?'

'You're not gonna be able to wait for them.'

'You are not very reassuring.'

'Just stay calm. We can do this.'

Creed's voice reminded Jason of his sergeant's just before the IED went off.

'Easy for you to say. You're not in the son-of-a-bitchin' car.'

'Not really easy. I'm driving about seventy miles an hour with one hand on the wheel and in pouring rain.'

Rain. Damn!

No wonder Creed had told him he didn't have time for the forensic team. If rain started battering down on the car, would the snake feel even more threatened? For the first time, Jason risked taking his eyes off the snake to glimpse up at the sky. Still overcast and dark.

'Corals don't tend to be aggressive,' Creed said, 'unless you step on them or pin them down. Then you've got a problem. They don't just strike once, they'll strike over and over again, rapidly in a sideways motion. And if they connect, they hang on.'

'You're not making this better.'

'I just want you to be prepared. They might look small but they are the most virulent. All they have to do is attach to a piece of skin.'

'Still not helping.'

'Is there anything in the car – blanket, towel?'

Only then did Jason notice that Agent O'Dell had left a lightweight jacket on the passenger seat.

'A very thin jacket.'

'Good. Listen to me carefully, because you're gonna need to put the phone down in order to use your hand.'

Jason hadn't even thought about his new disadvantage. Suddenly he became acutely aware of everything. He could feel the wet back of his T-shirt sticking to the vinyl car seat. He gauged the tight space between his thighs and the steering wheel. He'd never be able to move quickly enough. It didn't matter how many hands he had.

'Jason.' Creed's voice brought him back to attention.

'Go ahead.'

'Is the snake's head still in the bag?'

'I think so.'

'This is what you need to do. Drop the jacket over the opening of the bag. Then open your car door at the same time that you lift up your left foot. Bring that foot all the way up to the car seat.'

'How the hell—' He had to stop himself to lower his voice and grab hold of some composure. 'My leg's never going to fit.'

'Sure it will,' Creed told him as calmly as if he were asking him to try on a new pair of shoes. 'The open door will give you more room. Just do all of this slowly. Then lift yourself and slide over to the other side of the car. You'll have to decide when to bring up the other foot.'

'You've got to be kidding. I'm not jumping out the door?'

'Not that door. You're going out the passenger door.'

Jason looked at the gearshift and console that separated the seats. There was too much to get over. He'd never be able to do it. The car was too small. He wasn't a big guy, but how the hell could he drag and bang himself all the way to the other side and do it faster than a snake that could crawl up and at him in a matter of seconds?

'That's your plan?' he asked Creed.

'You got a better one?'

That's when the first raindrop hit the windshield.

43

There wasn't a day that went by that Jason didn't think about – or have nightmares about – those 164 seconds that changed his life forever.

Without prompting, he could taste that dust in his mouth and feel the rock against his cheek as he lay helpless, not realizing at that moment that his arm had been severed and blown completely off his body. All he could see was his sergeant, no more than ten feet away. Jason hadn't been able to take his eyes off the bloody pulp that used to be the man's face. But he was still alive. Somehow they put him back together again, just like they did with Jason.

Humpty Dumpty sat on a wall. Humpty Dumpty had a great fall.

Some days – most days – Jason wished they had let him die.

Then there were days he contemplated rectifying their decision. It'd be so easy. Some of his friends had done just that.

So now, sitting here trapped in a vehicle with a poisonous snake at his feet, he actually thought, *How bad could it be?* Why not just let the snake bite him? How much could it hurt? It'd probably be a few minutes of intense pain. He'd already been there, done that. *Piece of cake.*

He toyed with the idea. Hell, Creed's idea might get him bitten anyway. Rather than try that, he could grab the thing.

He watched the tail slink farther out of the sack and was surprised by the panic in his gut. Was that a good sign? Had today – tracking through the woods, finding death – given him some strange purpose? What was he waiting for? He had the perfect opportunity. A poisonous snake. No gun, no blood, no mess for his mom.

No, with his luck he wouldn't die, again.

'What are you waiting for?'

The voice startled Jason. He'd forgotten that he had put the cell phone in his pocket but hadn't disconnected. Creed wanted him to stay on the line to make sure he was okay. He'd clicked on the speaker option.

'Can snakes hear?' Jason asked with his chin on his chest to get his mouth close to the phone.

'I think they feel vibration. So they might be able to feel your voice.'

'Then shut up.'

He was waiting for a comeback, but Creed was actually listening, which made Jason more nervous that the snake could probably hear him even breathing.

He slowly lifted his hand while getting ready to lift his left leg. It took him too long to find the door handle, making him more anxious. He gripped the lever, squeezed, and raised it almost in slow motion. The door clicked and he started raising his foot when he noticed movement in the burlap bag. A second tail poked out.

'Holy crap! There's more than one.'

'Easy, you can do this.' He heard Creed's whisper in his pocket.

Jason swung open the door and jerked his foot up. With his other boot he swept at the burlap bag. It was instinctive, like kicking out a live grenade. He watched the bag tumble out the door as snakes started twisting and falling out. Both his feet were on the car seat and he was standing, his back against the roof as he watched them hit the ground.

'What the hell's happening?'

Jason climbed over the console, knocking his knee and scraping his ear on the overhead light. Somehow he managed to get out the other door. His boots hit the ground, and he ran up the steps to the front porch. From there he could see the snakes getting untangled and winding out. His fingers were shaking when he pulled his phone out of his pocket.

'I'm okay. Looks like there were three sons of bitches in the bag.'

'Sheriff Holt is sending someone to get you,' Creed told him. 'You did good.'

He breathed a deep sigh of relief, and it surprised him how good it felt to still be alive.

44

Amanda watched from her window perch. She had overheard Hannah talking on the phone. There had been an urgency in the woman's ordinarily calm voice. It made Amanda's heart start to race even before she heard Hannah say something about an FBI agent.

Were they calling in the feds to take her away?

Every time she tried sneaking out of her room she could hear Hannah at the end of the hallway, as if she was purposely watching for and guarding against Amanda's escape. Wasn't it just yesterday that she didn't care?

Other than the clothes she had worn at the airport, the only belongings she had were in the small square purse that had been strapped across her body. Hannah had left it on the nightstand, but Amanda figured the woman had gone through it. Didn't matter, except that the passport was issued under her real name. Leandro had said it was easier that way, and since her mother obviously didn't care about Amanda, she'd never report her missing. As far as she was concerned, Amanda was out of her house, and that's exactly what she wanted.

She stretched and grabbed the purse without leaving her lookout post. There wasn't much in the small bag: her passport, a few bucks (Leandro didn't want her carrying more than twenty dollars), some throat lozenges, a lip gloss (though she never used it, but Zapata said all teenage girls carried one), and the new iPod Leandro had given her.

He had presented the iPod to her the last night they were together. She had always wanted one but couldn't remember ever telling him that. He could be so considerate like that. On the flight to Atlanta she had listened to some of the music he had already downloaded. Maybe she expected Spanish love songs. She admitted she was disappointed that most of them were salsa, with no lyrics, or hard rock with words she couldn't decipher. He had also downloaded a few videos and games and a bunch of apps. Amanda had no idea what some of the apps were for.

She turned the iPod on and watched it go through the process of powering up and connecting to whatever it connected to. Her eyes were more interested in the length of driveway she could see through the trees. She didn't want to miss Ryder Creed's Jeep when it brought the FBI. The dings from the iPod startled her – one after another, a succession of them. She glanced down to see the message box icon with the number 9.

How was it possible that she had nine messages?

Her palm began to sweat under the weight of the gadget. She didn't want to look. She didn't want to see what they were telling her, the names they were calling her, the threats that were being made. Maybe they were Leandro telling her he loved her. She had thought of him as her knight in shining armor when she first met him. Now she wasn't sure if she was feeling sick because she was excited that he might be missing her, or if she was still scared of him.

And just as easily as she had turned the iPod on, she pressed the button and listened to it shut down. She was shoving it back into her purse when Hannah came barging into the room.

'Don't you ever knock?'

'It's my house.'

'Even when you have a guest?'

'You're not a guest.'

Yet even as she said it, Amanda watched the woman drop a set of clean towels on the corner of the bed. She had certainly taken care of Amanda as though she was a guest, but Amanda wouldn't push the point. Besides, she needed to think of herself as a prisoner instead. She couldn't be caught off guard.

'You're ratting me out to the FBI.'

Hannah made a clucking noise with her tongue and shook her head.

'You've been eavesdropping,' she said. She wasn't surprised.

'But it's true, right?'

'Child, the FBI's not coming for you.'

'I don't like you calling me child.'

'And I don't care what you like or don't like. Until we can get ahold of your momma, you'll—'

'Oh my God! You're not trying to call my mom, are you?'

Amanda could see in Hannah's surprise that she had revealed too much panic. She wished she could take it back and tried to steady herself and her voice when she added, 'My mom won't come for me, so you're just wasting your time.'

'And why is that?'

'She doesn't want me. She told me to get out of her house.'

'Child, sometimes parents say things they don't mean.'

'Oh, she meant it.'

'All you've been through? She wouldn't have wanted that.'

'She doesn't care. Besides, she wouldn't believe it. And I won't go back there.'

Amanda only now realized she had pulled her feet up onto the chair and she was hugging her knees to her chest, rocking back and forth. She saw the concern in Hannah's eyes and she hated that this woman might pity her. Shock would be better than pity, and that's why she said what she did next. Because she wanted to wipe the pity off Hannah's face.

'I'd rather swallow cocaine balloons than have her boyfriend continue to stick his dick down my throat.'

THURSDAY

45

O'Dell thought she had gotten good at disconnecting from pain. She had definitely had enough practice. Life was about sorting and tucking away and compartmentalizing feelings, emotions, and yes, even pain. It was supposed to be as simple as mind over matter. She needed to tell her mind to go somewhere else, to separate from the physical discomfort.

Simple, unless you couldn't swallow. Unless you found it difficult to breathe. Every time she opened her eyes, her vision blurred, creating two-headed monsters, then lights swirled until there were only ropes of colors racing around in her head.

She squeezed her eyelids tight and fought against the

damp chill that drenched her body. Any movement – a bump and slide – made her nauseated. Hands grabbed at her and she swatted them away. But they insisted – touching, dabbing, another sting. This time a needle. And so she went somewhere else in her mind. She tried to access sunny skies. Ocean waves. The sounds of seagulls overhead.

But the dark and the pain triggered other memories. A flood of them.

Suddenly she was in a dark forest. Red eyes watched her, hunted her from every direction. The electrical jolt of a Taser brought fresh pain. And the paralysis lingered, making her feel even more helpless. She felt herself curl into a bed of leaves that crumpled. The wet soil underneath made her cold – so very cold.

Then a gunshot made her jerk. Searing pain raced along her scalp, tearing, ripping, burning, until she could smell the scorched flesh. This memory was worse than the scorpion stings, and it pushed her to the surface of consciousness.

This time when O'Dell woke and opened her eyes she was able to focus. There were no trees, no forest. A high ceiling with polished wood planks. She was in a bed surrounded by cool sheets. Someone stirred behind her, and the panic grabbed hold for a second until she felt the wet tongue on her bare shoulder. She reached back, comforted by the touch.

'Hey, Grace.' She petted the dog as she relaxed back into the pillows.

Her eyes searched her surroundings. The bed was at the far end of a large loft apartment. A wonderful scent of something cooking came from the kitchen at the other end. She lifted her arm out from under the covers and in doing so saw that she was wearing only her panties and an oversized T-shirt, the V-neck stretched out and slipped down off her shoulder. The backs of her hands and her arms were covered with a sticky white paste. She could feel it on her neck and her cheek, as well.

Grace now sat on the edge of the bed staring at her. O'Dell's eyes searched the apartment again: the over-stuffed sofa, the wall of bookshelves, the desk in a corner.

'Where's your owner?' she asked Grace.

The dog cocked her head.

'Where's Ryder?'

Grace's ears slicked back and she started to wag. She jumped off the bed and glanced back over her shoulder, ready to lead O'Dell to what she had asked for.

She was surprised to find her head quite clear. No swirling. Just a slight throb at her temples. There was no longer the deep, burning pain. Only an ache and soreness. Her knees didn't wobble, and she was able to stand without assistance. The T-shirt's hem came only to mid-thigh, and immediately she looked around the bed for her clothes.

Grace scampered across the room, her entire hind end wagging impatiently for O'Dell to follow her.

'You have any idea what happened to my pants?' she asked the dog.

Grace's only answer was a two-step prance and twirl.

'No, I didn't think so.' O'Dell couldn't help but smile.

Grace led her to a door off the kitchen that had been left open.

The stairs were polished wood and spiraled down to a balcony that ran the length of the outer walls. It overlooked an atrium of a large warehouse-like building. Despite the open rafters and silver air-duct piping along the ceiling, windows at the top brought in streams of sunlight that sent shadows dancing across the earth-toned walls and the stamped cement floor.

The place could easily be someone's warehouse-style home. It was obviously the living space for Creed's dogs.

From her stance on the balcony's landing, O'Dell could see a full kitchen in one corner with stainless steel commercial-sized appliances and shiny counter-tops. But instead of a table and chairs, rows of different-sized bowls were arranged on the floor with decorative mats underneath.

There was a buzz and she saw a line of dog doors, several going up electronically now as dogs came in and immediately looked up at her. In the opposite corner, kennels lined the wall; more than a dozen dogs were sleeping or watching Grace and O'Dell from dog beds that were scattered around the floor. And in the middle of them she spotted Creed curled up – shirtless with only jeans on – nestled up between two large brown dogs. His head lay against the bigger dog's back.

Despite the tousled hair and bristled jaw, she couldn't help thinking how much he reminded her of a young boy, fast asleep and at peace among the friends he knew he could count on and trust most.

46

She had been stung by scorpions and awakened from a black fog, and yet the first thing she said to him was, 'I couldn't find my clothes.'

Creed stifled a grin. He didn't want her to feel any more self-conscious than she obviously was. Already her fingers were tugging down the hem of his favorite T-shirt, stretching it out beyond repair and making it even more of a favorite.

'They were pretty dirty. Hannah took them to wash.'

'Hannah?'

'My partner.' He saw her glancing around his apartment and added, 'She lives at the main house with her boys. You met her last night, but I'm not surprised you don't remember.'

They had come back up from the dog kennels, though he certainly wouldn't have minded lying there a bit longer. He'd managed to get maybe three hours of sleep. When he woke to see Maggie standing on the balcony above, he thought he was dreaming. The sunlight streaming down on her had made the white T-shirt practically transparent. She had looked like an angel – a quite shapely angel – totally unaware that he could see more than the bare thighs she was now trying so desperately to cover.

'She offered to bring your freshly laundered clothes back with some lunch.'

'Lunch? But you have something smelling wonderful here in your kitchen.'

'Oh, that's actually for the dogs. I've got one with kidney disease. It's always a challenge to get him to eat. And we have two new boarders who are missing their owners.'

'Ryder's Dog Café?' She smiled at him, and he was glad to see she appreciated his effort rather than thinking he was silly. 'Boarders? I didn't realize that was part of your business.'

'It's not. Hannah volunteers at a place called Segway House. They take in runaways, recovering drug addicts, pregnant teens, and a lot of returning military. They can't have their dogs while they're living there. A couple of our boarders are dogs whose owners have been deployed and there were no family members to take the dogs in.'

She was staring at him, and for a moment he thought perhaps she wasn't feeling quite as well as she initially thought she did. 'Wow!' she finally said. 'That is really ... admirable.'

And that was the last thing any man wanted to be called by a half-naked woman in the middle of his apartment.

'Sometimes it's a pain in the neck. I end up with a dog I didn't want.'

'The owner doesn't come back for the dog?'

'Or he comes back in a flag-draped casket.'

'Oh.' It was obvious she hadn't thought of that.

At the kitchen counter he filled glasses with orange juice, then led her to the sofa, pointing to the blanket draped over the back. He waited for her to settle in while he held her glass. She tucked a bare foot up underneath herself, revealing even more than she intended before yanking the blanket over her lap.

She'd been feverish last night but the crimson today was definitely a blush. He hated that she was uncomfortable and hated it even more that he found it sexier than hell. Especially after what she'd been through. He'd had plenty of women come to his loft apartment, some stayed the night, others just several hours, but this was more intimate than anything or anyone before, and he hadn't even touched her.

Then he realized that she probably thought he had.

'Just for the record, Hannah and Dr Avelyn undressed you last night. They put the baking soda paste on the stings.'

She held up her hands and stared at the backs of them. The swelling was gone. A few welts were still visible under the paste. It was remarkable how, less than twenty-four hours later, Maggie looked almost back to normal.

'You're sure you're feeling okay?'

'I feel good,' she said as she took the glass of juice from him. Her eyes caught sight of his welts, and she reached up and touched the back of his hand. 'Looks like you got stung, too.'

Her fingertips meant to caress, but Creed felt only the unexpected electrical charge. He shrugged and pretended the stings and her touch were no big deal. He asked, 'No pain?'

She shook her head. 'I guess I'm a little bit achy. It feels like I have a hangover. But otherwise ... I feel amazingly good.'

'Dr Avelyn gave you something for the pain and to help you sleep when she gave you the antivenin.'

'Dr Avelyn?'

'Avelyn Parker.'

'You have a doctor who makes house calls?'

'She's not an MD. She's a veterinarian.'

She smiled, then nodded as if she should have guessed. And she didn't seem bothered by the fact.

'This type of scorpion doesn't inject enough venom to be lethal, but you had about eighteen stings. Actually, this particular type of scorpion doesn't usually sting unless disturbed or threatened. You did kind of disturb them.'

'All I can remember is that I couldn't breathe.'

'You had an allergic reaction. The symptoms come on quick and furious.' He reached out to touch her arm but stopped short, remembering the impact of her simple caress. Instead, he pointed to where the swelling had gone down on her shoulder and only a red mark showed through the paste. 'Without the antivenin you could have died.'

'It was meant to be a trap or another torture chamber, wasn't it? Just like the fire ants.'

'Most likely. The forensic team said there was a screen over the top to prevent the scorpions from escaping. The hole was lined with burlap to keep it moist. Someone had dumped rotted wood with enough termites to keep the scorpions fat and happy.'

'But Mrs Bagley didn't die down there.'

'No. I expect the coroner will be getting those details to you and Sheriff Holt when he knows the cause of her death. There is something else.'

He sat down in the recliner beside her, close enough that his knee brushed the blanket. He stayed at the edge of the chair, set aside his now-empty glass, and leaned forward, elbows on his knees, chin on his fists.

'Your rental car's been impounded by the forensic team.'

'What? Why?'

'Jason got your belongings from the trunk. He'll bring them when he comes to work today.'

'I'm not worried about that. Why did they take the car?'

'Someone left a burlap sack under the driver's seat. Jason found it when he tried to drive your car back yesterday. There were three coral snakes in the sack.'

She shot a hand up and ran fingers through her hair as she shook her head. 'Seriously, what is it with these people? Fire ants, scorpions, snakes?'

'Coral snakes have the most virulent venom of all the poisonous snakes in the States. One bite can kill a dog in a matter of ten to twenty minutes.'

Her hand came down to her lap and her eyes widened. 'Is Jason okay?'

'Yeah, he's okay. A bit shook-up. Corals are shy, not aggressive. They like to hide, but if they feel trapped, they'll strike.'

'Like the scorpions.'

He scooted closer. Drew her eyes to meet his. 'Normally I don't need to know everything from law enforcement except what'll help me and my dogs do our job. But this is one time I think you need to tell me what's going on.'

'I told you. We fished Trevor Bagley out of the Potomac. We think someone tortured him.'

'With fire ants. I got that. But why?'

'That's what I'm trying to find out.'

'But you have your suspicions.'

Her eyes left his and without a word they confirmed what he had said.

'Look, Maggie, the scorpions have been there for whatever crazy reason. Scare tactic, torture ... maybe somebody's screwed-up idea of a joke. But the snakes ... The snakes were put in *your* car on purpose.'

He waited to see that fact sink in. She looked tired. Her skin was still rash-red in places, and strands of hair stuck to the paste on her neck. He noticed that her eyes were slow to track, almost as if her mind was playing catch-up. It was probably the residual effect of the drugs that Dr Avelyn had given her yesterday.

'When?' she said. 'When could they have put them in the car? The sheriff and his deputy—'

'Already checked on that. Holt said they left for about twenty to thirty minutes to meet the forensic team and then lead them to the place so they wouldn't get lost. That's not a long time span. Which means someone not only knew you were at the Bagleys' place, but they were there somewhere – watching.'

'So you think they meant to scare me?'

'No, I think they meant to kill you.'

47

'DEA's descended on the Bagley place,' Sheriff Holt was telling O'Dell. 'Why the hell would you do that?'

He had left over a dozen voice and text messages for her. By the time she returned his calls, he sounded exhausted and furious.

'I didn't do anything. I only woke up a few hours ago,' she tried to explain.

'I apologize, Agent O'Dell. I don't know what I was thinking. I haven't even asked how you're doing. Are you okay?'

'Sore and a bit achy. My head hurts.'

'So if you didn't tell them, how'd the bastards even know?'

'Your forensic team? Maybe someone from the café?'

'Believe me when I say nobody in these parts calls the feds.'

Fortunately, in his anger he was treating her like one of his team. He had forgotten that O'Dell was a fed.

'They'll be able to help with some lab tests that we wouldn't be able to do.' She tried to keep positive.

'That's great, but they're not even letting us continue on the investigation.'

'What do you mean?'

'They were already there when we arrived this morning at eight. They ordered us off the property. We're not allowed to return.'

'You're kidding.'

'Do I sound like I'm kidding?'

'Let me see if I can find out what's happening.'

'In the meantime, what the hell do we do?'

'Did they ask for the evidence the forensic team recovered?'

'Not yet, but I'm told they barged in on our coroner. Shoved some badges in his face, then loaded up and hauled out Mrs Bagley's body.'

O'Dell couldn't say she was surprised. She'd had a gut feeling from the moment they pulled Trevor

Bagley's bloated corpse out of the river that this was a much bigger case. She just didn't realize how big.

'What other evidence did your team find?' she asked.

'After they recovered the body, they spent a bit of time in one of the sheds behind the house. No more bodies, but it'll make your skin crawl.'

She stayed quiet and waited. As angry as he was, she could tell this was something that was hard to digest.

'Looks like they kept some kids in there.'

Her stomach twisted in knots. 'Did the feds ask for the evidence?'

'Didn't ask and we didn't tell. I don't think they know how much we found. Maybe they don't even know about the kids. Seems they're more concerned about us busting up their drug case.'

'Did the forensic team find any drugs?'

'Not even a little.'

They discussed what to do with the evidence the team had collected, then promised they'd be in touch. It wouldn't be the first time that O'Dell found herself on the side of the local law enforcement rather than her colleagues on the federal side. What was adding one more clash with her boss?

When O'Dell clicked off she scrolled down to the messages she had purposely ignored from her boss. Now she punched in the last one and listened to his voice message: 'O'Dell, where the hell are you? I need you in my office first thing in the morning.'

She checked for the day and time stamp. Today at 10:00 AM. By the current time on her cell phone, she saw that she'd never be able to catch an evening flight back to DC. It would take driving all night to get there by 'first thing in the morning.'

She dialed his number, and when his secretary answered – the secretary whose main job seemed to be playing interference and denying access – she passed O'Dell through so quickly O'Dell thought it had to be a mistake. Turns out Assistant Director Kunze was that anxious to chew her out. She let him rant for several minutes. Past experience had taught her that he tended to reveal important information during his angry outbursts. This time was no different.

In those brief minutes she learned that she had encroached on a classified case that the DEA had been working on for months. She had to bite back the fact that she had pointedly asked him about this being a drug hit. Now she wondered what exactly Kunze knew and when he knew it.

'I want you back here in my office tomorrow to explain to the DEA what exactly you found.'

'Wouldn't it be easier to talk to them right here?'

'Excuse me?'

'From what I understand, they've taken over the Bagley property. The county sheriff and his forensic team that were working the scene have been denied access and told to leave the property. They even raided the county coroner's office and took Mrs Bagley's body.'

Silence. So Kunze didn't know everything.

'Another floater was pulled from the Potomac this morning.'

That surprised her. But it probably explained part of Kunze's fury.

'A second package,' she said.

'Stan Wenhoff thinks the victim died from poisonous spider bites – like dozens of bites all over his body.'

O'Dell couldn't stop a shiver from sliding down her back. She could still feel the scorpions on her skin and in her hair.

'Driver's license?'

'Don't know yet. Mouth's duct-taped shut. Stan won't remove it until he does the autopsy tomorrow. I want you to be there. How soon can you get here?'

At that moment Creed came back to the apartment, entering through the door from the kennels below. He had left to work with the dogs. He saw that she was on the phone and offered a wave and a nod.

His T-shirt was drenched in sweat and stuck to him like a second skin. His jeans were mud-stained and his hiking boots must have been, as well, because he had left them behind somewhere and came in with bare feet. He carried what must have been another of Hannah's casseroles. The aroma reached O'Dell clear across the loft – something wonderful with garlic.

She watched him carefully place the glass dish on his stovetop, then instinctively lick one of his thumbs that accidentally grazed the masterpiece. She found herself smiling, then surprisingly caught herself thinking, *I could get used to this place ... to this man.*

'Agent O'Dell, did you hear what I said?'

Kunze startled her back to attention.

'Stan will start as soon as you can get back. Agent McCoy will be in my office tomorrow afternoon at three. You need to be back here in the morning. Is that clear, Agent O'Dell?'

He was actually waiting for an answer, as if it made a difference. Maybe he expected her to argue. Instead, she simply said, 'I'll be there.' And she ended the call.

48

'I don't want to put you out of your bed for a second night,' Maggie told him.

Creed didn't make the suggestion that he wanted to make. The bed was, after all, big enough for the two of them. Grace could sleep in the middle and supervise. Though it wouldn't matter. He knew he'd never be able to get any sleep in that bed as long as Maggie O'Dell was anywhere in it. So he did the gentlemanly thing and prepared the sofa with a blanket and pillow for himself.

He realized Maggie probably wondered why Hannah didn't offer for her to sleep at the main house. It was huge. Even from the outside there was no hiding the fact that it housed at least three or four bedrooms. But he couldn't risk her running into Amanda. It wasn't that he didn't trust Maggie; he refused to get her involved. Also, she was an FBI agent and would probably want to do the right thing. Creed didn't think they'd agree on what the 'right thing' was right now.

They finished Hannah's casserole and the salad Creed had made for them. Maggie insisted on doing the clean-up. Grace and Rufus offered their undivided help and attention, both of them following and then sitting within feet of Maggie.

She stopped to scratch behind their ears. 'I miss my dogs.'

'They must be with somebody you trust.'

'Yes, they are.'

She met his eyes and then suddenly her eyes left his and darted around, as if she had been caught doing something she shouldn't be doing. There was electricity between them. There was no denying that. Just now he could have heard the crackle if he'd listened hard enough. But he knew he shouldn't. He knew he ought to let her go back to tooling around his kitchen without any more of an explanation. For some reason he couldn't. Not after what they'd just been through. He needed to know.

'The guy who takes care of your dogs, does he also have your heart?'

When she turned back around to look at him, she looked surprised at first. Like she hadn't really thought of it that way. Or was she just surprised that Creed would ask so blatantly?

Then something passed over her and he swore to God she looked sad. That was the only word that came quickly to mind. He hated like hell that his heart leaped and rejoiced in the seconds that followed.

'Ben and I are ...' Her voice trailed off, as if she were trying to figure it out as she was telling him. 'I'm not sure what we are. It's complicated.'

Creed stood and took a step around the counter. It was more instinct than anything else. She took a step back and he stopped. But only for a few seconds. In the next steps he felt the jolts as much as a magnetic pull. He was kissing her before she had a chance to think, before she could retreat. There was nothing about her lips or hands on his chest or her hips pressed against him that told him this guy Ben had a hold of her heart. But when she pulled away, her eyes said otherwise. There was want and need, but also a hint of guilt.

'I can't' was all she said, almost a whisper. Then a bit stronger, she added, 'Maybe I shouldn't stay here tonight.'

He brushed her hair from her face. He let his hand caress her cheek, and he heard her breath catch.

'It's okay,' he told her. 'I'm a big boy. Takes a lot more to hurt my feelings.'

Just when she looked like she might change her mind, and Creed knew he'd never be able to pull away a second time, he pointed at Grace and Rufus, who had been staring at them the whole time.

'Besides,' he said, 'Grace would never forgive me if you left early.' And he made his way to his sofa, thinking it was going to be a hell of a long night.

FRIDAY

49

'I really don't want to talk about this right now, Hannah.'

Creed didn't want to talk, period. He had taken O'Dell to the airport early in the morning. He didn't like the way it felt watching her leave – actually, he didn't like that he felt something, and he was trying as hard as hell not to think about it.

The minute he got back he'd wanted to get to work on the new security system he'd stopped off to buy on his way home. He'd come to the main house to install cameras, not argue about their houseguest. Even if the houseguest was the reason he was installing the cameras.

'What'd the electrician say?' Creed asked, trying to divert Hannah from the direction he knew she was headed in.

'He looked over everything, said it looked fine. You're trying to change the subject. You seem to trust Agent O'Dell. I'm just saying it wouldn't be such a bad idea to tell her about the situation. She's FBI. She could probably help. Maybe even fix things.'

'I already told you, I don't want another person involved.'

'We work with a whole bunch of law enforcement people. Any one of them might be able to help. Make this all go away.'

She waved her hand at the packages he had loaded under his arm.

'And what happens to Amanda?' he asked.

'That's not your concern.'

'It's not? She came to me, Hannah. She chose to trust me to help her. How can I just hand her off to someone else?'

'They'll come for their merchandise. And not just the drugs. They consider *her* merchandise, too. *Their* merchandise.'

'I understand that. You're not telling me anything I don't already know.'

'And you're willing to risk everything?'

'I'm taking care of things.'

'By making this place some kind of fortress?' She pointed at the cameras now. 'This is not the way I want to live, Rye. It's not the way I want to raise my boys, always looking over my shoulder, afraid some-one's watching. Maybe just waiting to hurt one of them.'

'If you show someone that you're scared of them, then they've already won,' he said. 'You told me that when we first met. You remember that?'

She crossed her arms and released a heavy sigh. She shook her head and said, 'This is different, Rye.'

'Is it? Or are they just a different kind of bully?'

He didn't wait for her response. Instead, he grabbed the tool bag he'd brought with him along with one of the cameras and headed to the kitchen. For a minute he thought she had given in, but he knew her better. He decided to wait. He set every-thing down on the kitchen table and grabbed a banana from the counter. Hannah would need to have the last word. Sure enough, he heard her coming up the hallway. He leaned back, peeled the banana, and took a bite.

'I understand why you don't want to get Agent O'Dell involved. You're sweet on her. But there are others who would help us.'

'I don't get sweet on women I work with. "Sweet on"? Really? Does anyone use that phrase anymore?'

'Well, I'm glad to hear you have standards.' Then suddenly she frowned at him. 'Where did you get that banana?'

'From the counter? What, you're mad at me so I can't have one of your bananas?'

'I didn't buy no bananas. I haven't been to the store yet.'

She came over to the counter, staring at the bunch as if they were foreign objects. He went to take another bite and she grabbed his wrist.

'Put it down.'

'Hannah, come on.'

'What's that white stuff?'

She pointed at one of the bananas on the counter, and he saw what looked like a puff of cotton attached to it.

'Okay, so they might have a little mold. No big deal.'

He poked his index finger at the spot to rub it off. That's when the puff of white erupted.

'Oh my dear God!' Hannah started screaming as dozens of tiny spiders burst out of the white web and raced across the countertop in all directions.

When he looked at the banana in his hand he saw a similar patch of white at the bottom of the peel. And now it was bursting open with tiny white spiders spiraling onto his hand and up his arm.

He searched the counter and grabbed a half-eaten loaf of bread. With one hand he popped open the bag and dropped the bread on top of the mass of spiders. It stopped those underneath, and suddenly the others turned and started coming back. In seconds the bread was swarming with the creatures. He swatted those on his hand and arm back down onto the countertop to join their friends.

'Get me a garbage bag,' he told Hannah, who stood paralyzed and deaf, watching with wide eyes and her hand over her mouth. 'Hannah, where are the garbage bags?' He didn't want to move too much and start banging cabinet doors in search of something that she knew exactly where to find.

Finally she turned slowly, mimicking his slow

movements. She reached down and carefully pulled out a heavy black garbage bag from under the sink. As soon as she handed it to him, he gently unfolded it, never taking his eyes off the slices of bread that were now covered completely by tiny spiders. He couldn't tell whether they were devouring the bread or simply attracted to it.

How the hell could so many spiders come out of such small pieces of web? Neither patch looked any bigger than a Q-tip head.

Hannah saw what he was planning and she shifted and bent down to the same cabinet where the garbage bags were. She brought out a short-handled squeegee. She nodded at him, then took a position, holding the squeegee up and ready, though he could see her hand shaking a bit.

Creed aligned the opening of the bag against the lip of the countertop as close as possible to the mass of creatures, dog-piling one another on top of the bread.

'We'll only get one chance,' he told Hannah.

She didn't take her eyes off the spiders. He saw her fingers tighten on the squeegee handle. 'Let's do it. You ready?'

'Ready.'

He was still holding the bread wrapper in case she missed. He'd sweep them in with his hand, too, if necessary.

'Dear Lord, give me strength,' Hannah said, and then she slammed the squeegee on the countertop and swiped hard and fast. Several spiders fell off but Hannah was faster than them, pounding the squeegee down again and sweeping them into the bag. She even swept the rest of the bananas into the bag and was ready for more, but there didn't appear to be any.

Creed twisted the top of the garbage bag closed and held it tight, searching the floor for escapees.

'Did we get 'em all?' Hannah wanted to know, squeegee still gripped in her hand.

'I think we did.'

'Lord have mercy.' She released a huge sigh and stared at the garbage bag. 'What you gonna do with them?'

He shrugged. He hadn't thought that far in advance.

'Go ahead and mix them in with those bastards' cocaine balloons.'

In the seven years he'd known Hannah, he had

never heard her say a curse word even close to 'bastard.' Suddenly he laughed, then watched the realization cross her face. She tried to give him her best scowl, but instead, she started laughing, too.

50

Creed couldn't help thinking that if he'd already installed the cameras, he'd know exactly who left a bunch of bananas with spiders hatching onto Hannah's kitchen counter. His best guess was the electrician, although Hannah insisted he was wrong. Tony was staying at Segway House, she told him.

'No way, no how, did that young soldier do this.'

But Creed saw in her eyes that she was questioning her own words. He didn't have to confront the young man because he knew as soon as he left the house that Hannah would be on the phone interrogating whoever had sent him.

On the way to the kennels he stopped off at the

building they had just finished for Dr Avelyn Parker's clinic. Hannah still complained that it was an incredibly expensive investment. The equipment alone had required a chunk of money, but Creed knew it would pay off in the long run with all the dogs that would be cared for.

Having a facility out here on their property was as much about convenience and saving time. And having Dr Avelyn on staff – even if it was for a limited number of hours so she could tend to her own practice in Milton – was more than worth the money.

He dropped off the garbage bag filled with spiders and deposited it in a metal trash can with a note attached. One great thing about the woman was that she knew almost as much about the creatures that dogs had to watch out for as she did about dogs. By the time he reached the kennels, he saw her black Tahoe coming up the long driveway.

Most likely the spiders were meant to send a message. Someone was trying to tell him what he already knew all too well – that despite the isolation of their facility, and despite Creed's best efforts to keep strangers off his property, they were able to walk right into the house and leave a bunch of bananas.

Simple as that.

If they could do that without anyone noticing, what else were they capable of doing? And suddenly he thought about the kennels and the dogs. Immediately he started searching every inch of the facility for anything that looked a bit out of place.

What occurred to him and bothered him most was that whoever took the risk to come here didn't seem the least bit concerned with finding or taking Amanda or the cocaine. Maybe they just didn't have time. Or wanted to learn the layout of the entire place for when they came back. And that made him realize this was just a prelude. There was more to come, and they wouldn't stop until they were satisfied with taking or destroying whatever they wanted.

Creed heard the electronic buzz of the back door and turned to see Jason coming in. All the doors were ultrasonic-sensored, allowing only those wearing the infrared bracelet with the coded signal to come inside without using hands. The same technology opened the six electronic dog doors. As long as the dogs had on their coded infrared collars, they could come in and go out to the fenced yard as they wished. It also meant that no one had access to any of his buildings without a bracelet to trip the sensor, and Creed was very careful about who he allowed to have one.

He watched Jason struggle with a load of training buckets despite the door opening automatically. The kid had been working his ass off. And yet Creed caught himself wondering how much would it take for a cash-strapped amputee to betray him? The best way to get to Creed would be through someone he'd never feel threatened by. Someone he was supposed to trust.

No, he stopped. Even if by chance Jason was the one someone had paid to plop a bunch of bananas down on the kitchen counter, no drug cartel would use this kid to finish the job. They would use a hit squad, wouldn't they? And if they came here, they were on his territory.

He scanned the ceiling, the sprinkler system, the doors, the kennels, and the windows that lined the very top of the building, two stories up. He'd positioned them purposely too high for anyone to come through or for a scared or manic dog to jump through.

'Everything okay?'

Creed turned to find that Jason had put down the training equipment and was now ten feet away, staring at him. The kid actually looked concerned. Or was it guilt?

'Everything's fine. Why wouldn't it be?'

Creed's cell phone started ringing before Jason could respond. He grabbed it out of his pocket and took a quick glance. It was a number he didn't recognize.

'This is Ryder Creed.'

'Creed, hi. It's Liz Bailey. From the Coast Guard.'

'Rescue swimmer Bailey, how are you?'

He didn't remember giving her his phone number.

'Sorry to call you like this, but there's something you should know. Can you talk?'

He shot a look at Jason, but the kid had already retreated out of earshot, going on to his next task. 'Sure, what's going on?'

'This isn't public knowledge yet. I heard it very unofficially. There was a body fished out of the Potomac.'

He almost stopped her to say he had already heard about Trevor Bagley and the possible drug connection. But she surprised him with what she said next.

'He was pulled out yesterday morning. Tortured with spider bites all over his body. Gagged and dumped in the river. They think he might have still been alive when he was thrown in.'

'How do you know this?' He checked his wristwatch. Bailey had to be talking about the second floater. The autopsy that Maggie's boss wanted her back in DC for. Was it possible they already had an ID on the guy?

'Our crew's been working with the DEA for a while now,' Bailey said. 'The *Blue Mist* isn't the only fishing boat we've been tracking that Choque Azul might be using. But I think everybody was surprised with the cargo we found. Seems to be sending a shock wave even through the cartel.'

'Are you saying the body in the Potomac is connected to what we found?'

'The victim was the captain of that fishing boat.'

That surprised Creed.

'DEA thinks there's a hit list. We all might be on it.'

'Seems to me they're eliminating their own employees.'

'That's what I thought. Not such a bad thing, right? Look, this is just talk at this point. You know how talk starts, even in organizations that aren't supposed to talk. But you might want to be careful.'

'I already know.'

'Excuse me?'

'I know I'm on their hit list.'

51

Stan was waiting for O'Dell. He didn't bother to hide his irritation. The body was ready on a table. The medical examiner bent over and prepared his instruments.

'I have no idea what Assistant Director Kunze thinks you'll be able to witness or report back to him that wouldn't already be in my notes.'

'Your guess is as good as mine. I would have much rather stayed in bed this morning.'

He glanced up just as she was taking off her jacket to gown up, and then he did a double take when he saw the welts on her arms.

'What in the world happened to you?'

'Scorpions.'

'Seriously?'

'Seriously,' she said, and joined him on the other side of the table, trying to ignore his staring. He was waiting for an explanation. She raised an eyebrow at him. 'I thought you were in a hurry?'

'Something tells me your scorpion story is related.' He put down a scalpel and crossed his arms. For the first time since she'd met the man, he looked genuinely concerned about her.

'Actually, it's your fault.'

'Mine?'

'I went searching for the original crime scene and fire ants.'

She gave him a quick rundown on how she found scorpions instead. She caught him wincing twice.

'DEA.' He said it like he had a bad taste in his mouth. 'They must have known when we pulled Bagley out of the river.'

'Do you know who received the call about the first package?' O'Dell asked as she let her eyes examine the bloated victim. This guy hadn't been in the water as long. 'You mentioned it that morning. Did it come into your office?'

He shook his head as he picked up the scalpel and a hemostat. Gently he began to tug at a corner of the duct tape on the victim's mouth.

'We were simply told. I believe the call that came in to us was from someone at Justice.'

'In the Department of Justice? Not someone at the FBI? Or maybe the DEA?'

'I can check. I'm sure we track such things.'

'That's why you were surprised to see me there?'

'I guess neither of us should be surprised at too much anymore.'

Stan had worked off most of the tape now but stopped when he saw what looked to O'Dell like a thin black thread overlapping the lower lip. At first, she thought it might be a suture. Then it moved.

'Holy crap!' Stan jerked back.

O'Dell stared and watched, mesmerized, but she didn't dare get any closer. The object poking out of the corpse's mouth was made up of small segments and moved almost in robotic twitches back and forth.

'Seems I spoke too soon,' Stan said as he looked

around his workspace. He grabbed a large Ziploc bag and shoved it at O'Dell.

'It's not a spider leg.'

'No,' Stan agreed. 'I'm guessing antenna. The bastard's sticking it out to get a sense of his new surroundings.'

'Are you thinking what I'm thinking?'

'The one primitive species that has survived for millions of years and can survive anywhere on earth and probably in hell. Yes, I'm sure we're thinking the same thing.'

He twisted around to his tray and plucked up tweezers and a bigger hemostat while O'Dell pulled on a pair of latex gloves. She had left the gloves in her pockets since she hadn't intended to touch anything. Stan was a stickler for no interference. That he was suggesting she assist him was a breakthrough she could actually do without. Still, she took the plastic bag and followed his instructions.

'He'll either retreat when he sees the lights or he'll race out,' Stan told her as he donned headgear that provided magnification and a stream of LED light. Then he bent over the victim, fingers ready.

'What makes you think there's only one?'

He looked up at her over the contraption as he flipped the light switch and shot the beam of light in her eyes, making her blink.

'Just be ready to play catch,' he told her. 'I don't want a bunch of cockroaches running around my autopsy suite.'

52

O'Dell had gotten to Quantico with only forty-three minutes to spare before the dreaded meeting with AD Kunze and Agent McCoy.

While she printed out the autopsy photos of this latest floater, the images of the cockroaches reminded her of the scorpions. It would take a long time to forget that feeling of them skittering over her body.

She rubbed at the backs of her hands. The swelling was completely gone this morning. Dr Avelyn's sticky paste mixture had reduced the welts to mere red marks, no more noticeable than a mosquito bite. A small amount of makeup and her hair covered the ones on her neck and cheek. She'd keep her jacket on, though, to avoid any more reactions like Stan's. Although she was pretty certain the attention wouldn't be on her after showing these photos.

Stan had removed a total of five cockroaches from the victim's mouth. Only one hadn't come out willingly and had to be extracted. The other four had raced out as soon as he pried the lips apart. One almost escaped up the medical examiner's hand before O'Dell swept it back into the plastic bag, which she had tried to wrap tight against the victim's bloated face. The trick was that Stan had to keep the tweezers and at least his fingers inside the bag to open the mouth. He was fast but not as fast as the roaches.

O'Dell had to admit, she had a newfound respect for Stan. He hadn't flinched. If he had, all five roaches would probably have been long gone in the corners and cubbyholes of his meticulous autopsy suite.

Only after Stan was convinced there were no more cockroaches had he dug deeper and worked carefully to remove the other object that had been stuffed down the throat – the man's driver's license.

Before she left the District to head to Quantico, she had typed 'Robert Díaz' into several searches available to her. Those were also waiting for her to print out.

When she arrived five minutes before three o'clock, she was surprised to find everyone waiting for her. And even more surprised to see Senator Delanor. She was seated in the same chair across from Kunze's desk, where O'Dell had found her the last time. AD Kunze introduced O'Dell and Agent McCoy with no explanation about the senator's presence, and Senator Delanor made no motion to leave. She was obviously a part of this meeting. And immediately, O'Dell felt her guard go into place. She seemed to be the only one here who had no clue what the hell was going on.

'Agent McCoy was just filling us in about what happened at the Bagleys',' Kunze said, as he waited for O'Dell to take the chair next to the senator. McCoy evidently had chosen to stand.

'Yes, how are you doing?' Senator Delanor patted her arm. 'How dreadful.'

Before O'Dell could respond, Kunze added, 'You should have told me about the scorpions when we talked yesterday.'

And there it was – already the sympathy had been converted to blame.

'I'm fine, thanks for asking,' she told the senator. To McCoy she said, 'So you knew about Trevor Bagley?'

'Oh, he and his wife have been on our radar for some time.'

'Would have been nice if you had shared that when we pulled his body from the Potomac.'

'Agent O'Dell,' Kunze scolded.

'No, that's okay.' McCoy smiled and waved a hand at Kunze, dismissing O'Dell and her comment even before adding, 'I've already heard she's a pistol.'

O'Dell had checked him out, too, learning everything she could, though there wasn't much available. In the last twenty years, Agent McCoy had been promoted up the ranks, starting out as an immigration officer before moving to the DEA.

Somewhere she had read that he was a Texan, and she half expected a big and bold cowboy with a southern accent. Even in the confines of the office, he still managed a swagger, but there were no other signs. No Stetson, no cowboy boots, no decorative belt buckle. She was almost disappointed. Agent McCoy looked very much like an official government agent – square shoulders, a standard steel-blue suit to match his tie and eyes, polished black leather shoes, and slicked-back hair with just enough gray at the temples to make him look seasoned.

'What happened is unfortunate, Agent O'Dell, but we could hardly expect that you'd be running out to Alabama and tromping all over the Bagleys' property, now could we?'

'I'm curious why not?'

'Excuse me?'

'If you knew it was Bagley in the river, and this was such a sensitive case, why weren't your people at the Bagleys' before me?'

This time Kunze didn't hush or scold her. At a glance, she could see that her boss was also interested in the answer.

McCoy used that moment to sit down on the corner of Kunze's desk, ignoring the assistant director's look of disapproval. His perch kept him higher than everyone else, establishing an air of authority and making the rest of them all look up to him. It was an old trick. O'Dell had used it herself sometimes when questioning suspects. However, she had never done it with a colleague.

'We tend to measure our moves carefully, instead of running half-cocked.' He shot an irritated look at

Kunze. McCoy no longer seemed amused by this 'pistol,' though he didn't mind continuing the metaphor. 'We've known that Mr and Mrs Bagley were running drugs. We were waiting for the right time to raid their property so that we could use them to help make our case against George Ramos. We wanted to do as much damage as we could to Choque Azul. Are you familiar with them?'

'Agent O'Dell was responsible for putting Ramos behind bars,' AD Kunze said, and for the first time in a long time O'Dell thought she heard a hint of pride in her boss's voice.

'Ah yes, that's right,' McCoy said. 'You went out to rescue him and his kids on his houseboat during a storm and ended up interrupting a drug pickup in the middle of the Gulf.'

He had to already know that. O'Dell couldn't figure out why he was pretending it was news to him. She glanced at Senator Delanor. George Ramos had been her husband. He was the father of her children. She was the one who used her influence as the junior senator from Florida to get Kunze to send out O'Dell and the Coast Guard to rescue her family. It couldn't be easy listening to McCoy talk about it so flippantly.

After all, the woman had winced when O'Dell accidentally called her Senator Delanor-Ramos just days ago. But she was a professional politician, and somehow she managed to keep her face impassive. O'Dell saw that the senator kept her hands in her lap, and she noticed that the interlaced fingers were gripped tightly together, almost in a stranglehold.

'It wasn't until Ramos's arrest that we discovered not only that he was a part of this Colombian cartel, but that he was the *jefe*, the boss man, for the entire southeastern region. His arrest last fall caused all kinds of shifts and tensions. We've learned that his son has been trying to take over in his absence.'

'His son?' Kunze asked, and looked to Senator Delanor.

'I knew George had a previous life,' Senator Delanor said. 'In Colombia, long before I met him. Of course, I didn't know until recently that he had a wife and a son. Or that he was still in touch with them ... and taking care of them.'

'So did Choque Azul decide to get rid of the Bagleys before you got to them?' O'Dell asked.

'That's what we thought initially, when you pulled Bagley's body out of the Potomac. This cartel is known for their creative warnings. Torture and kill a stoolie, then dump him where he's easily found. Keep any other members from even thinking about flapping their mouths to the feds. But they didn't just dump Bagley and let him be found. They announced that they left a package in the Potomac.'

It only just occurred to O'Dell, and she looked at Senator Delanor. 'You got the call.'

The woman's eyes confirmed it before she said, 'Yes, it appears it's me they are warning.'

—————

53

When O'Dell described the spider bites on Robert Díaz's body, Agent McCoy nodded as if he had already seen or expected the wounds he was looking at in the photos.

'They call him the Iceman,' McCoy said with an odd look on his face.

'No one knows who he is or what he looks like. I've been tracking him for almost a decade now, ever since I came to the DEA. He's like a ghost. Those who claim to have seen him, or know something about him, end up dead before we can get to them. He's Choque Azul's assassin. These two floaters – I recognize his trademark. These were his.

'The Zetas and Sinaloas – their assassins use shock

and fear by leaving the dismembered bodies of their enemies hanging near school yards or from bridges. The Iceman likes to be subtle. He seems to enjoy making his prey squirm as he tortures and destroys them slowly.'

'And the cockroaches?' O'Dell asked. 'What exactly were they for?'

'Cockroaches?' McCoy sounded genuinely surprised.

She pulled out the photos.

'Robert Díaz's mouth was duct-taped shut. When the medical examiner pulled it off, we found these five cockroaches in his mouth.'

'Oh my God!' Senator Delanor stared at the photos.

'Were they still alive?' Kunze wanted to know.

'Yes, very much so.'

'How is that possible?' the senator asked.

O'Dell was watching McCoy the entire time. 'Hard to explain, but I've seen it before.' She couldn't decide whether McCoy couldn't believe that the Iceman would deviate from his MO or he was trying to figure out what it meant. 'So are you still sure this was the same assassin?' she asked him. 'That both of these victims were connected to Choque Azul?'

McCoy nodded. 'Killers change up their signatures. As a profiler, you know that, Agent O'Dell. I'm still very certain both Bagley and Díaz were killed by the Iceman for Choque Azul. We already suspected the second package might be Díaz. He disappeared days ago, after some of our agents questioned him. He was captain of a commercial fishing boat that we've been keeping an eye on. A seventy-foot long-liner named the *Blue Mist*.'

He smiled at that. 'It's a subtle trick we're finding they like to do. Choque Azul is "Blue Shock" in Spanish, or something to that effect. They think it's clever wordplay to use "blue" or "electric" or "shock" for various names or codes. Even George Ramos's houseboat ...' He glanced at the senator, and O'Dell thought he looked like he enjoyed the woman's slight grimace when he added, 'It was christened *Electric Blue*.'

'So my very first instinct was correct when we pulled Bagley's body from the river.' O'Dell looked at her boss. 'You told me it didn't have anything to do with drug cartels.'

'I honestly didn't know.'

'That was my doing, I'm afraid,' Senator Delanor

said. 'When the message about a package in the Potomac came into my Senate office, I had no idea either, but I suspected it had something to do with George. So I asked for Raymond's help. George has made it no secret that he expects my help or he could cause me trouble.'

'Trouble? He's in prison.'

The senator looked at O'Dell, and for a brief moment her porcelain veneer cracked enough to show the exhaustion and something else close to the surface that she was trying hard to suppress. Something she definitely didn't want to be seen because she crossed her arms and sat back. She turned her head away as she said, 'It's complicated.'

She expected that to be enough explanation, which only made O'Dell angry. 'Is it complicated or just embarrassing?'

'Agent O'Dell, you are out of line.' It was Kunze again.

'I could have been killed. I think I deserve more of an explanation. How exactly can he cause you trouble when he's in prison?'

'You obviously have no idea.' Senator Delanor glared at her now. O'Dell had hit a nerve with the senator and she was glad. She was tired of the political bullshit.

'Being in prison hasn't severed any of his connections,' the senator continued. 'If anything, his arrest only strengthened and invigorated his henchmen ... or whatever it is you call them,' and she shot a glance at McCoy. 'George has always had a less-than-subtle way of getting my attention. His trial is coming up.'

'And your reelection.'

'Agent O'Dell, I'm warning you.'

'It's okay, Raymond,' and this time she put up one of her delicate and manicured hands as if to stop him. 'Probably both, Agent O'Dell.'

'But the Iceman is involved.' McCoy brought the attention back to him. 'We don't believe he was brought in just to deliver a few warnings. He's cleaning up. And there's a good chance these two victims are not the only two on his hit list.'

_____

54

'Trevor Bagley and his wife were doing more than running drugs for Choque Azul,' Agent McCoy told them. He looked at O'Dell. 'I understand you found a piece of child's clothing in the woods.'

'That's right. It looked like it was bloodstained.'

'We suspected that the Bagleys were keeping several children against their will.'

'And yet you didn't do anything about it.'

'We were building a case.'

'While they were trafficking children.'

'Wait.' Senator Delanor was sitting on the edge of her chair. 'What are you talking about? There were children involved?'

'Choque Azul's newest business venture.'

'George would never be involved in something like that.'

'Really?' Agent McCoy stood up from his seat on Kunze's desk so he could stand in front of the senator. 'This is exactly what George is making sure that his people cover up. Because his precious trial is coming up and he doesn't want any evidence connecting him to human trafficking. So his Iceman is eliminating the evidence.'

'I don't believe this. Why haven't I heard about it?' Senator Delanor asked.

'We've been trying to keep it under wraps.'

'While you build a case,' O'Dell interrupted. 'Who cares if a few kids die in the meantime, as long as you build a *strong* case.'

This time she was surprised that Kunze didn't reprimand her. She glanced at him, expecting it, but when he met her eyes she realized he hadn't signed on for something like this. McCoy, on the other hand, was glaring at her, no longer amused and unable to contain his anger.

'You have no clue what it is that you stepped into, Agent O'Dell,' he told her.

'If it wasn't for me, it sounds like you'd still be investigating, while the Iceman takes care of everyone on his list.'

'How do you know, Agent McCoy, that George's cartel has started trafficking children?' The senator seemed to have regained her composure. 'Maybe the Bagley couple were doing something illegal with children on their own?'

In that moment, O'Dell was stunned to realize Senator Delanor was still protective of her ex-husband. O'Dell was there the night they arrested him aboard his houseboat. He had taken their two children with him during a raging thunder-and-lightning storm. If that wasn't dangerous enough, George Ramos didn't seem to mind bringing his kids along while he picked up a shipment of cocaine in the middle of the Gulf of Mexico.

Now O'Dell wondered if Ramos was delivering messages and packages for his ex-wife because he knew he still had some kind of hold on her. If she was willing to use her political power and influence to ask for help from Assistant Director Kunze, what else was she willing to do?

Agent McCoy, however, wasn't so willing to appease the senator.

'A week ago, the Coast Guard stopped Captain Robert Díaz's commercial fishing boat – the *Blue Mist* – in the Gulf of Mexico,' McCoy continued. 'They brought on board a dog and its handler, expecting to sniff out cocaine under the full load of mahi-mahi. You know what they found instead? Five kids – three girls, two boys – all under the age of thirteen. American kids, from the States.'

'But the Bagleys – ?'

'For the past year Trevor Bagley has been working as a fisherman off and on, independently contracted to the *Blue Mist*.'

O'Dell listened to Agent McCoy and couldn't help thinking he was enjoying making Senator Delanor squirm a bit as he dealt out information piece by piece. She wondered what their past relationship was.

'So potentially everyone who was involved in this raid on the fishing boat could be on Choque Azul's hit list? Is that correct?' O'Dell asked, but there was only one person she was concerned about. Agent McCoy had mentioned a dog handler. Somehow she knew it had to be Ryder Creed.

'Yes, we think that's a possibility.'

'Tell me something, Agent McCoy. On the Bagley

property there was evidence found that children may have been kidnapped and held against their will.'

'We believe so, yes. In one of the outbuildings there are signs that they may have been keeping several people against their will.'

'Your team that's taken over – have they found any drugs?'

'Drugs? No, I don't believe so.'

O'Dell looked at Kunze. 'Sir, with all due respect, this isn't a case for the DEA. This sounds like something the FBI should be in charge of.'

'What?' McCoy asked.

'Actually, Agent O'Dell is right.'

'Sir, I'd like to go back down and finish what I started.'

55

Hannah was surprised that Amanda didn't argue with her. Either the girl did still have a healthy dose of fear of the people she had run away from, or she was used to taking orders. And doing so with much urgency.

Ryder had convinced Hannah to take the girl and leave. Dr Avelyn had been able to identify the spiders that had hatched on Hannah's counter. She had come to tell them the news as soon as she recognized them. Ryder heard that they were poisonous – the most lethal of all spiders – and immediately he had been anxious and pushing for Hannah to leave quickly, as if a hurricane were coming ashore.

It didn't help matters that Dr Avelyn said these

spiders were rare in the States. According to her, these spiders usually take refuge in clusters of bananas grown in Colombia. She guessed that this bunch hadn't accidentally made it past inspectors, but rather had been especially picked.

Now Hannah worried that Ryder had something crazy and dangerous in mind, but she realized that staying would not change his plans. This time she knew she wouldn't be able to talk him out of it. She recognized that look in his eyes when he told her to pack her bags. Actually, she already had one packed and in her car. She had done it the night Amanda arrived. Even then she knew she might need to leave at a moment's notice.

She had convinced Amanda that they needed to change her appearance before they left. It was a five-hour drive and she didn't want to take the chance that someone might be looking for the girl or happen to recognize her.

The box of hair color turned her into a brunette, making her look older, which seemed to please them both. Hannah thought she had done a nice job with the haircut – she kept the bangs and cut the rest chin-length to help hide Amanda's face. As did the large-framed eyeglasses. Then there were the clothes – no more designer jeans. Hannah had borrowed from Andy – from her days as a vet tech – a blue smock uniform top and a pair of khakis. Even Amanda seemed surprised at the transformation. She no longer looked like an emaciated teenager but rather a young woman either coming home from or going to her job.

Hannah promised Ryder that she would call when they arrived at their destination. They had been on the road for only thirty minutes when they crossed the bridge over Escambia Bay. From the minute they'd gotten into the car, Amanda had been slouched in her seat with her earbuds in and her iPod on, but suddenly she sat up straight and asked, 'Can we go see Pensacola Beach?'

'No,' Hannah told her. 'We don't have time for any sightseeing.'

'But it's such a gorgeous day and I've been cooped up for forever. What will it matter if we're a few minutes behind? We're just going to some stupid hiding place.'

Hannah shouldn't have been surprised that transforming the girl's appearance would do nothing to change her attitude. She was still a whiny teenager.

'No,' Hannah said again.

The girl crossed her arms and pouted, staring out the window. Traffic on I-10 was crazy, as usual. No more than five minutes went by when Amanda sat up again.

'I have to pee.'

'Seriously?'

'I've done everything you asked me to do. Can't you just stop and let me pee?'

Hannah checked her rearview mirror. With this much traffic it had been impossible to notice if anyone was following them. She took the exit for the first rest stop and kept her eyes darting back to her mirrors. Two vehicles followed them. She drove down the road designated for cars, slowed to a crawl, and watched as she passed several parking places. Both of the vehicles parked, but Hannah continued past the restrooms and headed back up the entrance ramp to the interstate.

'Hey!' Amanda twisted in her seat. 'What are you doing?'

'I have to make sure no one's following us. Don't get your panties in a twist. There's a truck stop just a mile up. I'll stop there.'

This time only an eighteen-wheeler trailed them

down the exit ramp. The truck stop was much busier, with three sets of gas pumps, a large shop that boasted showers for truckers, and a dine-in restaurant.

'I'll top off the fuel tank,' Hannah told the girl.

If she had to stop she wanted to make sure they didn't have to again anytime soon. She pulled alongside the pumps, satisfied that no one had followed them off the interstate. The shop door was well in her view. She nodded to Amanda, giving her permission, then watched the girl. For someone who had to pee, Hannah thought she sure was taking her sweet time, doing more looking than hurrying.

56

Amanda couldn't believe how paranoid the woman was. She was driving her crazy. It was bad enough that she had to wear these stupid clothes, but she swore she'd scream if she had to spend another four hours in the car with her.

Granted, the woman had fed her well. And she had actually been pretty good to her. She had even brought her antibiotics that made her stomach and throat feel better. Plus, the woman hadn't asked her to do anything weird or ... Until today, she hadn't asked Amanda to do anything.

Amanda pretty much figured she'd need to change her looks if she ever wanted to go out into the world again and didn't want Zapata finding her. That woman had eyes everywhere. And she was a spiteful old woman. She'd be pissed as hell with Amanda. No telling what she would do. And suddenly Amanda felt like she was being watched. Silly, really. Hannah's paranoia was probably wearing off on her. She'd seen how easily Lucía had been replaced. No way Zapata cared what happened to her.

Amanda crisscrossed the aisles to a hallway underneath the RESTROOM sign at the back of the store. No one paid much attention to her. Of course they didn't. She looked like a total nerd in this outfit. She was used to men at least noticing her. The new haircut and color made her look older and more mature, but the wardrobe canceled out any of the haircut's benefits.

As she made her way down the hall, she glanced back. Maybe there was some advantage to not being noticed, to being sort of invisible. Maybe she would be able to have a real life after all.

She found the door for the women's restroom at the end of the hallway. Just as she put her hand up to push the door open, someone grabbed her from behind. An arm came around her waist as a hand came over her mouth. Before she realized what was happening, she was being pulled back into a dark closet.

She tried to struggle, tried to kick, but no one was even close by to see or hear her feet stomp against the now closed door. Then suddenly she could smell him – his greasy hair gel mixed with his sweat.

Leandro.

'I love your sexy new hair,' he whispered in her ear.

'How? How did you even find me?'

'You did not think I would forget about you, did you? Remember, I told you whenever you listen to your music, I would be there with you.'

He let her turn around to face him. Her eyes started to adjust in the dark. He still gripped her wrists and pulled her against him. He kissed her on the lips, slow and gentle like a lover.

And Amanda kissed him back.

57

Hannah went in to pay for the gas and picked up a couple of cans of soda, only because it took her to the back refrigerators. She glanced down the hallway to the restrooms, then checked for other exits. There was only one. It was in the opposite corner and it was an emergency exit. So the girl would have to leave through the front of the store.

She wasn't sure that she cared if Amanda sneaked away. But Ryder cared, and he had entrusted Hannah with her safety. She browsed and picked up a few more items, then paid and went back outside to the car. Then she sat and watched the front door to the store.

Ten minutes later, Amanda came out, her face flushed. Hannah wondered if the girl had gotten sick.

'You okay?' she asked when she climbed in and busied herself with the seat belt.

'I'm okay.'

'Took long enough.'

'I got my period.'

'Oh, okay. Did you want me to buy some pads or tampons for you?'

'No, I ... I got one from the machine in the rest-room.'

She was lying. Hannah's two little boys were better liars than this girl. But she wasn't sure why she'd lie about a thing like that. Maybe Amanda had thought there would be a back door, and when she realized she couldn't escape or come up with a better plan, she had to deal with the fact that she'd have to get back in the car.

Hannah didn't bother figuring it out. They were stuck with each other. The sooner they got back on the road, the sooner she could rest, at least for a while.

Traffic was still busy, but Hannah knew I-10 would be like this all the way to Biloxi. She kept in her lane, drove the speed limit, and paid little attention to the cars zooming past her. Her fingers were tight on the steering wheel but not clenched. As she approached the first bridge, she didn't notice the black SUV coming up alongside her. Vehicles had come and gone for the past hour. But when he stayed beside her for too long, Hannah did glance over. The young man grinned at her as if that was exactly what he had been waiting for. And then, without warning, she saw him pull his steering wheel hard to the right.

The first crunch shoved Hannah's car. She held on, even though it pushed her vehicle onto the shoulder. She took her foot off the gas pedal but the car was still going too fast. Her first instinct was to brake and brake hard, but she knew that might roll the car.

'What's happening?' Amanda yelled.

'Hold on,' she told her, but even as she prepared for the second hit, it rammed the car so hard the steering wheel spun out of her hands.

She grabbed on again and pulled to the left, only to be met with another crash of metal. This time it sent her car off the highway. Both of Hannah's feet were riding the brake as her vehicle plunged over the guardrail and kept flying.

58

Creed found Andy stopped in the middle of her training session with Chance. He was bringing her a glass of iced tea. She had messaged him earlier to come see the progress she had made.

The big German shepherd stared at him but stayed seated without Andy telling him to. The fact that the dog didn't want to rip out Creed's throat was impressive in itself, and he was surprised to see him so quiet.

'He's calm.'

As soon as Andy turned to face him, he could see that she was not. Her eyes and nose were red. She'd been crying and was still holding her cell phone at arm's length. Creed guessed it was the source of her upset.

Before he could ask, she said, 'There's been an accident. Actually, I don't even know if it was an accident.'

'What are you talking about?'

'Hannah and Amanda. Someone ran them off the road.'

Creed squeezed the glass of iced tea so hard it burst in his hand. Shards flew. Several stabbed into his flesh. Chance jumped up and barked.

'Chance, sit!' Andy told him, and immediately he complied, though now he panted, anxious and watching. 'Creed, you're bleeding.'

'What happened? Are they ...?'

'No, they're not dead. But both are in critical condition. Some guy in a black SUV rammed into them. Witnesses said he didn't even stop.'

They stared at each other, neither one needing to say what they both knew may have happened.

Against Creed's better judgment, Hannah had insisted they tell their senior employees about Amanda and how she had come to them. Hannah said they deserved to know, and it would help to have them watching for anything out of the ordinary happening on the property. Now Creed was grateful that he didn't need to explain his deepest fear, because Andy already knew.

'I can hold down the fort until you get back.'

He nodded.

'You want me to wrap that for you?'

Only now did he look down and stare at his hand as if it belonged to someone else. Two chunks of glass were embedded in the palm. He shook his head as he pulled them out. He made a fist and held his hand up against his chest.

'I'm okay,' he said as blood dripped down his arm.

'Call me as soon as you know something.'

He nodded again, though he honestly didn't hear the rest of what she said over the throbbing in his head. With every step, he felt the anger brewing. In all his plans, in all his stupid strategy to protect and defend, he never thought they'd attack somewhere else. Or someone else.

Now he understood. They'd done their homework. They knew that to torture and hurt him would be too easy. And they knew that terrorizing and hurting those he loved – including his dogs – would be exactly what would rip his heart out. What would truly destroy him.

59

Creed had his elbows on his knees and his face planted in his hands. He didn't care that his makeshift bandage had bled through. He kept his eyes closed and was hoping the throbbing in his head would quiet down, when suddenly he felt someone standing over him.

'We have to stop meeting in hospitals.'

'And in holes in the ground,' he answered, before looking up at Maggie O'Dell.

She didn't smile as she sat down beside him. Months ago, a case they'd worked on had landed them in a ravine and twice in hospital waiting lounges. Creed supposed it wasn't something either of them was ready to joke about.

This waiting lounge had been full just minutes ago. Or maybe it was hours ago, because now he saw that darkness filled the windows where sunlight had been when he arrived. Only an elderly couple remained, clear on the opposite side of the room. They were staring blankly at the flat-screen television on the wall.

'How's Hannah?' she asked.

'Still in ICU. They won't let me see her or inform me about her condition because I'm not family.'

'Does she have family?'

'Her two boys are with her grandparents.'

She was waiting for more. When he stayed quiet for too long, she said, 'You didn't tell them yet, did you?'

'They're five hours away. Hannah wouldn't want them driving here.'

He didn't add that Hannah wouldn't want to risk placing the boys in harm's way. She'd trust Creed to make sure that didn't happen. But he didn't think Maggie would understand. It probably sounded strange that he wouldn't even call her family.

Truth was, he and Hannah were each other's family. The two of them were used to making decisions that would influence each other's lives. By the time Hannah had met and married Marcus Washington, Creed and Hannah had been business partners for several years. They had been through things that had already bonded them thicker than blood. As a consequence, they watched out for each other and cared for each other with no conditions, no terms. That's just the way it was. He couldn't explain it to Maggie. Hell, he couldn't explain it to the ICU warden either. Once in a while, when Hannah got upset with him, she'd tell him he was 'depreciating the business.' But even then he knew it had nothing to do with the business. She didn't care about that. She said it only as a way of telling him to straighten up.

Marcus came to accept him as one would accept a brother-in-law. And when he left for his tour of duty in Iraq, he told Creed that he never had to worry because he knew Creed would take good care of Hannah and his sons.

But this time, Creed had let Hannah down. He should have listened to her when she felt so strongly about sending Amanda somewhere else. He'd let his emotions and memories of his sister override Hannah's instincts, and Hannah had paid the price.

'You should have told me about the girl,' Maggie said, surprising him.

'And maybe you should have told me that the Bagleys were trafficking kids for a drug cartel.'

'How do you know about that?'

'How do you know about Amanda?'

She sat back, crossed her arms, and sighed with frustration. But Creed didn't care who knew what anymore. Hannah was fighting for her life. Nothing mattered right now except maybe the throbbing anger that was building up inside him.

'I just found out about the fishing boat and the kids,' Maggie said. 'I wasn't even sure about the cartel connection. My politically inclined boss was stonewalling me. All I was doing was looking for the original crime scene so I could figure out what happened. Turns out I pissed off a bunch of people.'

'Welcome to the club.'

That made her smile. He sat back in his chair until he was even with her. Crossed his arms and leaned his head against the wall.

'I didn't want anyone else involved,' he told her. 'That's why I didn't tell you about the girl.'

'And it appears I'm already involved.'

She went ahead and explained what she knew about the Bagleys kidnapping and trafficking children for Choque Azul. Now that she had the case file, she knew much more. One of the three girls Creed and the Coast Guard had rescued on the fishing boat had already identified Regina Bagley from a photo lineup. It happened during their debriefing a week ago. So Agent McCoy knew that the Bagleys had kidnapped at least one of the children, but O'Dell said she had asked McCoy why he didn't question them or even arrest them – and she wasn't thrilled with his answer. Something about building a stronger case.

She said the stories the children told during their debriefing were all different. One was taken from a mall. Another from a truck stop. She stopped when she saw Creed wince.

'Were they using them like Amanda? As drug mules?' he asked.

'I'm not sure. I don't know if anyone knows. Less than forty-eight hours after the captain of the *Blue Mist* was released from custody, he went missing. They pulled him out of the Potomac.'

'Spider bites. I know.'

'How could you know that?'

'Let's just say someone heard about it and told me.' He ignored her second sigh. 'So what are you doing back here?'

'For some dumb reason I took the case back.'

He turned to look at her and raised an eyebrow instead of coming right out and asking if she was crazy.

She smiled again and shook her head. 'I know, it's insane, right? But this asshole of a DEA agent pissed me off.'

And that made Creed smile.

'What did you do with the cocaine?' she asked in a low voice, though the couple on the other side of the room weren't paying any attention to them.

'How the hell do you know there was any?'

'They said she was carrying.'

'They?'

'Agent McCoy. The DEA guy.'

'And how would he know?'

That stopped her, and Creed could see she was now wondering the same thing.

'He said something about security cameras in the airport terminal.'

Creed couldn't believe that the DEA knew all along

that he had been harboring a drug mule. Was that possible?

'The DEA already has an agent outside her ICU room, waiting for her to regain consciousness.'

He shot her a look of alarm before he could stop it. And Maggie noticed.

'You can't keep protecting her. The information she's able to share could put away some really bad cartel guys.'

'Or it could get her killed.'

'Or it could get you killed. I'm just trying to help.'

'And I'm just telling you that I don't know what you're talking about.'

'Are you serious?' She jolted to the edge of her seat. 'Do you think I'm wired or something?'

'No, I don't. But I don't want anyone else hurt. This is my fight.'

He stayed sitting back, head against the wall, eyes forward, even though he could feel her staring at him ... hard.

Then suddenly she said, 'Your fight? Let it go, Ryder. You can't win this one.'

'Spiders and snakes' – he pursed his lips and shook his head – 'they don't bother me as long as they don't

hurt my dogs or anyone else I care about. But this . . . '
And he jerked his chin in the direction of the ICU door.
'They're not getting away with this.'

'You're kidding, right?' She glanced around them,
then scooted closer until her knees were pushed against
the side of his leg and she could make him look at her.
'Let the DEA and the FBI handle these guys. You
cannot win a fight against them.'

'That's nice, but it's not like I have a choice.' He
finally met her eyes. 'I know I'm on their hit list.' When
she tried to look away, he gently took her chin with his
fingertips and brought her eyes back to him. 'But you
already knew that, didn't you?'

'Agent McCoy only mentioned a dog and handler
when he told us about the kids you found. Now that
I know about Amanda . . . All the more reason for you
to leave it for the DEA and FBI to handle.'

'Other than you, I don't see anyone from either of
those agencies running to my rescue.'

He dropped his fingers from her face but held her
gaze until she looked away. She moved back to her
original position. They sat quietly, side by side, for a
while. Then suddenly Maggie got up.

'I'll be right back,' she said.

He watched her walk across the waiting room and head directly to the woman behind the window. The one who guarded the RESTRICTED door, who had told Creed she couldn't let him see Hannah, nor could she even give him any information about her current condition because he was not family. The woman was black and she must have known that Hannah was black because while she told him he wasn't family, she looked him up and down as if she were giving him a warning not to try to get that one by her.

Now he saw Maggie pulling out her wallet to show the woman something. No, it wasn't her wallet – it was her badge. He couldn't hear what she was saying. Maggie turned and pointed to him. The woman craned her neck, practically standing up to look out her protective window with the slot at the bottom. When she saw who Maggie was referring to, Creed saw her make a face. Maggie continued talking, and soon the woman was nodding, then she handed her something over the desk and through the open slot. He had no idea what it was.

Maggie walked back and gave him the item. He looked at the laminated badge, fingering the lanyard that was attached.

'You can see Hannah anytime you want. Just show that to whoever is at the reception window.'

He stared at her.

'The doctor overseeing her case will be in checking on her in the next hour. He'll be sure to update you.'

'Always good to have the FBI on your side. Thank you.'

He didn't want to ask for anything else, but there was one other thing he couldn't do on his own.

'Would you mind checking in on Amanda? I don't want her to think I deserted her.'

She made it easy on him. Didn't even hesitate.

'Sure, I can do that. I'm staying on Pensacola Beach while we finish working on the Bagleys' property. You have my cell phone number. Call me. I can give you an update on Amanda and you can let me know how Hannah is doing.'

He nodded.

'I know you're too stubborn to ask, but despite falling into scorpion pits, I actually might be able to help. I'm pretty good with a badge ... and even a gun.'

This time he smiled as he watched her leave. But he already knew he wasn't going to let anyone else he cared about risk getting hurt.

60

Creed hated to leave Hannah. She looked so fragile with all those tubes and needles poking into her. Thanks to Maggie, he had been able to sit by her side and hold her hand. The doctor had told him her condition was stabilized, but they were keeping her in ICU overnight. No matter what the doctor had said, nothing could have made Creed feel better except maybe Hannah opening her eyes or squeezing his hand. Neither of which she was able to do.

He had promised Liz Bailey that he would meet her at Walter's Canteen on Pensacola Beach.

'I heard about your business partner. How is she doing?'

'She's a tough lady. Doctor said she's stabilized.' He scooted his chair closer. The place was full and loud. He didn't add that Hannah certainly didn't look anywhere near stabilized.

'Maybe this is how they intended to hurt you.'

Liz Bailey said out loud what Creed already knew. He figured it was definitely part of their plan, although he didn't think for a second it was over. More than anything, he didn't want anyone else involved or concerned, so he told Bailey, 'Yeah, maybe this was their strategy.'

She filled him in on what she knew about the children they had rescued. All five had been returned home to their families. She said she had visited the little boy, whose name was Rudy, and he asked about Grace. Rudy's parents had asked her to pass along their contact information.

'They want to meet you. To say thank you.'

'We were all just doing our jobs.'

She slid a piece of paper over the table.

'All I promised was that I'd make sure you got it. You can do with it what you want.'

Bailey's phone started vibrating and she grabbed it. She took one look at the text message and frowned.

'I'm sorry. I gotta go. My night to be on-call and they're calling.'

'It's okay,' Creed said.

She started pulling out a twenty-dollar bill and he stopped her.

'But I invited you,' she said.

'Doesn't matter,' he insisted. 'Last time we were here, your dad picked up the tab. It's my turn.'

She shook her head as she grabbed back the piece of paper she had slid across the table and wrote a second number down.

'If I can help, let me know. Or if you just want to talk.'

He couldn't tell if she meant it flirtatiously or just as a colleague. She left as he tucked the paper into his wallet.

He finished his drink and zigzagged through the crowded bar. He was almost to the door when he noticed a commotion at the other end of the packed room. He recognized Jason in the middle of the mess, but he didn't know the four men who had just started to shove Jason around.

61

In another lifetime – pre-Afghanistan – Jason would have enjoyed exchanging punches with these assholes. Most likely they were college boys on summer break with their perfect white teeth and all of their suntanned limbs still in place. Among the four of them there was enough bulk and brawn to cause some serious damage. So maybe he should have let it go when the one who looked like their leader for the night bumped into their table.

The guy was drunk. That was obvious. The place was crowded, wall to wall, standing room only. He probably didn't mean to knock into them and topple their beer glasses, but Jason was drunk, too, and thought the guy owed them an apology.

'Hey, watch where you're going,' Jason told him.

The guy saw the spilled beer and smirked at him. 'Tough break.'

Jason knew the type – the guy probably wasn't used to anyone telling him what to do. He wore cargo shorts and a crisp new tank top with PENSACOLA BEACH emblazoned across the front. Sunglasses hung from the shirt's crew neck, and Jason could make out GUCCI on the side. He recognized the designer flip-flops, too. He didn't know why it made him mad, but it did.

That's when Jason stood up and shoved him.

Immediately he saw his mistake. The guy had three friends at the bar who saw what had happened and came pushing their way through to his defense. Jason had Colfax and Benny, who stared into their empty beer glasses. They looked completely miserable. He could see that they didn't want to do this. They probably thought they couldn't do this. And maybe that was another reason why Jason needed to do this. But tonight Tony wasn't even here to give them a fighting chance.

'Come on, Mike, don't bother with those losers.' One of his friends tried coaxing him away.

He didn't listen to his friend.

'Don't shove me, asshole.' And he gave Jason a shove.

'You owe us an apology.'

Instead of an apology, Mike pushed him again, this time harder, sending Jason slamming into one of his buddies. Before Jason could regain his balance, he was being shoved back the other way.

Mike was in Jason's face, about to yell something when he winced suddenly and jerked backward. Ryder Creed had the guy by the back of the neck. He stood several inches taller than Mike and was able to pull him not only back but also up. The grip reminded Jason of the way Creed might hold a dog by the scruff of the neck.

'What the hell?'

'I thought I might join the fun,' Creed said. 'Since it was a bit uneven. Four against three.' He let go of the guy and stood between them, glancing around and waiting.

'Nobody grabs me like that, man.'

'Nobody shoves my friends around. So why don't we call it even and go home.' Creed shifted his weight, and Jason couldn't believe he thought it was that easy. That it was all over.

Mike's face had gone crimson, a combination of anger and humiliation. His friends were watching him, ready to move if and when he gave the word. Jason balled up his fist. He could still hit and kick, and he wanted to hit this guy more than ever.

Then Mike made his move. He reached his hand up to shove Creed the same way he had shoved Jason. Only his hand didn't even make it to Creed's chest. In less than a second his fingers disappeared in Creed's palm. Suddenly the guy was on his knees, screaming in pain. Creed had his hand twisted and locked at an unnatural angle. It looked as though one more ounce of pressure and bones would snap.

His friends didn't move. They stared at him and Creed as if they couldn't believe what was happening. And all the noise seemed to get sucked out of the room, the vortex starting in the radius surrounding them.

Jason recognized a couple of the bartenders. They separated the crowd for the gray-haired man who was making his way into the inner circle as others backed away. Mike's scream had been reduced to a whine, then almost a whimper. The old man looked at Creed, and that's when Creed finally let go.

'That bastard almost broke my hand.'

He held it up for everyone to see. Jason didn't think it was broken, but it was already starting to swell and turn blue.

Jason glanced over at Colfax and Benny, who looked even more miserable, if that was possible. He couldn't help noticing that Ryder Creed didn't look the least bit remorseful, and the old guy seemed to take note of that, too.

'I want the police called.' Still on his knees and cradling his wounded fingers, Mike was still giving orders.

That's all Jason needed, a police report. The military would never give him a new hand now.

'Did you four come over to buy these veterans a drink and thank them for their service?' the old guy asked, surprising all of them with his casual tone.

'What? What the hell are you talking about, old man? He broke my hand!' Mike pointed at Creed.

'I may look like an old man, son, but I own this establishment. If you'd like to file a police report, you're welcome to do that. You might want to put some ice on that hand.' He shook his head as he looked at it for the first time. 'Probably should be soon. That doesn't look too good.'

Then he turned to one of the bartenders. 'Help these fellas find a place out on the patio, Carl.'

'Wait! You're kicking us out?'

'Just putting you outside to get some fresh air.'

'But you're kicking them out, right?' Mike asked.

Jason watched the old man's eyes go from Creed to Colfax and Benny, and then they stopped at his. Something told Jason the old guy knew he deserved to be thrown out. But then he said something that floored Jason: 'Hell no, I'm buying these veterans a round on the house.'

SATURDAY

62

O'Dell walked across Pensacola Beach from her hotel room to Howard's Deep Sea Fishing Marina. It was still early and the beach was already crowded and the sun already hot. She carried her flip-flops in her hand for the part of her trek that was sand. It reminded her that she could use a few days of sand between her toes and the sound of breaking waves. Maybe when all this was over, she'd come back.

The two-story shop was whitewashed with a marlin painted on the sign below the orange and blue letters. A boardwalk ran the width of the shop and connected to a long pier where boats of all sizes occupied some of the slips. On the boardwalk were bistro tables with umbrellas and chairs. She noticed the small oyster shack attached to the far side of the shop. It had its own sign: BOBBYE'S OYSTER BAR. It was closed but the chalkboard out front already advertised that night's specials.

O'Dell stopped and watched the pelican sitting on one of the posts. Seagulls screeched overhead in a blue sky that didn't show a hint of clouds. From somewhere she could smell the heavenly aroma of food on an open grill, and her eyes started looking for the café or restaurant before she reminded herself why she was here.

The man behind the counter had to be six-foot-five. His broad shoulders and chest filled the lime-green and yellow boat shirt with a marlin across the front that matched his sign out front. He wore white linen pants, as white as his mustache and the thick mass of hair on his head.

The first thing she noticed was the shelf that ran along the walls, about a foot from the ceiling. Miniature model boats were displayed, tightly packed end-to-end. There had to be hundreds of them.

'A hobby that has become an obsession,' the man said in a rich baritone that could have been intimidating if it wasn't accompanied by the crinkles around his brilliant blue eyes.

'They're beautiful.'

'Thanks. What can I do for you?' he asked.

'Ellie Delanor sent me.'

She watched his smile come slow and easy as he said, 'I'll get something cold to drink.' Without hesitation, he flipped the sign in the window to CLOSED.

They spent the next hour at one of the bistro tables on the boardwalk. O'Dell sipped raspberry tea and listened to Howard Johnson tell her what he knew. It was hard to believe that this mild-mannered gentleman had once been a top drug dealer for the Gulf cartel back in the 1990s. When Senator Delanor had asked O'Dell to talk to Howard, she said that he knew more about George Ramos than anyone. The two had been best friends twenty years ago, before they both decided to go straight and clean. Only, Howard didn't realize at the time that George wasn't serious, never even attempted it.

'George was convinced,' Howard said, 'that I had kept millions of dollars of the cartel's money. He even told the DEA. I had one agent hounding me for years. The guy started out in immigration as an ICE agent.

That's how George got his ear in the first place. Tried hard to destroy me. I always figured he tried to destroy George, too.'

'And Senator Delanor?'

'Oh jeez, we were all in love with Ellie. But she chose George.' He looked at O'Dell, waited for her eyes. 'And now George is going to destroy her completely, isn't he?'

63

Creed had given everyone the weekend off. If Jason was right, Choque Azul's hit squad would be coming for him either tonight or tomorrow night.

After his friends Colfax and Benny had left the bar last night and it was just the two of them, Jason told Creed about Tony. A guy named Falco had convinced Tony to leave the bananas on Hannah's kitchen counter. Somehow Falco knew that Tony had been hired to go out and check the electricity at Creed's facility. He swore he didn't know about the spiders, and Jason said he believed him.

He also said his friend was still pretending to be interested in doing more work for Falco. That's how he knew about the raid. From what Tony had shared with Jason, Choque Azul was used to hiring ex-military members to do quite a bit of their dirty work. And unfortunately, many of them were lured in, just like Tony had been, by the large amounts of cash they were paid and the promise of much more. Jason offered to help. Creed declined. He told him not to take it personally. He simply did not want anyone else to get hurt. The information he had given was more than enough.

Creed took the entire day to prepare, and needed every minute. Then he waited for darkness. He knew they wouldn't come until they had the cover of night.

In some strange way – and Hannah would probably add 'some sick way' – Creed was impressed with the show of force that Choque Azul thought was necessary to bring him down. On his iPad he watched the men approaching – which made it look like he was playing a bad video game. The infrared cameras he had placed on the dogs' collars jerked a bit more than he'd like, even though the dogs were doing their best stealth tracking of the men who were now invading his property.

All three dogs were war dogs. Two male, one female. Cheyenne was a muscular pit bull mix; Diesel, a sleek, bronze boxer; and Nuru was a blue-eyed husky mix. They had been trained for military work and could track independently behind enemy lines without constant instruction and with little guidance from their master.

The cameras on their collars were accompanied by a GPS and another device that emitted a series of high-pitched signals. Only the dogs could hear and react to the signals. Creed was able to give them directions by punching in commands using special apps on his iPad and his cell phone.

The dogs understood they were to track the intruders while remaining unseen and unheard. It looked like quite the challenge, because from what Creed could see, the men were equipped with infrared goggles. So far, the dogs were following behind or alongside in the trees and brush and keeping low to the ground.

Suddenly one man stopped to listen. He spun around to look behind them.

Creed held his breath as he watched.

The guy called out something to the other two men with him, and they stopped up ahead. Creed couldn't make out what was said. For all the wonderful technology of the camera, it had a crappy microphone that filled Creed's ears with only his dog's sniffs and pants.

The man swung his gun and his bandanna head with goggle eyes from side to side, looking up at the branches and into the trees. For some reason he didn't bother examining the tall grass or anything closer to the ground. Thank goodness, because from the angle of Cheyenne's camera, Creed knew the dog had dropped to its belly.

The man decided there wasn't anything, and he waved to his buddies. They continued to sneak through the trees.

Again, with another app, Creed pulled up a map of his property. Three lights were blinking within the borders – one green, one yellow, and one red. Each light identified a dog and his or her location. Cheyenne was the green light, tracking the group that came in from the road.

Creed could also access the other cameras he had planted around the property. A touch of his iPad screen and he could choose to see in real time what was in each camera's viewfinder. Of course, he couldn't monitor the entire acreage, but he had views of almost every possible approach to any of the buildings on the property, especially the one with the dog kennels and his apartment.

In addition to Cheyenne's team of three that he was following, Diesel had two in his sight coming through the forest behind the main house. Nuru's group from the west included two more. From the camera up in a tree at the end of his driveway, Creed could see a vehicle parked off the road with its headlights off. Once in a while he saw what he believed was the red-orange tip of a glowing cigarette behind the steering wheel.

None of the other cameras had shown any movement for the last hour. So Creed put the count at seven, with one outside the perimeter. He wondered if the guy who had run Hannah and Amanda off the road was here tonight. He hoped so.

What Jason had told him appeared to be correct. Most of the men looked like ex-military. But they also looked like a ragtag assortment. Some were dressed in camouflage. A few wore bandannas around their heads. A couple chose ball caps.

No helmets. That was good.

It meant no advanced communication system, and he didn't see any radios strapped to their arms or any jawbone microphones.

What surprised Creed – and should not have – was the firepower. Two of the men looked like they were carrying AK-47s. The others had serious semiautomatic handguns. One guy wore an ammo belt strapped across his chest. Another had what looked like grenades hanging from a belt.

This seemed like overkill.

Maggie O'Dell had said that Trevor Bagley and the fishing boat captain had been tortured by fire ants and spiders, then dumped into the river. Neither had been shot or stabbed or blown up. They had been killed by the cartel's hired assassin, a phantom nicknamed the Iceman. He preferred to torture his victims. Creed wondered why they had sent an entire military-style hit squad to kill him.

And then he realized the answer to his question, and he felt a knot twist in his stomach. Suddenly he was questioning his entire strategy. These men had probably been ordered to capture him for the Iceman. The heavy artillery wasn't for him. It was to take out his dogs.

64

Creed's second cell phone started to vibrate. Diesel's crew had tripped the motion sensor at the back door of the main house.

Creed grabbed his iPad. He punched the app that brought up all the dog collars and their communication devices. He opened Grace's and tapped three times. She didn't have a camera – just the communication gadget. He'd be able to watch her from the cameras already in the house. He touched the app for the interior and brought up the camera views from inside. And sure enough, he saw Grace scurrying into position.

The two men entered the kitchen at a crouch. Diesel knew not to follow them inside unless or until Creed gave the command. From Diesel's camera, he watched the men disappear inside. And from the kitchen camera, he saw them moving in.

The lights were on in the house. In every room, every possible bulb burned bright, so the two men removed their infrared goggles. From camera to camera Creed watched them sneak from room to room. He adjusted his earbud. The microphones on the cameras in the house were much more sensitive.

'Did you hear that?' the man in the lead asked his partner.

'Sounded like it came from that way.'

Just at that moment, Creed saw Grace peek around the corner, letting the men see her.

'It's a dog.'

Gunfire blasted in Creed's ear, sending him to his feet.

Damn it!

Frantically, he punched at icons, bringing up cameras to follow the men when he really just wanted to run to the house. As soon as they got to the hallway that Grace had disappeared down, Creed pulled out the remote from his pocket and began clicking buttons, one after another, sending the entire house into darkness.

'Holy crap! What the hell!'

He could hear the men as he watched them screech to a halt. There were only two doors down this way. He kept a faint light on in the room at the end of the hall, which had been Amanda's room. But it was difficult to see because the other door halfway down the hall was fully open and obstructed the view of the rest of the hallway.

'This is the way the dog went.'

'Come on, let's get this little bastard.'

The one in a hurry raced to the open doorway with his friend close behind. He rushed through and the scream and crash stopped his buddy in the threshold.

'Craig, what the hell happened?'

Too late! The heavy metal door swung into the man's back, sending him down. Creed turned the lights back on in time to see Bolo, with his big front paws still on the door, keeping it closed as Creed hit a button and heard the bolt slide and click into place.

'Sorry, guys. Hannah's been nagging me forever to put steps down to that storm cellar.'

Then he turned on his microphone for the communication system in the dogs' collars and said, 'Good job, Bolo.'

He saw Grace come from the end of the hallway to join the big dog.

'Good job, Grace.'

He watched their ears go back and he knew they had heard him.

'Grace, Bolo, go hide.'

Both of them stood there a moment, as if they expected him to come into the house. That was the only part of this that he hadn't perfected – no pats, no rewards. Only audio praise. Not until the end ... if there was an end.

They still hadn't moved.

'Grace, Bolo, go hide.' He used a sterner voice and the two took off.

Two down, Creed thought. *Five to go.*

And his cell phone began to vibrate again. One of the groups had just breached the motion sensor at the corner of the kennel warehouse.

Creed readjusted his gadgets and wiped his forehead.

Come on in, guys.

65

Falco waited in the SUV at the end of the driveway, exactly like he was told to do. But he wasn't happy about it. He was getting tired of being bossed around by Leandro.

As an apprentice to the Iceman, Falco knew that he needed to stand back and be ready for when the hit squad captured the dog handler. And he actually looked forward to what the Iceman had planned – a brilliant combination of insect bites and stings in an arena-style setting of challenges that the Iceman promised would be worthy of the ex-marine.

Still, Falco longed to be a part of the men who were now sneaking through the woods like savages hunting prey. He was reminded again of those stray dogs in his hometown. The mayor had hired his own hit squad to round up the mutts. He even gave permission to shoot them in the street, although that plan backfired. No matter how much the people of the village wanted the dogs gone, they did not want to witness such savagery – or be caught in the line of fire.

Falco had volunteered for the mayor's hit squad, and the man laughed at him.

'You're not big enough to even hold a rifle,' the mayor told him, and then laughed again, humiliating Falco in front of the others.

He felt like Leandro was always trying to do the same thing to him. Always pointing out to the others how young and inexperienced Falco was. Not that Falco wanted to shoot dogs. He actually felt sorry for the beasts. They didn't stand a chance against the weapons these men had chosen to bring. It was a bit ridiculous.

When Falco had helped recruit these men for this mission, he left it up to each man to bring the weapon or weapons of his choice. Leandro said that was best. Make them account for their own weapons. Ex-military guys never seemed to have a problem getting their hands on a wide assortment of firepower.

Leandro had even insisted that this be part of the contract. That way, if any of the men were caught by law enforcement during any part of the operation, the weapons could never be traced back to Choque Azul, and instead, made each man look responsible.

Okay, so sometimes Leandro could be smart. Although many of the men Falco worked with said that Leandro's father was still the mastermind, even from behind prison bars. There was even talk that the Iceman might be taking over.

Falco tapped out another cigarette, impatient and wanting to calm his nerves. He'd need to turn the engine on soon and cool off, again. He didn't dare open the car windows because he knew he'd have more mosquitoes than he would have breeze.

He had pulled the vehicle off the main road and onto a patch of dirt that connected the neighboring pasture to the road. Trees and shrubs gave him cover on one side. He could still easily see the long driveway, but he had given up trying to see the men through the woods.

He was about to light the cigarette when he thought

he saw a flash of light in the rearview mirror. That was impossible. He was backed up to the pasture. Nothing but cows, and even they had left. The dark and the quiet were starting to make him imagine things.

Then suddenly someone knocked on the passenger-side window. Falco startled with a manic jerk that banged his knee into the steering wheel. He fumbled for the revolver under the seat but stopped when he recognized the face – the scarred face – staring in at him with a crooked smile.

He turned the switch and hit the button to lower the window. He remembered the guy from Segway House – Colfax was his name.

'Did you decide you wanted to be a part of the action after all?' Falco asked him.

'Something like that.'

A flood of light hit Falco in the face. This time when he reached for his weapon, Colfax shoved the barrel of his handgun through the open window.

'Might not be such a good idea.'

The floodlight shut off, and it took Falco's eyes a few seconds to adjust to the dark. When they did, he could see a strange contraption five feet in front of his SUV. It resembled a wheelchair, only with caterpillar tracks that made it an all-terrain vehicle. In the raised seat was the crippled guy also from Segway House. He had a rifle pointed directly at Falco's head, and he was grinning.

66

'Look at that.' A giant of a man came into the kennels' warehouse after a good ten minutes of peering around the corner of the open garage-style door. 'This should be easy.'

Creed saw him point at the dogs in their kennels at the far end of the building.

'It'll be like shooting rats in a barrel.'

Creed swallowed bile and let himself feel anger instead of panic. He stayed calm and he stayed hidden as he continued to glance at his cell phones and iPad and watch the giant's two buddies venture inside behind him.

The giant stood at least six-five and weighed three

hundred pounds of solid muscle, by Creed's estimate. With his gear he looked like a space monster. The infrared goggles were pushed up into a thick mass of dreadlocks, making him appear to have eyes on the top of his head. He was dressed like his buddies, in a black T-shirt and camouflage pants.

This was Cheyenne's group. Creed recognized the small guy in the Kevlar vest with the bandanna wrapped around his head. He had taken off his goggles and let them dangle on his chest. The third guy – suntanned and wavy blond hair – looked like he could have stepped off his surfboard and strapped on a military belt, with the knife still in its scabbard and the automatic revolver in his right hand.

The second group – Nuru's – had just tripped the sensor over at the pool and training house. Bad timing. Creed wouldn't be able to give both his attention.

Creed felt sweat slide down his back. The gear hanging from his neck suddenly felt heavy and in his way. He swung it slowly and quietly around to hang down his back instead of his chest until he needed it.

'They aren't even barking at us,' the surfer guy said. 'Look at them. They're so quiet and calm. Do you think they're drugged or something?'

The other two guys looked nervous. Even the giant stopped grinning and started craning his neck to examine the balconies above.

On his iPad, Creed could see Nuru's crew of two enter the pool and training house. He noticed that Nuru had already left them, and he couldn't help but smile and think silently to himself, *Good dog.*

'His apartment is supposed to be on the second floor of this place.' The big man pointed his chin at the landing in the middle of the atrium. 'Looks like there's a door.'

Creed watched the two men inside the pool and training house. They both wore red – one a red bandanna and the other a red ball cap. Either they were bold enough to wear red or too stupid to know how well it showed up in the dark. Now in the pool and training house lights he saw how young they looked, even with the black paint smeared on their faces, and he decided 'stupid' was probably correct rather than 'bold'. Although either one was dangerous when you combined it with semiautomatic weapons.

'No one's around,' the surfer guy said down below. 'Maybe the other guys are having more luck in the house.'

'Oh, he's here,' the one in the Kevlar vest told them. 'Falco said he followed him home. Watched him go from his vehicle into here.'

Creed had noticed the tail, although he had to admit, Falco was good. He wondered if Falco was the one who was waiting at the end of the driveway.

He saw that the red bandanna and the red ball cap had reached the duffel bag he had left on the floor in the middle of the training facility. Just as they came up on either side of it, Creed clicked his remote twice. He didn't have the sound turned on to hear their screams as the floor opened up and swallowed them.

Deep graves under floorboards were always an excellent training tool for cadaver dogs.

Two more down.

The three in the kennel warehouse were right below Creed now. Two of them started climbing the stairs at opposite sides of the building.

Creed put the whistle to his lips and blew. Only the dogs could hear it. They came out of their kennels and headed for the dog doors. The electronic buzzes startled the men.

'What the hell?'

'They decided to leave.' The Kevlar vest guy thought it was funny and started laughing. 'They probably don't like the way you smell,' he told the giant, and the surfer guy laughed now, too.

That was a better reaction than Creed expected. The dogs' leaving would actually make their jobs easier.

Last dog out the dog door was Kramer, a Maltese who Creed didn't use as a scent dog because he was too small, even smaller than Grace. He was one of those heartstring dogs that Penelope Clemence had talked Creed into saving. Andy had trained Kramer to do a number of tricks, and before the dog left the warehouse, Creed gave two short blows and one long blow on the whistle. Kramer leaped up and tapped a small box about three feet off the ground.

'What did that dog just do?' The giant noticed and swung the rifle off his shoulder.

On the other side of the warehouse, the garage door they had come through started to close, and all three men jerked their heads in that direction as Kramer scurried through the dog door.

'Did that dog just close the door?' It was the surfer guy.

All three men came back toward the door, eyes and

guns darting across the warehouse. Yet none of them retreated or even tried to stop the door.

As soon as Creed was certain that all the dogs were gone, and when he heard the door hit the floor, he put on the contraption that had been hanging from his neck. Then he used his remote once again. Two clicks and the sprinklers in the ceiling burst open.

'What the hell.'

Creed watched the clock on his cell phone. It would take several seconds for the men to realize it wasn't water being sprayed down. He poked up from his hiding spot to sneak a peek at them down below. The giant saw him and raised his rifle. Creed had to duck as bullets ricocheted. They dinged off the metal railings on the balcony. Something ripped open Creed's cheek under his right eye. More bullets slammed into the metal bin as Creed belly-crawled back to his hiding place.

Okay, too soon. That was stupid. And he squeezed himself against the wall behind the bin.

'Stop, Adam. We're not supposed to kill him.'

'Damn it! What ... the hell is this ... stuff.'

Creed could hear the Kevlar vest guy struggling to get the words out. He stayed tucked away and watched the clock. His gas mask protected him. The other men should be knocked out in less than a minute. But he hadn't calculated someone as big as the giant. Adam, the giant, would probably take longer.

And that's when Creed heard someone coming up the steps.

67

A huge mitt of a hand grabbed Creed by the ankle and began to pull. The man didn't seem fazed by the mist that should have at least started to knock him out.

Creed kicked at the fingers with his other foot, smashing his own ankle but not discouraging the giant's hold.

'You bastard,' the man cursed at him, and Creed noticed the words weren't the least bit slurred.

He let go of his electronic devices to free up his hands. But instead of grabbing onto anything, Creed allowed the man to drag him out from his hiding place. And he did it as roughly as he could, seesawing Creed's leg and sending his head bouncing against the floor.

But out in the open, the gas mask surprised and stopped the man. Creed took advantage of the brief slip. He balled up his fist and slammed it into the giant's throat. The guy gasped and grabbed his neck, finally letting go of Creed's ankle.

Creed scrambled to his hands and knees as the man reached for him, again. Only, this time he collapsed. Finally the fumes had overcome him.

He gathered up his cell phones, leaving the iPad behind. By his calculation, there was one man left to deal with – the guy sitting in the vehicle at the end of Creed's driveway.

He had already switched off all the dog doors so none of the dogs could come back in until he could air out the building. With his gas mask still in place, Creed collected the three men's weapons, patting them down and finding knives and brass knuckles in boots and back pockets. He left each man where he had fallen to save time, but zip-tied their hands and feet, then duct-taped their mouths.

Finished, he stood over the pile of their weapons. He'd learned a long time ago that only a fool depended on weapons to save his life. But an even bigger fool wouldn't take advantage of one given to him. Creed picked up a pistol he actually recognized, though they had only recently been issued to the marine special ops. The Colt M45 was desert-tan and felt small in his hand. It was meant to be a close-quarters battle pistol, which was exactly what he needed right now. He lifted his sweat-drenched T-shirt and slipped the gun in his waistband.

He was already headed for the back door when he heard dogs start to bark. He froze in his tracks. Barking was not good. Every single dog had obeyed his commands all night. Barking was not allowed. Creed had gotten through this far with anger fueling him, but now for the first time panic kicked him in the gut.

The dogs' outdoor pen ran the length of the warehouse. He continued to use the back door as planned, letting himself out and keeping his body pressed against the building. He pulled off the gas mask, setting it down and sucking in the humid but fresh air. A gentle breeze reminded him that he had also gotten soaked by the spray. He filled his lungs with the damp night air, then he moved on.

He crept in the shadows, trying to listen beyond the barks. Night birds he didn't recognize seemed to fill the air, possibly stirred up by the dogs' barking. He was almost to the corner of the building where the pen began when he heard a man call out for him.

'You just as well come out, Mr Creed.'

The deep voice had a heavy Spanish accent. That surprised Creed. He expected the Iceman to blend in better. The dogs had quieted, and Creed had to step slower and softer without their barking to cover his approach. His fingers started to pull the pistol out of his waistband when he heard a dog cry out in pain.

He recognized that cry. It was Grace.

68

The man had Grace tucked under his left arm. In his right hand was the end of a short rope. The other end was tied around Grace's neck. A slipknot allowed the man to pull it as tight as he wanted.

'Put her down,' Creed said, as he came out from around the corner of the building, holding his hands up in front of him. Anger and panic made it difficult to keep calm when he wanted to race straight ahead and rescue her.

'This is the little bitch that started this whole mess. Is that not correct?'

The man grinned at him with white teeth made brighter by the dark stubble on his jaw. He looked about Creed's age – middle to late twenties, brown skin, and greased black hair. He wasn't dressed like his hit squad. Instead, he wore blue jeans and a designer T-shirt that he had never intended to soil on this night.

'I'm not sure what you're talking about,' Creed said, while he tried to make eye contact with Grace.

He wanted to tell her it would be okay, even if he knew it might definitely *not* be okay. The man kept the rope tight around her small neck, so tight she didn't move in his grip.

'The fishing boat. This little bitty thing. Who would have guessed she would be the start of so much trouble. Such a mess, and no one to clean it up except me.'

'Put her down and I'll do whatever you tell me to do. It's really me you came for. Not her.'

'Oh, the Iceman will still have you to himself.'

'You're not the Iceman?'

This made the man laugh.

'My name is Leandro Ramos. If you were not so stupid, you would know that. I run Choque Azul in these parts. You took something of mine. It is only fair I take something of yours.'

'I didn't take anything off that boat.'

He laughed again. 'Not off the boat. At the airport.'

'You mean Amanda? If you wanted her back so badly, why'd you run her off the road?'

He shook his head, the grin still in place. 'I was done with her anyway. And by running away, she got you to bring her here and led us right to you.'

'So then you must mean the cocaine?' Creed told him. 'I can get it for you. Just put the dog down.'

'Yes, of course, you will get me my cocaine.'

Creed started to breathe a sigh of relief just as the man named Leandro dropped his arm out from under Grace. She jerked, then dangled at the end of the rope. Leandro now held up the other end, letting the slipknot bite into her neck.

Creed's hand went for the pistol at his back. Before he could yank it free, Leandro's left knee exploded, sending him to the ground. Without even looking to see where the shot had come from, Creed rushed to scoop up Grace. He didn't even notice that while Leandro was screaming in pain, he was reaching for his own pistol.

This time Creed saw a flash of fur, then he heard a snarl. Somehow Chance had gotten out. He grabbed Leandro's arm and made the man scream.

'Don't let go, Chance.'

He heard a growl, then the big dog shook his head. Leandro screamed even louder.

That's when Creed felt a lick on his hand. Grace looked up at him and he massaged her neck. Had it really been only a second or two that she had dangled at the end of the rope? It had felt like minutes.

'You okay?' he asked her. And she started to wag.

'How about you?' someone asked from behind Creed.

He turned to see Jason and another man coming out from the woods. Both were dressed in fatigues. Jason had a rifle with a scope swung over his shoulder.

'Go check on him, Tony.'

The other man was already going to take care of Leandro, but stopped when Chance growled and shook again, and Leandro screamed.

Over his shoulder Tony said, 'He screams like a girl.'

'I know you said you didn't want any help, but we just happened to be in the neighborhood,' Jason said with a grin that Creed had never seen on the kid.

Creed hugged Grace closer. He pointed at the rifle. 'Was that you?'

'Oh yeah, I guess I might have forgotten to mention. The army trained me as a sniper. Amazing what you can still do with only one hand.'

SUNDAY

69

O'Dell greeted Agent McCoy as he came up the Bagleys' front porch steps. Behind her the forensic team was finishing up. She could see the other FBI agents waiting for her by the outbuilding where the children had been kept.

'Is this your first time here?' she asked McCoy.

'First time in Alabama.'

'Really? But this was such an important case.' She held the screen door open for him.

He maneuvered around her into the entry, and she noticed his eyes darting around the place.

'It's called delegating, Agent O'Dell. You should try it sometime.' He stuffed his hands in his pockets, obviously impatient with her. 'So what's so important that you brought me all the way out here and on a Sunday, no less?'

'I appreciate you taking the time.'

'Yeah, well, be sure not to waste my time. I wouldn't be here if your boss wasn't busting my boss's chops. Now that we have George Ramos's son in custody, my people are anxious to close this sorry-ass case.'

'It's just too bad they haven't found the Iceman.'

He shrugged. 'According to Leandro Ramos, the Iceman's apprentice was supposed to be at the scene last night, too. And we haven't found him yet either.'

'Maybe he's a ghost, just like his boss.'

She thought she saw a spark in McCoy's blue eyes. She wasn't sure if it was more impatience or perhaps a flicker of respect that both the Iceman and his apprentice had beaten them all once again.

'So what's so important?'

'It's upstairs in the master bedroom.' She pointed to the open staircase, then she led the way up, stopping for one of the forensic team who was coming down.

'They should be finished,' McCoy said as they passed another tech in the hallway.

'Pretty much.'

The door to the master bedroom was open. She stepped in and waited for him. She watched him glance at the altar, then scan the rest of the room as if he were looking for what it was she thought was so important.

'Something's been bugging me about the altar the Bagleys set up for Santa Muerte.'

'I hate to tell you this, O'Dell, but I've already seen this altar in the case photos that were taken. And believe me, they had all kinds of angles and close-ups, so please don't tell me you brought me all the way out here to find what's bugging you about this.'

'Have you looked at very many other altars to Santa Muerte?'

He let out a long sigh of frustration and said, 'No, I can't say that I have.'

'All of them leave gifts, and there's some variation but there are a few things that seem to always be the same.'

'And I can't wait for you to tell me what those are.'

'Almost all of them leave tequila. Seems strange to me, but all of it seems strange so why not tequila, right?'

He glanced at the altar.

'Sometimes the whole bottle is included. Sometimes

not. But always, if there's tequila at all, there's some poured into a glass or several glasses.'

'That's so very interesting, O'Dell, that you're putting me to sleep while I'm standing up.'

But she didn't think he looked bored. For the first time since he entered the house, Agent McCoy looked a bit uncomfortable.

'I've checked with some experts.'

'There are experts?'

'Oh yeah, it's crazy, isn't it? They all say the tequila is poured and ready or it's not an official offering. Sometimes people will refresh what's in the glass, but never will they leave a glass empty. That would be disrespectful. Actually, an insult.'

She waited for his eyes to check out the glass, even though he certainly already knew it was empty. The glass was the only thing set off to the side. She hadn't allowed the forensic team to touch anything else.

'Your prints are on the empty glass, Agent McCoy.' She said it bluntly, as a matter of fact. 'I'm just wondering how that is possible when you've never set foot in this house. No wait, you haven't even been in the state of Alabama.'

'I don't know what you're trying to pull. I pissed

you off, so this is your way of getting back at me.' He shook his head as if he were disgusted by her. 'You're a sorry piece of work, O'Dell.'

'You've gotten away with it for so long that you got a bit cocky. You didn't think anyone would notice. Especially if you had your own team in here cleaning up after you.'

'You don't know what you're talking about.'

'You're a ghost, right? No one knows what you look like. You've been able to arrest or kill anyone who might.'

His eyes flashed at her. Blue eyes. Ice blue.

'But your apprentice knows.'

'*My* apprentice? What the hell are you talking about?'

She pulled out her cell phone and hit SEND on the text that she had drafted, letting her team know it was time to come on up.

'What are you doing? What did you just do?'

'You and George Ramos have been friends for a long, long time.'

'You have no idea what you're talking about.'

'All the way back to the days when you were a simple immigration officer working for ICE. You helped him come to the States. When you got promoted and went to the DEA, you even tried to bust his old partner in the Gulf drug cartel.'

He shook his head again, but he didn't stop her. She wondered if he was trying to figure out how she knew this or if he was plotting what to do with her.

'Howard Johnson went straight. And no matter how hard you tried, you couldn't bust him. But your buddy George got involved in a new cartel, Choque Azul. Somehow he convinced you to come along for the ride.'

'You don't know anything.'

'You're right about that. There are a whole lot of holes I haven't filled and dots I can't connect. But I've seen the way you look at Senator Ellie Delanor. Did you come in second to George with her, too?'

'Shut up, O'Dell. You really don't know what you're talking about.'

'When I ended up busting George on his houseboat, he put his son Leandro in charge. You thought it should have been you, right? After all, weren't you the one that came up with the new idea of trafficking kids?'

'That was Leandro, not me.'

She kept quiet, staring at him and waiting for him to realize his slip. When he finally did, she saw the anger before he tucked it away and replaced it with a smile.

'You can't prove any of it.' He pointed at her chest. 'What, are you wearing a wire? Thinking I might confess to your crazy-ass theory?'

'What about the fingerprints?'

'You planted those.'

'Then what about the one man who can identify you as the Iceman?'

'What are you talking about?'

McCoy's back was to the open door when the two FBI agents brought in the young man named Falco. McCoy turned, and she watched his face fall, along with all his carefully maintained composure. From what she knew about the Iceman, he had taken great pains to put away, destroy, or kill anyone who had ever seen his face, and he had been able to do that all the way back to the days when he was an ICE agent. But McCoy didn't know that Falco had been captured last night, so how could he get to him?

'Sorry, boss,' the young man told him. 'They tricked me, too.'

THREE DAYS LATER

70

Creed grabbed the last box from Jason's car. It was heavy, and he wondered how the kid had intended to move it on his own. Everything else he owned he'd packed into black garbage bags – the kind with the drawstring handle that could easily be carried with one hand or tucked under the arm. Sadly, there weren't that many bags.

After talking to Hannah, they decided to offer Jason a trailer they kept on their property. It had been empty for only a few months, after Felix, one of their dog handlers, took a job on the West Coast to be closer to the new love of his life. Coincidentally, Hannah had already reserved Jason's room at Segway House, because an available room there, no matter how small, was a commodity.

As soon as they had moved Hannah from ICU to a regular room, she insisted on being taken to Amanda's bedside. Maggie had replaced McCoy's DEA agent, who had been waiting to interrogate the girl, with an FBI agent to stand guard and protect her.

Creed could only imagine Hannah's conversation with Amanda. It wasn't often she misjudged people, and she would make sure that she made it right. He knew that she had promised Jason's room at Segway House to Amanda, and Amanda had accepted. It was a start. She'd be safe there and well taken care of by not only Hannah, but the entire staff.

The trailer wasn't luxurious, but Creed figured it was a considerable step up from a room at a rehab center. Jason seemed genuinely speechless at the gesture. But as Creed watched him place a gallon of milk and a carton of eggs in the refrigerator, he thought he saw a hint of a smile.

'What do you have, a load of bricks in this one?' Creed asked as he hauled the box into the living room.

'No bricks. Books. Put it down anywhere.'

'I wouldn't have pegged you for a reader.'

'It was my secret escape when I was in Afghanistan.'

Creed nodded. He slipped his hands in his pockets and stood in the middle of the double-wide. He remembered when they first met. The kid had a chip on his shoulder as big as Texas. Hannah kept saying Jason reminded her of him, and he didn't see it. Refused to see it. But now he did. They had both been damaged in ways that would take a lifetime to heal.

'I can't thank you enough for this,' Jason said.

'You might not be so thankful when it's two o'clock in the morning and I'm pounding on the door to have you help me with a sick dog.'

'I don't sleep that much, so that'll be okay.'

And yet another thing they had in common.

'You saved Grace's life,' Creed said. 'Probably mine, too. I wish there was more I could do to repay you.'

'You already have.'

'A job, a place to sleep . . . ' Creed shrugged, as if it weren't enough. Certainly not comparable to saving two lives.

'No, you gave me a whole lot more.' Jason's eyes got serious, and it looked like he needed to swallow hard to get the next part out. 'You gave me a purpose.'

Creed understood that, too. It was exactly what Hannah had done for him.

'But there is something else I'd like, if you don't mind,' Jason said.

'Sure, whatever you need.'

'Can I have one of those black Lab puppies?'

That shouldn't have surprised Creed, but it did. 'I'm guessing you already have one picked out.'

'The runt of the litter, of course.' Jason's eyes lit up as he pointed to the box at Creed's feet. '*To Kill a Mockingbird*'s one of my favorite books. Already picked out Scout for the name.'

'From what I remember, the runt of the litter is a boy.'

'I figure he doesn't need to know he's named after a girl.'

'Your secret's good with me,' Creed told him as he started to leave. 'I've got to go pick up Hannah.' Before he got to the door, he turned back. 'Hey, Jason.' He waited for the kid to look up at him. 'Welcome back to the world.'

As Creed took the hospital elevator, he tried to untie the knots that had invaded his gut. Yesterday Hannah still looked so fragile. The bruising and swelling on her face had gone down, but there was something in her eyes that he wasn't used to seeing. It wasn't pain or fear. It was something worse – he was afraid that a piece of her spirit had crumbled away.

At the end of the week he was going to pick up her boys from her grandparents' farm. It was a five-hour drive each way. No way she could come along, though she had already protested. Maybe seeing them would be the best medicine.

But then he heard her voice – boisterous and full of life. Even from down the hall, he could hear her telling someone, 'Girl, you haven't eaten paradise until you've had my ham hocks, collards, and black-eyed peas with a nice slab of corn bread.'

'Stop, you're making my mouth water.'

And Creed stopped short in the middle of the hall. He recognized the second voice, too. The knots began twisting again but for a whole different reason.

He found Maggie O'Dell sitting in a chair pulled up close enough to the bed that she was holding Hannah's hand. Both women looked up at him, and their smiles slid off their faces.

'What?' he asked when they looked at him as if he had walked in and spoiled their party.

'Is it that time already?' Hannah asked.

'I thought you'd be anxious to get out of this place.'

'Oh, sweetie, I am. I just lost track of the time. We've been having ourselves a good chat.'

The two of them exchanged a glance, and Creed knew he had been at least one subject of their 'good chat.'

'I think I just convinced Maggie that she needs a vacation. She's coming back next month for a week—'

'Maybe a few days.'

Hannah shot her one of her looks and continued, 'Like I said, she's coming for a week on the beach, and she's gonna come over and have dinner with us.'

Maggie looked up at Creed. 'She can be very convincing.'

'Yes, she can.' He smiled and caught Hannah nodding at him as if to say, 'You're welcome.' Then to Maggie he said, 'Maybe you can bring your dogs so you won't need to leave them with anyone.'

ACKNOWLEDGEMENTS

As with each of my novels I have quite a few people to thank and acknowledge.

Thanks go to:

My publishing teams: Nita Taublib, Ivan Held, Meaghan Wagner, Kate Stark, Alexis Welby, and Stephanie Hargadon at Putnam. And at Little Brown/Sphere: David Shelley, Catherine Burke, and Jade Chandler.

My agent, Scott Miller, and his colleague Claire Roberts at Trident Media Group.

Martin and Patti Bremmer for a friendship that includes dropping everything and literally coming to the rescue, holding down the fort, and taking care of the pack in a moment's notice.

Dr Stephen Cassivi and the wonderful staff at the Mayo Clinic in Rochester, Minnesota, for making 'cancer' not such a scary word. I look forward to the day that Clare can read my books and maybe one day when I might read hers.

My friends and family put up with my long absences and still manage to love me and keep me grounded: Patricia Kava, Marlene Haney, Sandy and Fred Rockwood, Patricia Sierra, Sharon Kator, Maricela Barajas, Annie Belatti, Nancy Tworek, Patti El-Kachouti, Diane Prohaska, Cari Conine, Lisa Munk, Luann Causey, and Patti Carlin.

Special thanks to my friend Amee Rief for feeding us through some terribly sad and stressful days.

My fellow authors and friends who make this business a bit less crazy: Sharon Car, Erica Spindler, and J. T. Ellison.

The experts who I know I can call or email with the strangest questions and the oddest requests: Leigh Ann Retelsdorf, Melissa Connor, Gary Plank, and John Beck.

Ray Kunze, once again, for lending his name to

Maggie O'Dell's boss. And for the record, the real Ray Kunze is a nice guy who would never send Maggie on wild-goose chases.

Penelope La Lone and Penny Clemence for donating to a charity event for Gloria La Lone's continued fight against cancer. They won the auction to have a character named for them. Penelope Clemence is the dog rescuer who convinces Creed to take a chance on Chance.

My pack depends on some amazing veterinarians, and now they've become friends as well as invaluable resources for writing this series. Special thanks to:

Dr Enita Larson and her crew at Tender Care Animal Hospital, and Dr Tonya McIlnay and the team at Veterinary Eye Specialist of Nebraska.

An extra thank-you to Dr Larson for allowing me to name my fictional veterinarian after her children: Avelyn Faye and Ayden Parker. We'll see Dr Avelyn Parker in each of the Creed novels.

Thanks also to the booksellers, book bloggers, and librarians for mentioning and recommending my novels.

A big thank-you to all of my VIR Club members,

Facebook friends, and faithful readers. With so many wonderful novels available, I'm honored that you continue to choose mine. Without you, I wouldn't have the opportunity to tell my twisted tales.

And, as always, a special thank-you to Deb Carlin and the rest of the pack: Duncan, Boomer, and Maggie. They are my heart and soul.

Now read the beginning of
Ryder Creed and K9's next
rescue operation ...

1
___

HAYWOOD COUNTY, NORTH CAROLINA

Daniel Tate clenched his teeth and looked away just as the needle pierced a vein in his arm. He'd spent two tours of duty in Iraq and one in Afghanistan. He'd been shot at, dodged IEDs, and escaped a grenade. But needles – damn, he hated needles.

'This will help relax you,' Dr Shaw told him.

When she walked in the door, Tate had been relieved to see a woman. But she had barely introduced herself before pulling out a stainless steel tray with vials and surgical utensils and, of course, several syringes. Her black hair was pulled back tight, leaving only long bangs that overlapped heavy-framed glasses. She was younger than he expected, with smooth brown skin that hadn't yet earned wrinkles at the corners of her mouth or eyes. And she was attractive, but instead of looking at her now, Tate let his eyes scan the room. He didn't want to even see the needle so he stared at the walls.

It was a strange room, empty except for the examination table. The drywall looked spongy, like the foam mats you'd find at the basketball court tacked up under the basket for overenthusiastic athletes to bounce off. Only these mats weren't tacked onto the walls, they *were* the walls – whitewashed and seamless. The term 'padded cell' came to mind.

There wasn't a single thing displayed. Didn't medical exam rooms have diplomas or something on the walls? Not that it mattered. Tate's chance of backing out had passed. He knew it as soon as he signed on page seven of that ass-long contract they'd handed him when he first arrived.

He didn't even know where this place was. It had been pouring sheets of rain the entire hour and a half from the airport. That was yesterday, or at least he thought it was. His wristwatch and cell phone were two of the personal items he had to surrender. Other than not knowing the time of day, he didn't mind. But Tate couldn't understand why he couldn't wear his own shoes or underwear. The blue scrubs were comfortable, but the paper booties drove him crazy. He felt like he was shuffling, the sound reminding him of the old people in the nursing home where his wife, Susan, worked.

'After I administer the drug, I'll ask you a series of questions,' Dr Shaw said.

He glanced at her and held back a grimace. She was loading another syringe. Served him right for not reading all seven pages. All Tate cared about was the three thousand dollars he had been promised, and he'd double-checked that it was in the contract.

He hated that Susan worked an extra shift once a week just to make ends meet. Their oldest daughter, Nikki, had started waiting tables at the coffee shop. Even Danny Junior had a paper route. But Tate hadn't been able to get a job.

Not true. He hadn't been able to *hold* a job since he'd been back. The doctors called it post-traumatic stress disorder. But all Tate saw when he looked in the mirror was a perfectly healthy man. Nevermind that his mind twisted pieces of information, and insomnia kept him pacing the streets of their small town. He needed to start contributing and helping to take care of his family. Even if it meant a few needle pokes.

This time it didn't matter where he looked. As soon as the metal slipped into his vein, he felt the liquid rush into his body. A heat wave crawled up his arm, over his shoulder, and spread throughout his chest. It took his breath away, and he felt his body shudder.

'You may experience a tightness in your chest,' he heard Dr Shaw say, only now it sounded like she was talking to him from the next room.

He turned his head to look at her, and just that movement made him nauseated. He tried to find her eyes through the blur. The small rose tattoo he had noticed earlier on the side of her neck had grown legs and started to inch along her skin like an insect. Tate blinked hard, trying to focus. Sweat beaded on his forehead and upper lip.

'Nosebleeds are not uncommon,' Dr Shaw continued in her calm, cool manner. 'I'm going to ask you some questions, Daniel.'

Tate, he wanted to tell her everyone called him Tate, but he couldn't take his mind off the bug digging into her neck. His heart galloped in his chest, and it was difficult to breathe.

'Daniel, can you count backward from one hundred for me?'

His mouth had a metallic taste and it took effort to make it move. Teeth and tongue seemed to be in the way of him activating his voice.

'Daniel, can you count backward from one hundred?' she repeated.

Suddenly he heard himself say, 'That would be difficult to do because I don't like rice.'

Even as he said it, he knew it wasn't the correct answer but already he'd forgotten the question. Nothing mattered except the black insect on her neck. Why couldn't she feel it digging under her skin?

'Dr Shaw.' A voice called from the doorway.

Tate's entire body jerked before he saw the man. His head was shaved and gleamed almost as bright as his long white coat. Tate had to look away. The brightness hurt his eyes. Just as they were starting to focus, the light sent stars and sparks like electrical surges and he knew he couldn't trust them.

'I'm in the middle of a test,' Dr Shaw told the man.

'It's gotten worse. They're talking about landslides. We really must evacuate.'

'I've lived through hurricanes, Richard. This is just a rain.'

But she left Tate and joined the man at the door. Neither bothered to keep their voices down. In fact, they seemed to forget about Tate. They didn't even notice that he was panting now and wiping erratically at his eyes and sweat pouring down his face.

'The water is almost over the bridge.' Richard sounded panicked. He was loud and gesturing. 'If we don't leave now, we risk being stranded here.'

Dr Shaw was turned away from him, and Tate could no longer see the insect on her neck. He began checking his own hands and arms.

'We're safe here,' Dr Shaw was telling the man. 'This place is built like a fortress.'

Tate tried to see if there were any bugs on the man. His eyes were finally settling down, when he saw a flash of green and black fur behind the doctors. It looked like a small monkey running up the hallway.

'Well, I'm leaving. With or without you.'

'That would be a mistake. Let's talk about this.' She glanced over her shoulder and when she called out to

Tate, it sounded like a bellow echoing across the small room. 'I'll be right back, Daniel. Stay right here.'

She joined the man in the hallway and tried to close the door. When it didn't seem to fit the frame, she opened it wide.

'See, that's not a good sign,' Richard told her. 'Doors and windows tend to stick right before. It's bad, I'm telling you. We must leave.'

This time she pulled the door with such force it slammed.

Tate sat listening to the thump-thump of his heart. It was beating inside his head and he put his hands over his chest to make sure his heart hadn't moved. It wasn't long after the doctors had left when he heard a loud crack. So loud it jolted him off the table.

It sounded like an artillery shell. Was that possible?

He crawled under the examination table, his body scrambling in twitches and jerks. Then he listened for more artillery shells. The room started to sway and tilt. Was it the drug? Had it screwed with his equilibrium? His ears popped and instead of thumping of his heart, he now heard only a rumble.

He felt it, too. A vibration rattled the doctor's instruments, shaking them off the tray. The floor tiles lifted and rolled beneath him, and Tate grabbed on to the examination table.

That's when he saw the whitewashed walls crack and buckle. The walls were actually caving in, as if a bulldozer were on the other side shoving them in. Tate felt something coming down from the ceiling. He ducked his head back under the table. He watched, not sure whether to believe his eyes. It was raining dirt and gravel. He could smell the wet earth.

The rumble grew to a roar. Forget the bulldozer, a freight train was headed down on top of him. He covered his head with his arms and curled into a tight ball.

More crashes. Metal shrieked. Light fixtures exploded.

In the darkness Daniel Tate couldn't see. The floor became a roller coaster. He clawed to hold on to the steel table, as the world around him shattered and roared and collapsed on top of him.

SILENT CREED

Ryder Creed and Bolo's second adventure

When Ryder Creed responds to a devastating mudslide in North Carolina, he knows the difference between finding survivors and the dead – is time. Heedless of the dangers, Creed and his best search-and-rescue dog Bolo frantically wade through the chaos of twisted tree limbs, crumbled cement, and unrecognizable debris.

What they get from the mud reveals secrets that run deep, pointing to a possible serial killer and unexpectedly dredging up painful, hushed-up pieces of Creed's own past.

The mysteries unearthed will bring Ryder Creed face-to-face with his past loyalties, deeply embedded survivor's guilt, and a powerful figure from his past. He'll have to rely on his dogs if he wants to make it through alive ...

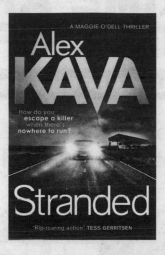

A MAGGIE O'DELL THRILLER

Alex
KAVA

How do you
escape a killer
when there's
nowhere to run?

Stranded

'Rip-roaring action' TESS GERRITSEN

For decades, tired travellers have stopped at rest areas on America's epic highways to rest, refuel and get a bite to eat, but little do they know that one man's rest stop is another's hunting ground. For years the defenceless, the weary and the stranded have been disappearing along the highways and byways, vanishing without a trace.

When FBI special agent Maggie O'Dell and her partner, Tully, discover the remains of a young woman in a highway ditch, the one clue left behind is a map that will send Maggie and Tully on a frantic hunt crisscrossing the country to stop a madman before he kills again.

As the body count rises and Maggie races against the clock to unmask the monster who's terrorising the nation's highways, she turns for help to a former foe who seems to have an uncanny knack for guessing what the killer's next move will be. But as she gets closer to finding the killer, it becomes eerily clear that Maggie is the ultimate target.